THE
RAINBOW MURDERS

ALSO BY
CHRIS COAD TAYLOR

THE
RAINBOW MURDERS

A NOVEL

CHRIS COAD TAYLOR

JOHAZEL PUBLISHING
LAND O 'LAKES, FLORIDA

The Rainbow Murders©

JASON GALEHOUSE and MICHAEL WACHOLTZ were my inspirational seeds for writing this fictional story.

In 2003, their disappearance and death captured the attention of the city of Tampa, Florida. I hoped that writing this novel might open prejudiced eyes and show the reader that each person is an important part of the world. My sympathy goes to the Galehouse and Wacholtz's family and friends.

Acknowledgments

Thank you to my many friends and critical readers of my first edition, Daine Darling, Maureen Bethke, and David Roth, with The Examiner-Tampa for his review of my first edition. The help of artist, Gainor Roberts, who helped me with the first cover of my first edition of this book.

Another thank you must go to Tampa-born resident and long-time friend, Mary Lozano, who spent hours touring me around the streets of Tampa and Ybor City and relaying its history. She helped me with my research of the cigar factories and shared yummy lunches with me at the Columbia Restaurant.

To author and friend, Paul Dubose, who was my constant mentor and friend but now is no longer with us. I will dearly miss you.

Lastly but as always, goes my appreciation to my husband and family. Without them, I would not be inspired to create or be so happy.

PROLOGUE

Kassandra

My name is Kassandra and I am a Soul Follower. My story is not about me, it's about murder.

Each living person has a Soul Follower assigned to him or her. There are over seven billion Soul Followers and my assignee's name is Amber Moon. This story is about her—and evil.

A Soul Follower is forbidden to interfere in the life of a human. Any intrusion could cause a ripple or a flutter effect, which could change the universe. However, interference could save lives.

Most humans never feel or hear us, although they believe in our existence. Our speech travels time on a different frequency than the human ear can hear. Often we attempt to whisper or nudge our assignees to help or guide them. A rare few are sensitive to us, the "Special Ones," like Amber's mother, Suzanne.

Amber may be a Special One like her mother; however, she has a logical mind and does not listen. If she hears me, the killing in Tampa could stop. If my nudges are not felt it could be fatal for many and evil will remain.

Touch of Evil

His perverted mission was to fight sinners and to bring decency back into the world.
The notes spoke of atonement and penance. He claimed his actions exposed the sinful.
He petitioned the righteous to fight wrong. Yet, his words possessed the very essence of
EVIL.

* * *

Amber fumbled with her key at the door. The light of the half-moon illuminated the knob for a few seconds then the clouds passed over and darkness fell again. She shuddered as an eerie feeling cloaked her.

As the fog thickened, the night took on a bizarre sensation. The last few weeks Amber had been receiving harassing phone calls of deadly silence except for the heavy breathing that could be heard from the other end of the line. Seconds later a click would follow, disconnecting the call, then dead silence. The strange atmosphere of tonight made her jittery. Still, her stubbornness caused her to refuse to accept that she could be vulnerable and defenseless.

The local news reported of murders by a possible serial killer dubbed, "The Rainbow Killer." A killer on the loose in Tampa proved that life could be interrupted in a nanosecond. Still, Amber felt she was immune from the danger and thought her nervousness was unwarranted. The Rainbow Killer targeted gay men—she was a straight female.

1

The anxiety of her close homosexual friends proved contagious though. The same as Typhoid Mary had infected people around her with a deadly disease; Amber's friends had unintentionally infected her with their morbid perspective and fears.

A homicidal maniac in the city was enough to plague her gay friends with worry even though they only casually knew the first two murder victims. It was obvious that a tidal wave of fear had engulfed the entire homosexual community and was overflowing on Amber.

Before entering her small Florida bungalow, Amber flipped on a wall switch to light the living room. When she took a step inside, she kicked something with her foot. Looking down, she saw an envelope. She bent down, picked it up, and took a closer look. No return address or postmark, nothing unique just a white envelope with her name scrawled in pencil. The writing was legible but consisted of thick jagged lines that formed her name and seemed written with an intense, heavy hand.

Holding the envelope in her hand, Amber walked over to a cherry, Queen Anne desk. It had been an extravagant purchase but one she never regretted. The desk was where she relaxed every day with her morning coffee before work, her *tranquil place*.

Amber placed her purse down and opened the center drawer to retrieve a letter opener. As she looked down, her auburn hair fell forward. "I can't see anything with this hair," she muttered. Frustrated, she dug into her purse and produced a barrette with opals, gold beads, and amber crystals, one from her mother's design line, a "Suzanne Exclusive." After pinning her hair back, she picked up the envelope to examine it.

The phone rang. She stopped to answer it.

"Amber?"

"Mom, what's the matter?"

"Are you okay?"

"Of course. Why wouldn't I be?"

2

"I was afraid you weren't safe," Suzanne said.

"Safe? Mom, what are you talking about?"

"Well, the police keep finding bodies dumped in town. It's dangerous now for a woman living alone. I just felt . . .." Suzanne stopped. "Forget it. It's probably nothing. I'm just being a mom. I wanted to make sure you got home and locked everything up."

"Mom, you worry too much. Not all your feelings are premonitions." Amber looked at the envelope as she spoke.

"I know. But . . .."

"Mom I hate it when you do this to yourself."

Suzanne let out a heavy sigh. "I understand. I felt the same way about it until—"

"I'm not going to debate this tonight. I know Grandma believes you have a sixth sense. I don't know how I feel about what happened before, maybe you do have a gift, but you must stop dwelling on every gut feeling that comes your way."

Suzanne used to ignore her feelings too, until five years ago. She described it as a whisper in her ear, softly nagging with warnings. She said it was only a nervous worry—not intuition. Certainly not a gift. Sure, sometimes she sensed little things, but so did others. Her life was normal. Not like her mother's, and not like the way movies portrayed psychics. She stood firm in her belief until what happened to Linda, her best friend.

Suzanne had a dreadful feeling about Linda and fought the urge to call her. To tell her to get her car checked by a mechanic. Suzanne ignored the whispers because Linda had just bought a new car, therefore, it wasn't logical to warn her.

A week later, Linda was dead. Her brakes failed and her car skidded into a semi-truck that was going sixty. After her funeral, Suzanne vowed never to ignore her feelings again. Suzanne started listening.

3

"Did you lock the door, Amber?"

Amber glanced at the unlocked front door. "Yes. Stop worrying."

Amber's stubbornness would not allow her to admit she had not locked the door immediately upon entering. Mentally she excused the lie, reasoning that she didn't want to upset her mother.

"You know I've been coming home alone to an empty house for years."

"I know," Suzanne said, almost sounding like a whining child. "But I just couldn't shake this feeling. I wish you had an alarm system."

Amber took a deep breath, pressed her lips together hard, and remained quiet. She exhaled slowly. "I'm fine, Mother. I need to go now. Talk to you tomorrow."

"Wait! Aren't you going to tell me about your day? What was the surprise?"

"The day was great. I'm tired and have a headache. We'll have plenty of time to talk tomorrow at the spa."

The day had been wonderful, perfect in fact. She hated to put her mother off, but she was curious to open the envelope in her hand. She hung the phone up with her eyes fixated on the envelope. Then a loud noise sounded from the back of the house. She jumped, dropped the note, and froze for a few seconds listening. Nothing.

Stepping lightly, she moved away from the desk toward the dark hallway, which led to her bedroom in the back of the house. At the hall threshold, she flipped the overhead light on in a quick motion lighting the narrow hall with the brightness spilling down into her bedroom. Amber inched closer and scanned the room as she approached. She reached around the doorframe, found the bedroom switch, and turned on the ceiling light.

No one was there.

She hurried to the closet door, grabbed the doorknob, and with one quick movement whisked it open, lunging forward, she flailed her arms about the clothes to feel for the Boogieman.

No Boogieman.

Turning around, she looked across the room. Her eyes focused on the window next to her bed. The window hung open about an inch. Sure, she had locked it, however, in her rush to pack for the weekend, she must've forgotten.

Amber crossed the room to the window and looked outside. The fog was dissipating, revealing the big oak trees and bushes. Nothing unusual. She pushed the window down hard and twisted the lock. The old sash windows in these aged homes always swelled and were difficult to shut. The fresh scratches in the wood around the window frame and the small chips of paint lying on the sill, evidence of jimmying damage from a screwdriver or knife blade went unnoticed.

Outside, a shadowy figure stood flattened against the wall of the house next to the window. She pressed her cheek to the windowpane and looked into the blackness. Looking first to the right and then left. Seeing nothing, she headed back to the living room.

Back in the security of the living room, Amber went to her desk and picked up the envelope. Her hand shook, still jittery from the unknown noise. The paper had a gritty, sticky feel and seemed to exude heat. She shuddered as a creepy feeling flowed over her as if an invisible insect had crawled out from the envelope and slithered up her arm.

She opened the desk drawer to retrieve an amber-handled letter opener—another gift from her mother. One of Suzanne's endless streams of gifts, Christmas or Hanukah, any holiday worked as an excuse. Since Suzanne was Lutheran and Amber's father was Jewish, it was justification in her mother's eyes to celebrate both religious holidays with gifts.

The envelope was addressed simply—Amber Moon. The heavy dark pencil printing pressed deep crevices into the fibers of the paper and seemed to reflect intense emotion. Amber's middle name was Moon, a fallout from her parent's hippie years. Amber felt lucky they had not named her Star, Winter, or Moonbeam. Several years ago, she legally changed her last name Rosenbaum to Moon. It made things easier, fewer explanations when signing contracts. Amber told her mother *Amber Moon Designs* would be more recognizable, besides it had a catchy sound to it. Suzanne admitted, for business purposes, she was probably right.

Amber slit the top edge of the envelope and pulled the note out. As she unfolded it, she gasped, dropping the paper as if it had instantly burst into flames. The exposed ranting fell to the desk face up.

> BITCH,
> Evil is among us. The unrighteous will not enter the Kingdom of God.
> Homosexuals deserve to die. Their souls belong to the devil.
> Amber Moon, you chose to close your eyes and mingle among them, the lost souls of the devil.
> Vic Richardson, Phillip Brooks, and your friends contaminate the world. Sinners will perish.
> Save yourself. I will fight the devil and exterminate evil. Your time to repent is now before it is too late.
> I Am a Shepherd of God.

Panic

Tears of panic came to Amber's eyes as terror pulsed through her body. Her mind raced. The words didn't make sense. Evil around her? There was no evil, she thought. Vic and Phillip were good and decent people. Amber's heart pounded as her mind reeled. She felt nauseous. Her thoughts jolted. She spun around.

"The door!"

She raced across the room with a hand reaching out in front of her, fingers extended. Touching the doorknob, her fingers fumbled at the raised bar in the center and turned it to a locked position. Amber twisted around and leaned against the door, with the look of fear on her face.

I need to call the police. She took a deep breath, trying to regain her composure. She didn't want to sound like a hysterical female on the phone. *Oh yeah, the police will have a good laugh about the little lady who's afraid of a scary note.* What could the police do? There wasn't anyone in the house.

After mentally battling with herself about if the police would think this was worthy of consideration, as well as figuring the police would take a call from a man more seriously, Amber finally decided to call anyway. She needed to make them listen to her; after all, someone had been there to slide the note under the door. A note that threatened Vic and Phillip. That alone was a matter for the police, plus the news reported that The Rainbow Killer left notes about sinners.

"Could this note be from that maniac?" Amber whispered. She hurried to the phone, picked it up to call, and stopped. Amber's logical mind crept back. "But the news said the Rainbow's notes were pinned to dead bodies," she half-whispered to herself. "I'm alive—scared—but alive."

The news didn't mention anything about notes of warning sent to people. Perhaps it wasn't connected to the gay killings. She put the phone down. *There's no need to come unnerved over a childish note.*

The string of murders in town could put Phillip, Andy, Saffron, or anyone of her friends in the group in danger. But, not her. She wasn't gay. The police probably would attribute the note to a wounded ex-boyfriend trying to scare her into coming back to him. She and Frank broke up long ago, and she hadn't dated anyone since. Frank had been upset. Still, threatening notes weren't his style. Then a thought rocketed into her mind—*Mom's premonition.*

Amber gulped as she pressed her hand against her forehead to think and forced back panicked tears. Her mother sounded so worried on the phone. She had been right about Linda—Vic needed to be warned. Picking up the phone, she decided to call the police first, then Vic. That way she could reassure him the police would take care of things. There was no need to scare him. He only needed to be informed so he could be alert.

Amber blinked back tears and punched the numbers. "Stay calm," she whispered as she looked around the room. The house had been checked out. She needed to be able to answer questions from the police rationally. As she waited for an answer, she glanced over to the hallway. "Oh no," she said faintly. She pushed the off button and placed the phone down on the desk. Her bedroom to the left and down the hallway was the only room she had checked. To the right, the guest bedroom in the front part of the house remained unchecked, and between the two bedrooms, a small bath. She hadn't gone to the kitchen either.

She tiptoed to the kitchen and flipped on the light—Nothing!

She let out a deep sigh and then went to a drawer, grabbed the biggest knife she could find, hurried back into the living room, and to the phone on the desk. She would call the police and then check out the front bedroom.

Cr-e-e-eak.

The sound came from the wood floor in the hallway, as if from the weight of a heavy footstep. There was no time to wait for help from the police. She steadied herself, pulled the knife up, held it out in front of her with two shaking hands, and moved forward cautiously. Approaching the hall opening, she looked to the right, and then to the left. No one was there. The bathroom in front of her was empty.

"I'm being hysterical," she said. "I need to get a grip! I almost called the police—how embarrassing that would have been." Then thoughts of the note flooded back and she started to shake.

"Someone's been here. Here, at my home, and he wants to punish me."

The Call

Amber hurried back to the phone and paused. Should she call 9-1-1 or the non-emergency number?

Amber picked up the phone and punched in 9-1-1.

Amber's assets were many, her internal strength one, however, clinging to independence with unbendable stubbornness in the light of danger was an astronomical defect. I felt her heart racing and pounding and heard her fearful thoughts. It was so difficult to remain detached. As a Soul Follower, we experience everything our assignees feel and think. Amber's body was tense in the "fight or flight" mode.

"Hello," a voice said from the other end of the phone line, then paused. "Hello? Is anyone *there*?"

"Vic. Is that you?" Amber couldn't remember actually punching in the numbers. "Did you call me?"

"What?"

She shook her head. "No, of course, you didn't call me. I called you. I guess I called your number automatically."

"I'm on your mind that much, huh? I'm not sure if I like being thought of routinely. I kind of like people to intentionally call me."

"Vic, listen."

"What's the matter? Are you okay? Did you get in a car accident?"

"No."

"Something's wrong. Where are you?"

Amber didn't answer, it was important to tell Vic about the note, but he didn't need to know she was scared. She didn't want to be one of "those" women, who expected men to rescue them whenever they were afraid. She hated that. Sure, she was frightened, that's why she wanted to call the police, but Vic didn't need to know about her fear.

"I'm okay."

"You sound shaky. What's the matter?"

Calling the police was not a sign of weakness she thought. Nevertheless, she didn't need Vic to play the male role and rush over. The police would come out. Vic just needed to be warned.

"Amber. Are you there?"

"Yes. You need to give me time to speak."

She and Vic had known each other for several months. They were close, but still, she kept her life private. They talked about the murders and Vic's worries about Phillip's safety. Amber supported Vic's attempts to fumble his way back into Phillip's life. Vic treated her as his equal, soliciting her advice, which was a compliment. Still, Amber insisted on remaining self-reliant. Her private way of thinking was very different then Vic's openness. I heard Vic often complain of Amber's arms-length attitude, but she refused to change.

"I . . . I meant to call the police."

"Police? Amber, what's going on?"

"I'm okay. It's nothing to panic about. It's only a note. I found it on my living room floor. I was calling the police because it may be connected to The Rainbow Killer."

"What! I'm coming over there." The sound of panic in his voice grew stronger. "Are you still at home?"

"Yes, but you don't have to come. I've checked the house. Everything is secure and I'll call the police."

"I'm coming," Vic insisted.

"Vic, wait. I needed to call you to tell you something about the note. Uh, it concerns you and Phillip. It talked about punishing sinners and me—"

"Punishing you? For what?" The panic sound in his voice grew stronger.

"Let me finish. The note said your souls belonged to the devil. And *sinners* needed to be punished."

"How'd the note get on your floor? Did someone break in?"

"No one broke in. You're yelling at me! Calm down." *Why is he scolding me? I'm not a child.*

Amber's heart pounded as fearful thoughts raced in her head. Her body was tense and the pressure almost unbearable.

"Were the doors locked?" Vic asked.

"Yes, my doors were locked," she said through clenched teeth. "He, or who-*ev-er*, must have pushed the note under my front door."

Amber approached every problem with logic. A problem represented a misplaced piece of a bigger picture—like a giant jigsaw puzzle mixed up.

Amber continued, "If whoever wrote the note is involved with the murders and if he knows about Phillip's *social relationships* . . ." Her thoughts jumbled with the words as she spoke. "And the three of us are connected, then the note makes sense."

"What did the note say," Vic asked.

"The envelope had my name on it." Amber was experiencing a mix of anger, for being so vulnerable, and regret, because of upsetting Vic, plus embarrassment for not being able to keep her house secure.

"Amber, you didn't answer me. What . . . did . . . the . . . note . . . say?"

"I was going to call the police," she explained as if not listening to his question. "So, they could see it, but I accidentally called you instead. I'm probably overreacting. You know, like Bennie is always doing—just being hysterical."

"Okay," Vic lowered his voice. "Amber, you're not hysterical."

It didn't matter now what the note said, it was obvious Vic was not going to let Amber handle the situation alone whether she liked it or not.

"You're trying to make sense of this note that could've been written by a murderer," Vic spoke slowly, "or at the very least, someone who is linked to the Rainbow Killings."

His calm tone was not helping Amber's nerves. To the contrary, fear swept over her and an involuntary tear trickled down her cheek.

"If that's so," Vic said. Amber's eyes searched the room as he spoke. "Then there's nothing sensible or rational about the situation. As the reporters have said, whoever is responsible for the murders thinks he is cleansing the world. I'm coming over. Understand? Keep the doors locked. And call the police!"

"Okay, but Vic, wait." She wiped her cheek dry. "Do you think the note could really be from The Rainbow Killer?"

"I don't know, you haven't read the note to me. Even if it's not him, he threatened you. Now hang up and call the police. I'm on my way."

"Vic . . ."

"What!"

"Please hurry."

Amber didn't want to believe it, but Vic said everything that had run through her mind. The murder count totaled eight, nine if Patrick was included. His body had never been located. Everybody's nerves were on edge in Tampa, even the straight people. A maniac roamed the streets.

Todd and Patrick were the first victims. Initially, Todd's death and Patrick's disappearance only merited two small spots in the local news. As the body count increased and the victim's names were reported repetitively in newscasts, the murders became more relevant to reporters, police, and John Q Public.

Vic hung up and Amber pressed the button to get a dial tone. She didn't care to think logically or try to compose herself anymore. Now she was terrified. Very terrified.

A man's voice answered, "9-1-1, what's your emergency?"

Even though Amber was not gay, knowing and having a circle of friends who were put a bulls-eye on her. The growing tally of victims made it obvious—

Hunting Season was Open.

The Intruder

A shadowy figure remained motionless outside Amber's bedroom window.

Seven houses down from the small frame bungalow, an old Ford pick-up truck sat at the curb. Two men in the front seat watched in the darkness staring in the direction of Amber's house.

"What is he doing down there?" the man in the passenger seat said.

"You think I can see in the dark? I'm not a bat, dip-shit."

The pint-sized man snickered. "Bats can't see. They're blind. And you call *me* stupid."

"Shut up," the skinny man said sitting in the driver's seat. He turned around, looked out the rear window, and then turned back. "Hurry up, come on and get your ass back here," he muttered as he drummed his fingers on the steering wheel. "Someone's going to call the cops if they see us sitting here."

"I say we leave him," the passenger said.

The man behind the steering wheel whipped his head around and glared at him. "You don't value your life, do you? We're not moving from here until he gets back."

Inside the bungalow, Amber had hung the phone up. The police dispatcher had assured her that a patrol car was in the area and would be there shortly. She stood for a minute, clutching the kitchen knife, then walked over to the couch and sat down to wait for the police. Vic would be there soon. She shouldn't have to wait very long.

Hope Vic doesn't get a ticket racing over here. If I know him, he'll be doing seventy through town.

15

Normally at this late hour, it would take Vic twenty minutes to get to Amber's house, but tonight he'd be there in ten.

Eight minutes passed.

The man hiding in the shadows outside the house relaxed his stance and looked around. He turned toward the window, inching his face past the window's edge to look inside. The bedroom remained lit but Amber was nowhere in the room.

He looked around the bushes for something to hoist himself up. Under the branches of a bush lay a large clay pot on its side. He bent down to grab it as a porch light came on from next door. He moved down into the bush to hide. A small, shaggy dog bounced down the steps as a man in a terrycloth bathrobe stepped out onto the stoop. "Hurry up Sheba," he called out.

The dog stood motionless at the grass edge and looked toward Amber's house growling.

"Sheba! Stop it. There's nothing out there," the man said. "Hurry up. It's probably that cat from down the street."

Distracted from her guard dog attempt, the fluffy animal lifted her floppy ears and looked back at the porch door with a perplexed look. A second later, she wagged her tail and turned back around, took two steps into the grass, and squatted. When she was finished, she bounded back up the steps and both man and dog disappeared inside. The porch light went out.

The figure hiding in the bushes grabbed the clay pot and set it underneath the window. He stepped onto the container and pulled out a nine-inch hunting knife from a sheaf attached to his belt. Balancing himself carefully, he pried the knife between the sashes where the lock was located.

Inside, Amber sat alert on the couch. She had never noticed how alive her house was with sound. Every inch of the old structure creaked. The expansion and contraction of the wood floor sent eerie sounds across the living room, characteristic of ghostly footsteps moving about the room to play mind games with her. The kitchen light hummed an irritating buzz, and the once calming sounds of crickets outside her window sang an unnerving melody.

She sat forward on the edge of the couch and watched the front door. The ceiling light, two table lamps, and a pole light near the desk illuminated the small living room. In fact, every light was on in the house. As she waited for the police, her mind began to whirl with the inanimate noises of the house. The human silence was ear piercing and she wanted to scream.

Amber tightened her grip on the knife and started to tap her foot, beating out a second-by-second countdown.

I should turn on some music . . . maybe the television. She looked around the room. "No. I need to be alert," she said aloud. "I won't be able to hear something with music on. I'm not overreacting. Like Vic said, I've received a threatening letter. That's reason enough to be concerned."

She tapped her foot faster, an unconscious effort to speed up time as her eyes darted from side to side, scanning the room. *I'm making myself more nervous just by sitting and waiting.*

Sounds of sirens in the distance interrupted her thoughts. *That's them—no, the police wouldn't put their sirens on to answer a call about a threatening letter.*

A frown crossed Amber's face. Then thoughts crept in that maybe the patrol car coming might have been sent to an accident first, but she dismissed the thought as silly. Certainly, there would be more than one patrol car in the area.

Hope Vic gets here soon.

There was a loud thump at the back of the house. She jumped, whipped around, and stood frozen. Facing the direction of the sound, she clutched the knife in her trembling hand. Her fear was as intense as the time her father talked her into riding the Ferris wheel when she was six years old. But this was not a scary amusement park ride—the danger was real.

The next sounds vibrated throughout the living room and windows shook as heavy, running steps outside raced around the house toward the front yard.

"Hey!" Someone shouted outside near the side window where Amber stood.

"That sounds like Vic," Amber said.

Streams of light pierced the sheer curtains, ricocheting about the room. The wooden floor shook repeatedly with more vibrations of running. The sounds echoed everywhere.

Three thunderous knocks hammered at her front door. Amber screamed.

"Tampa Police, ma'am, stay inside," a voice called from beyond.

Amber sat down. Her heart raced, her body trembled, but her fear disappeared as relief washed over her. The police were there . . . and Vic.

She waited for what seemed an eternity. After a few minutes, the police officer knocked again. Amber jumped up, hurried to the door, and opened it. She found a towering, stone-faced officer holding Vic's upper arm. He stood silently with his hands behind his back at her doorstep.

"Ma'am, I'm Officer Young. This man says you called him about the intruder?"

"Yes, I . . . uh . . . I called him right before calling 9-1-1."

"Then you do know him?"

"Of course."

The officer looked hard at Vic, holding his stare, then relaxed and pulled a small set of keys out of his pocket. "I'm sorry sir," he said. "I couldn't take your word only. I had two men running in the dark and there wasn't time to sort things out." He reached around

Vic's back and removed a set of handcuffs. Amber looked at Vic with wide eyes.

"Come in," she said. She turned and motioned the men into the house. They walked past her and took a seat on her camelback Victorian couch.

"There was someone hanging around the side of your residence," the officer said. He took out a small notebook and grabbed a pen out of his breast pocket while still glaring at Vic. "When I drove up, the intruder ran, and 'your friend' here took off with him."

Amber reassured the officer again that Vic had nothing to do with the intruder.

"All right then. I'll need to take some information from you." He took down Amber and Vic's names, their phone numbers, and the details about what had happened before his arrival.

Amber answered the questions and gave him the menacing note. Officer Young took the note, read it, and looked at the petite woman sitting in front of him. "Don't worry, Miss Moon, you were right to call us," he said in a softer tone. "I don't know if this guy is connected with the murders in town, but in any case, we need to take him seriously. He did more than just send a note, he showed up here. That's not your normal nut job."

"Do you think he'll come back?" Amber asked, terrified to hear the answer, but more afraid not to ask.

"No, I think he got scared off. Too bad I couldn't catch him." He turned to Vic and frowned. "Mr. Richardson, next time you need to stay out of the way of the police and let us do our job. When I pulled up, all I saw were two men running from the rear of Miss Moon's property. You were lucky you weren't hurt."

"Let you do your job?" Vic said. "I got here and that *nut job*, as you called him, was trying to get into Amber's bedroom window. I didn't know when you would get here. What was I supposed to do? Sit at the curb and hope she wasn't murdered?"

19

"Of course not. We're glad people step forward. However, we don't want any civilians to get hurt in the process. So, what I'm saying is, next time when the police arrive on the scene, back off."

"Next time?" Amber interrupted. "I thought he was scared off."

"Yes, ma'am, he's scared tonight and probably won't come back in the next few hours. Besides, I'm going to make my presence known."

The officer reached into his shirt pocket, pulled out a card, turned it over, and started writing. "I'm going to give you Detective Harrison's number. He's in charge of the investigation of the . . . uh . . . Rainbow Murders."

He handed the card to Amber. "I've written tonight's case number on the front and Harrison's number is on the back."

Robotic-like Amber took the card. The officer continued, "I'm not saying this guy had anything to do with those crimes. You probably won't see him again, but his wording in the note, well . . . it needs some investigation, that's all."

Officer Young stood to leave. Amber looked up at the tall uniformed man, her eyes wide and watery with tears forming. The young officer sheepishly smiled. As a trained professional, he needed to remain detached even though the beauty of the frightened woman sitting in front of him would have challenged the composure of the toughest marine.

"It's possible Detective Harrison may be of help," Young added. "We've been ordered to inform Harrison's squad of any kind of link, no matter what. You need to call him in the morning."

He turned to Vic, "Mr. Richardson, will you follow me outside?"

Amber gave a confirming nod to the officer's instructions and sat staring at the card in her hand. As the two men reached the door, she looked up and called out, "Vic, you're coming back in after you're done talking with the officer, aren't you?"

Her voice sounded like a child asking a parent to leave a nightlight on at bedtime.

"Sure," Vic said. He gave a little laugh and added, "I need to make certain this big guy gets to his car safely."

Outside, Officer Young turned to Vic, "Look, I'm sorry if I was rough on you in there. There may not be any connection, but with these murders in the city, every weirdo in town is coming out of the woodwork. I think Miss Moon needs to be very careful." He looked over Vic's shoulder at the house and frowned. "It wouldn't hurt if you stuck around tonight."

"Okay," Vic said. "I'll make sure she calls that detective first thing in the morning."

"Good. Don't tell her I thought you should stick around. It'll only scare her."

"No problem. I wouldn't think of telling."

The officer opened the door of the cruiser and got in. "She looked pretty frightened already. Good night, sir. I'll be driving by. I'm on duty until seven a.m."

He pulled away, disappearing down the narrow brick street.

The Devil's Servants

Moments earlier, the shadowy figure disappeared into the darkness as the police officer shouted at Vic to halt. Seconds after Vic had stopped, the sound of tires squealed off into the darkness.

The pick-up sped down Amber's tree-lined street and raced toward Dale Mabry. At the corner, it made a quick turn as the wide-eyed driver gripped the steering wheel. The dark-clad figure, who had jumped into the back seat of the getaway pick-up, sat breathing heavily. The tires squealed again as the vehicle curved onto the entrance ramp of the highway and headed out of town toward Ybor City. The men braced themselves as the truck fishtailed.

"Take it easy!" the man bellowed from the rear seat. "We don't need to get stopped for speeding."

Behind the wheel, the skinny man's eyes conveyed a sense of sheer panic. His sweaty palms held the wheel in a death grip as he slowed down. The front-seat passenger's face was ashen. The driver glanced in the rearview mirror at the man dressed in black. He sat muttering, his face hardened into a scowl, as he clenched a huge knife in his hand.

"The cop car passed us," the driver said. "I wanted to warn you, Samuel, but if I had honked that woulda' tipped him off. But, no way, would we leave you."

The front seat passenger let loose his grip on the dash and chimed in. "The road was dark. We couldn't see nothin'. But we heard the cop shouting." He slouched back into the seat, which made him barely visible through the front window. "What happened back there?"

"Her friend showed up and ran after me and the cop pulled his gun on him," Samuel answered. "I heard the cop shout, 'Freeze or I'll shoot.' That Richardson fellow would've caught me if cops weren't so stupid. Richardson stopped, and I kept running until I got to the truck."

"Cops sure are dumb." The small man laughed and snorted. "So, the cop didn't catch you peeping?"

The man in the back straightened up into a rigid posture and sneered at the man. "I told you, you idiot, I was delivering a message. Weekends, she usually doesn't come home until after midnight."

The skinny man behind the wheel shot a glaring look at his sidekick and shook his head warning him to stop talking. He then looked in the mirror at the man in the back. "Never mind what Pete says, he doesn't think. He couldn't think his way out of a paper bag."

Pete gave a dirty look to the driver, then slumped deeper in his seat and folded his arms in front of him as they drove on.

The man in the backseat said, "Did the cops see you parked?"

"Nah," answered the driver. "We ducked down as they drove by. Where to now, Samuel?"

Pete perked up and giggled, rubbing his hands together. "We gonna go do some fag bashing now?"

"You are really scum, aren't you?" Samuel said.

"What the hell," Pete sputtered. "You sticking up for them fags now? And I ain't scum."

"Not all the lost souls are gone forever. Some still have time to repent. Time to be born again. Even you Brother Pete." The man touched a silver cross that hung around his neck as he spoke. "Your purpose is not to serve the devil. You are just an instrument sent to me from God, to help me serve Him. We are all God's servants. My purpose is to lead his lost sheep back to Him. I warn you, Brother

Pete, stop serving the Devil. The Devil is my enemy. I vow I will strike him and his followers down."

"Shut up, Pete," whispered the driver.

Treasure

Six Months earlier in an Atlanta Boardroom

A group of thirty-something men sat around a mahogany conference desk. They were clones of each other, each in dark suits with silk ties and matching red pocket squares.

Bruce Whitehouse, President, and owner of the company walked in looking distinctively different, but then, he always stood out from the crowd. He never wore a traditional suit. Usually wore a sports coat, designer and the best tailored, of course. Tan was the color choice most often and typically a Joseph Abboud original. Only custom-made dress shirts would do to complete his attire, but no ties, never a tie, not even at a black-tie affair.

Ahead of Bruce walked Vice-president and co-owner, Charleston Black. He was born privileged, which provided him with the best Ivy League education money could buy. He always wore suits, gray or navy.

The group of men already seated at the table straightened in their chairs and watched Charleston as he entered. His thick, premature silver-gray hair gave him a commanding and distinctive appearance far greater than his thirty-two years should have warranted. Moreover, his family's money commanded attention.

"Glad everyone is here on time," Charleston said as he took a seat. "Bruce says he has something interesting for us again."

Bruce stopped to turn the lights out and walked over to a laptop at the head of the table. "Gentlemen, I present to you our next investment horizon."

On a pull-down screen flashed two written lines: *Tampa Bay, Home of the Bucs. The Future is Unlimited.*

Mumbles and chuckles rolled across the room from the six clones. Charleston put his hand up signaling the men. "Quiet." Silence fell. When Charleston spoke, everyone listened. "Look here, Bruce. I admit you're a genius when it comes to having a vision for investments—but you're not suggesting we purchase a football team, are you?"

"Of course not, Chip," Bruce said.

The Black family's lineage dated back to the days when Sherman marched through Atlanta. The family influence swayed decisions in town involving everything from the preparation of the events at the Georgia Dome to what the local country club would serve for Sunday buffet. Having the very name, Charleston Black III, meant authority and could pave the way for anything Bruce wanted. He knew if he sold his idea to him, the rest of the board would dutifully fall into place.

"I have my eye on an area east of Tampa," Bruce said, "an area that should interest you, too."

Bruce and Charleston had known each other for only five short years, and in that time, they had become close friends—but not by accident. Bruce's background was not only worlds apart from Charleston's family riches, but the two men's worlds did not even operate in the same galaxy.

Bruce's family had always been poor, generations poor. He was determined to separate himself from the humiliation that kept the poor down and beaten. Bruce vowed to change things and stop the ache he had inside, which came from wanting a future. A future like the one wealthy people took for granted. So, he did his research and that is what brought Charleston and Bruce together.

Bruce met Charleston for the first time on a hot and steamy Fourth of July. Dressed in clothes that took two weeks of paychecks, he was ready to meet Charleston. Bruce needed investment money, plus the clout that came with having a member of the Black family support.

He walked with conviction right up to the Georgian mansion that was Charleston's home, climbed the steps, and hammered on the front door. When the butler answered, Bruce said that he was there to see Chip. "Pronto!"

Bruce was a driven man and his actions required boldness. No one in all of Georgia ever called Charleston Black III—Chip. Never, ever! However, there was no time to waste. Bruce's plan was to be a millionaire by the age of thirty. That day, he not only got to see Charleston, he also persuaded him to finance him completely. By the third venture, both men had made a profit of ten times what Charleston's initial cash investment had been. They formed a steadfast partnership and Bruce even got Charleston to agree to name the company "Whitehouse and Partners, Inc."

After that day, Bruce led a charmed life. His plan to be a millionaire by thirty years old was altered slightly—instead, he became a millionaire a month before his twenty-eighth birthday.

"Okay, no football team. Show us what you have," Charleston said.

Bruce pushed a button on his laptop. A slide show of photographs started.

"I present to you, Ybor City," Bruce projected in a loud voice across the room.

Images of a street with boarded-up storefronts flashed on the screen. Bruce clicked the keys, advancing additional pictures.

Whispers and sputters rolled across the darkened room.

The next photos appeared of small frame houses flashed on the wall, followed by a large brick building with broken windows and a sign on the door, "Keep Out. Private Property."

"What! You want us to invest in this?" Blair Casey's voice soured the room. "Now we're in building renovation? Let Habitat for Humanity do it." He laughed and the men on each side chuckled. "We're more interested in things like Broadway and Manhattan. Give us a break, old boy." Blair narrowed his eyes and frowned. "You want us to lose our money as fast as you made yours?" He folded his arms defiantly and gave a disgruntled sound.

Bruce ignored him and switched on the lights. He expected negativity from Blair and always got it. Blair came from old money and resented that Bruce had been allowed into the elite circle of wealth. Blair was jealous that Bruce had a nose for investments and a natural, creative ability to make money. Something Blair never had. The more successful Bruce's investments got, although they made money for the board, the stronger Blair's hatred grew for Bruce.

"Gentlemen," Bruce said as he walked back to the table and flipped open a folder. He grabbed some 8x10 glossies. "Take a look." He moved around the table, tossing photos down of different angles of the brick building from the slide show. A photo in front of each man.

"Ybor City was once known as the 'Cigar Capital of the World,'" he said. "Those small frame houses make up a community that surrounds the business area of Seventh Avenue. This area is rich in Cuban, Spanish, and Italian backgrounds and steeped in history. The neighborhood people used to work hand-rolling cigars in factories like the boarded-up brick buildings in the slide presentation you just viewed. The area has deep roots, and it's as exotic as you can get. This is a virtual gold mine and all we need to do is wake up the sleeping dragon."

Charleston picked up a photo and examined it. Each man followed suit and picked up a photo.

Bruce reached over to the middle of the conference room table where a cloth draped over something. With the flair of a magician, he snatched the cloth off to reveal an elaborate model. It resembled the red brick building from the slideshow, with perfectly scaled windows, doors, and several floors high. Around the perimeter were painted patio areas, trees, and bushes forming gardens around a blue kidney-shaped area, which designated a swimming pool.

A slightly taller structure sat across a painted street. Square cut openings revealed scale-size cars on various floors inside, obviously a model of a parking garage.

"This is our next investment. You wanted Manhattan, Blair? Take a history lesson from New Yorkers. A bunch of New York artists seized the opportunity and took a rundown area in Manhattan with cheap rent, moved in, called it an exclusive artist's neighborhood, added shops, and named it SoHo. That started a trend that is now recognized across the country as the place to go. Blair, you like New York? Take a look at the next SoHo."

Bruce walked around the table again rapidly throwing more pictures down. Photographs of architectural details. Close-up shots of arched brickwork. Massive cornerstones and retro tile floors, still intact as if lost in time. He spoke faster as his excitement grew.

"Once, there had been over two hundred of these beautiful redbrick masterpieces in Tampa—the cigar factories. Now less than fifty remain. We can buy this 26,788-square-foot abandoned factory for peanuts. The renovation will be massive, but I propose after we get the Historical Society's backing, we will make history."

Charleston leaned forward, examining the model. "Okay, say we do this. What will the building be used for?" Charleston had a shrewd business sense, although he trusted Bruce's vision, he required answers before making any decisions.

"An art gallery will occupy half of the first floor. The rest of that floor will hold a stylish drugstore for essentials and a small gourmet shop with unique spices, fruits, and imported cheeses from around the world." Bruce's eyes sparkled as he was caught up in his enthusiasm. "The ground level will be for the management offices and a large fitness center for the residents. On the second floor, we need to lease to elite service businesses, such as a spa, beauty salon, and fashion boutiques. The remaining floors, we divide up into a handful of luxury apartments. To buy into the premier place to live, they'll fetch top dollar."

"You really think we can pull this off?" Charleston asked.

"Absolutely! And our key is getting this man on board." He pulled out a picture of Matt Connelly. "This man owns a gallery in south Tampa. His business savvy and connections in Tampa are extensive. With him, we have our SoHo."

Transformation

Months Later in South Tampa

A small stucco building stood with a closed sign on the door. The hand lettering on the window read *Connelly's Hidden Treasures and Art Gallery*. Inside, a tall, dark-haired man slid a massive oil painting into a carton. On the outside of the box in big letters read *Connelly-Ybor City*.

The final week of packing gave Matt Connelly bittersweet feelings. He was a part of the South Tampa location as much as the Spanish tile roof on the building. He had worked years establishing his spot in the community and shared a closeness with the people in the area. Although he had a loyal clientele, Matt knew that some regulars wouldn't follow him. Still, relocating to the cigar factory named, *Casa de Ybor*, was a wise business decision. Actually, only a fool would have turned down Bruce Whitehouse's offer. This opportunity of a lifetime offered all the benefits of an investor to Matt without requiring him to put up any money. That did *not* happen every day.

Matt picked up some files and placed them into an empty box. *This is the right thing to do.*

If he had not jumped at this opportunity, it would've been like turning his back on the goose that laid golden eggs.

Why a company in Atlanta thinks so highly of me, and my business ability to put all the money up to get my gallery in their building . . . I just can't figure it out.

Not only did Whitehouse's company pay for his move, they also consulted with him in all discussions that involved the build-out of the gallery and footed that bill, too. The space they allotted

31

for Matt's gallery was triple the size of his South Tampa location. The limited, elite condominiums would open possibilities beyond belief. To say Matt found the Golden Goose was an understatement.

The door opened and a slender blond-haired man sauntered in. "Oh, Matt, you have everything packed. You're really going to do it."

"Bennie, I told you it's a good move. Don't worry. You act like it's your gallery."

"I know. I need to butt out. I'm not strong like you. I worry about people. You're always so sure of things, confident, just like my Ken."

"Well, stop worrying. Man up a little and quit being such a woman."

Bennie was a good friend but it irritated Matt that Bennie was so openly gay. He had a way of talking with his hands—and his walk—he swayed. It seemed to be imprinted into his DNA, no different than the color of his eyes or hair. Hoping he would change was a futile wish.

Matt was not going to let a friend's apprehension spoil his excitement about what the future held for him. Most galleries struggled to stay open. Many had to rely on framing jobs entirely to cover monthly bills. Some galleries even stocked gift items like artist note cards and art-related books to help with expenses.

Matt had been blessed. He built a successful business with art sales enough to cover bills, which made his framing sales gravy. Now Bruce Whitehouse and his big Atlanta Company wanted him in on their plan to breathe life into Ybor City again. Yes, Matt Connelly was very fortunate. It was inevitable that life would change drastically in the year ahead and things would never be the same.

A Gentle Giant

Through a timeline of events, irreversible changes can alter so many lives. One chance meeting. The decision to turn left, instead of right, or walk into a new gallery. Minor details that change life's equation and a person's destiny is changed forever.

* * *

Amber hurried to her car. She put the color board, along with her laptop in the back seat and slid behind the steering wheel. Her watch hands read at three o'clock. If she didn't hit traffic, she could still make it over the bridge and to Ybor City before five.

Once on her way, she would call her mother. Traffic had already started to become heavy, however, each lane moved along at a steady pace. She grabbed her phone and held down the number one to speed dial, Suzanne. Her mother answered on the second ring.

"Hi, Mom. Thought we could talk while I'm driving. I just finished with the Carsons. Everything went okay, I suppose."

"You suppose? What didn't they like, honey?" Like most mothers, Suzanne knew when her daughter's tone spoke differently than her words.

"Oh Mom, it's so frustrating. They insisted on mass production prints for the walls. It's like giving them a famous Valentino gown and they insist on wearing sneakers with it."

"Honey, don't be a snob. Prints are fine. It's not like they wanted to put up a paint-by-number."

"Yeah, I know, but thanks to you and Dad I have great contacts. They could have some wonderful original artwork. I'm probably the only designer within a hundred miles—no, make that

33

a thousand miles, whose parents formed lasting friendships with great artists from their hippie backpacking days in the 70s. For goodness sake Mom, I have that original Andy Warhol on my living room wall personally signed to you! I could get them anything from expensive, to not so expensive, but nooo they want prints."

"Amber, don't be label-conscious. Remember what I told you when I gave you Andy's sketch? Money and things do not make you happy. Anyway, Andy was just a little too weird for me. If he was still alive now, I'm sure he would not be one of your contacts. However, he was so right when he said everyone has their "fifteen minutes of fame.""

"Yeah, but if the Carsons would have only listened to me about the art . . .."

"Their priorities are different than yours, not wrong," Suzanne said firmly. "Don't get too big for your britches."

"Okay, okay. You're right. Mom, I could care less about labels. Really. Anyway, at least, I talked them into allowing me to pick out the prints. I thought I would look at the new gallery, you know the one in the renovated cigar factory, Casa de Ybor. Maybe some local artists will have some giclées there to pick from."

"One of my friends had a one-man show at the old gallery in South Tampa. I met him, the owner, that is. The owner's name is Matt Connelly. Handsome man, and very nice. Friends of mine say anytime they do a show with him they sell. He's a terrific salesperson, but not a pushy type. People like him and buy because he's down-to-earth and sincere. My kind of person."

"Mom, I'm coming up on the bridge and I always lose reception there. I need to hang up now."

Amber closed her phone and slipped it into her purse. Traffic was moving. There would be plenty of time to get to the gallery. She had heard about the cigar factory renovation and the gallery relocation for months. It seemed the local news was obsessed with any bit of information about what was happening in Ybor.

A few minutes after crossing the bridge, Amber exited the highway and headed to the *Hidden Ybor Treasure Art Gallery*. She parked behind the building, across the street in a vacant dirt lot. After locking her car, she headed toward the gallery. As she left the dirt lot, she passed a posted sign, which read, *Future Parking Garage for Casa de Ybor*. Until construction was completed, the small dirt lot would have to do since work vehicles and barriers blocked nearby parking on the street. The area around the building was roped off and showed signs of additional renovation. Another sign was inside the ropes with the words, *Future Home of Casa de Ybor Luxury Condominiums* in big script lettering. This sign showed a picture rendering of the building with the outside patio areas and lavish tropical plants bordering a large swimming pool.

Once in front of the building, Amber stopped and looked at the stairs leading up to the massive double doors. "Wow! This gallery is sitting on a gold mine," she said. Even in its incomplete state, Amber couldn't help but be impressed. It was apparent it would be breathtaking once the whole project was completed. "Every person moving in will need artwork," Amber muttered as she climbed the outside stairs. "And who wouldn't want to buy a condo here?"

Amber entered the double doors, which led into an interior lobby. The tile floor was a black and white octagon mosaic. To her left, a wall of glass enabled her to see into the gallery. When she entered a soft chime chirped from an electric eye stationed at the door as she passed by it.

Twelve-foot, floor-to-ceiling windows stretched across the back wall. Wonderful natural light streamed in. The room had vignettes stationed around with half walls separating each, which enabled an extended view of the entire gallery. An easel posted the gallery's current exhibit of collective works of twenty artists. An array of different mediums from painting to sculpture to photography could be seen.

To the far-right side, a frame shop area displayed a huge wall of frame samples. From behind the wall, someone with a deep voice called out, "I'll be right out, Pumpkin."

Seconds later, Matt walked out with a warm smile. He towered every bit of six-foot-two, a powerfully built man. Husky, not fat, just solid and muscular with movie star looks.

"Oh, dear. I'm sorry," he said, looking a little red-faced. "I was expecting my daughter and my ex-wife. I thought you were them." He extended his hand. "Please forgive me."

His handshake was firm and friendly. But not one of those, vice-gripping, bone bone-breaking ones, that supposedly implies confidence while conveying importance.

"Welcome," he said with a pleasant smile.

Amber smiled, "Beautiful place you have."

"Yes, I love the light. It's a lot bigger than my old gallery, I'm still getting used to it—it's a little overwhelming for me." He smiled again and his hazel-brown eyes seemed to twinkle with the same penetrating soulful look that was characteristic of Johnny Depp. "I was organizing some new pieces that just arrived, and was in the back getting supplies to hang them." He looked at Amber intently. "You don't look familiar. Is this the first time you've visited either of my galleries? My old one was in South Tampa."

"Yes, I'm familiar with it, but never got in to visit."

"I didn't think so; I'm usually very good at remembering faces. What brings you in?"

"I have a client wanting some prints. I normally work directly with artists and don't get the opportunity to visit galleries much. I recently read about this gallery in *Tampa Bay Magazine.*"

"Great. I've gotten a lot of good responses from that magazine article." He turned back to the display of frames and walked over to a bin that held artwork. "I have matted prints from some of my Tampa artists here. They're very reasonably priced and a beautiful option for the client with a budget."

He flipped through the first few pieces, then hesitated as if he had forgotten something and quickly turned around to face Amber. "I've not introduced myself. I'm Matt Connelly."

"Nice meeting you, I'm Amber Moon."

Amber liked Matt instantly but didn't know why. Perhaps it was because he seemed so genuine and comfortable, like an old friend.

"Amber Moon, what an unusual name. Pretty . . . I know I recognize it."

"You may have seen my company name, Amber Moon Designs. *Tampa Bay Magazine* did an article the month before yours. They featured one of the homes I did over at Madeira Beach. They ran interior and exterior photos of the house. It had an old Florida look with turquoise palm tree cutouts mounted on the shutters, a white tile roof, and sat on the Intracoastal Waterway."

"Maybe."

"There was a picture of their yacht, the *Utopia.* The length of that boat was as long as the house was wide."

"We Floridians love our toys, don't we?" Matt said and then chuckled. "I know I must've seen the article but I just can't place it. What did the inside of the house look like?"

"Well, I guess what you would remember the most would be the room with the white baby grand piano. The piano sat in a typical Florida room with wall-to-wall Miami windows overlooking the dock. The wide-angle shot the photographer took showed the outside view, which made the room look much larger. In reality, it was small—all the rooms were. The project was a challenge but the house was very memorable. It turned out to be my favorite design job."

"I remember now. You put blood-red roses on the piano. I loved it. Simple, but elegant. Using the casualness of the rattan with the high-tech look of the glass accent pieces was brilliant."

He really does remember. Amber blushed. "Thank you."

They talked for a few more minutes. She was impressed with how Matt remembered every detail and was sure he noticed in the magazine photos that she only used one painting in the entire house. He never mentioned it, like other gallery owners would've done. He seemed to focus on the overall look. She respected that, and he never commented on how purchasing paintings from his gallery in the future would make her design jobs better.

After that day, Amber and Matt developed a strong friendship. She liked bouncing design ideas off him and grew to depend on his opinion. They would talk two or three times a week, but it was not only about design, they would chitchat like girlfriends. Still, Amber was not aware of all the expertise Matt possessed in marketing and event planning, nor was she aware of his extensive contacts in the business community. That knowledge would come later, after Matt's call about the fundraiser. That was when the proverbial "Pandora's Box" opened.

Deadly Spiders

Four-fifteen on a Wednesday afternoon, Amber's phone rang. She heard Matt's familiar voice, "Moonbeam. Do you have a minute?"

She had made it all through her childhood and teenage years without having the nickname, *Moonbeam*, from the 70s hippie generation pinned to her. Now for some reason, Matt chose to reserve it affectionately for her. However, it didn't bother her when it came from Matt, especially since he never called her Moonbeam in public.

"For you, of course, I even have five or ten minutes. What's up, Matt?"

"I'm organizing this *thing*. A fundraiser, in conjunction with a month-long art exhibit. I'm going to host a VIP party and auction to kick it off."

"Well count me in," Amber said and then jokingly added. "That is if I'm on you're A-list." She didn't hear any laughter resulting from her clever wit, only silence from the other end of the phone. "Matt, are you there?"

"I think . . . uh . . . you should know what the fundraiser is for first before you commit to it."

"Matt, anything you're hosting is okay by me. Unless it's . . . sleazy. Is it?" She laughed, but still, there was no laughter.

"Of course, not." After a brief delay, Matt said, "It's to raise money for AIDS Awareness."

"Oh. Okay. I'm all right with that. I mean I'm straight, but everyone knows by now that it's not just a gay disease."

"Good, then I'll send you an invitation. It's going to be August tenth. That's a Friday, at seven o'clock. It should be a great night.

And what goes around comes around Moonbeam. There are going to be some important people there. Good contacts."

"Now you're talking. You know, it's all about me."

"Oh, yeah. That's why we get along together so well," he said. "Thanks, I'll be in touch."

Matt had not shared much about his personal life, even with their closeness. Amber wouldn't have ever known he had a daughter or an ex-wife if he hadn't been expecting them the day she met him. She wondered why he chose AIDS for the fundraiser.

The spotlight on the disease had dimmed since the 80s when the movie star, Rock Hudson's homosexuality was revealed and the news leaked out about him dying of AIDS. That announcement turned AIDS into the charity of choice. Celebrities seemed to line up to host fundraisers. In 2009, a family member of someone who had been touched by the disease might do fundraisers or host benefits but other than those times, people didn't give the disease much attention. Amber didn't know what drove Matt's involvement. However, she didn't feel comfortable probing him for an answer.

In the weeks to follow, as Matt's plans continued, he called in favors by requesting some long-time business friends to help with the event. The number of people wanting to get involved grew daily. Some of the strongest supporters were prominent leaders of the community. Things were rolling along at lightning speed.

One week after Matt's call, Amber turned on the evening news.

"A few months ago, we reported about the excitement surrounding the renovation of a historic cigar factory in Ybor City," the voice blasted from the television. "The event of the year is now in the making. Legendary businessman and gallery owner, Matt Connelly, has announced plans for an art exhibit and auction /

private party to help kick off the sale of luxury condos at Casa de Ybor.

Co-hosting the event is Bruce Whitehouse of Whitehouse and Partners, the investment company doing the renovation of the building. Stay tuned to hear more after this commercial break. Our sources tell us the Mayor of Tampa is one of the people on the guest list."

"Whoa, Matt you weren't kidding when you said your party was going to be big," Amber muttered.

A few days later, Matt told Amber he was inundated with every business owner in town wanting to join the cause after the news reports. In the weeks that followed, every time Amber picked up the newspaper there was another article about the VIP party and art exhibit. A Presidential Inaugural Ball couldn't have gotten much more attention. It was the buzz of the city and predicted to be the event of the year.

Three weeks later. Downtown Tampa.
"Hi Sheri," Amber said to the receptionist on the fifth floor at one of the biggest law firms in Tampa. "Mr. Bennett wanted me to drop off this contract. It's for the art in his office."

"He's still in court."

"It's not a problem; he can just sign it and put it in the mail. Tell him I'll call him when the artwork is ready. It should be ten days, or so."

"Okay. I'll put the contract on his desk so he'll have it in the morning."

"Thanks. Have to run. I want to beat the afternoon traffic. I must get over to the Westshore area with some material samples I promised a client."

Amber hurried out and was on Kennedy Boulevard by 4:30. As she got close to the Channel 13 building, she noticed a large crowd carrying demonstration signs.

Wonder what this is about? There must be fifty or sixty people up there.

As she drove farther, angry screams from the crowd seeped in through the closed car windows. One protester called into a bullhorn, "Homo's don't need VIP parties. AIDS is your punishment. Leave Tampa, we don't want you"

As Amber passed, she saw one of the painted homemade signs.

Casa de Ybor Gallery
Give art back to the straight community.

Traffic slowed in front of her car as rubber-neckers passed by the protesters. Blue and red lights flashed in her rearview mirror diverting Amber's attention from the protesters. When she looked back at the sidewalk, she saw a smaller second group walking toward the volatile crowd.

"Homos don't need art to buy," the protestors shouted. "They need to go away and die."

The approaching group, with arms locked together, formed a wall of force. On the front line, in the middle, was a Latin-looking man in a pink T-shirt with, I'M GAY AND HERE TO STAY, printed across the front. He carried a bullhorn and led the group's chant:

"We're here! We're here!
Out of the closet and into the streets.
We're here!"

"Gosh Matt, you didn't just get the attention of the mayor and the business community," Amber muttered. "You stirred the pot up good."

Trouble was coming to a boil and fast. The fanatics were crawling out of the woodwork, as fast as a million hatching spiders.

Alone in Danger

The night of the gala, Andy pulled into the parking lot and checked his watch. *Good. Five o'clock, enough time to get the tables set up for the wine and refreshments.*

He wanted to be earlier but ran into unexpected traffic; still, there was plenty of time before guests would arrive. As Andy turned off the ignition, he noticed the yellow jeep parked two spaces over from him. *Saffron is here.*

The lot only had two cars in it, his made three. Andy didn't know the difference between a Cadillac and a Mazda—cars just weren't his thing. However, he knew Saffron's bright yellow jeep because it stood out from the norm. *I wonder why she's here so early. Maybe Matt is having her greet the guests at the door.*

Andy turned around and surveyed his back seat filled with supplies. Plastic bags crammed full with cups, napkins, linens, and party essentials sat waiting. On the back floorboard were boxes filled with an assortment of wines. Everything needed for the gallery grand opening and VIP fundraiser party. He figured that he would take in the paper supplies first, and then come back with help to carry in the bottles of wine.

As he stepped out of the car and turned around to grab the bags, he noticed a blue pick-up on the street creeping toward the parking lot. The right front fender of the truck was dull brownish-red. Andy recognized the sanded look of prepped metal for painting because his cousin did auto bodywork for a local garage.

The vehicle continued at a snail's pace.

"Wonder what's up with them," Andy mumbled as he gathered five bags in each hand.

Keeping a watchful eye on the truck, he pushed the car door shut with his hip. The unknown men sat on the sides of the truck bed staring hard in Andy's direction. A cold chill went up his spine as their eyes met.

They look like bad news to me, Andy thought. He moved briskly toward the corner of the street. Call it paranoia if you like, but his instincts screamed, "Beware!"

The Ybor City streets at this early hour were normally deserted. Andy sensed the men didn't belong there. Ybor City partygoers didn't start showing up for the bars and clubs that lined Seventh Avenue until long after sunset. Once night fell, even the empty side streets would come alive with activity.

As Andy hurried, his mind locked onto the scruffy-looking men in the back of the pickup with their gray-white t-shirts and patched jeans. *They definitely are not dressed for the gallery's VIP party.*

The driver was well-groomed and dressed in a button-up black shirt and noticeably better dressed than his companions. Nevertheless, instinctively something still bothered Andy about him.

"Even if the driver is dressed like Johnny Cash, I'm sure he's *not* on the VIP guest list any more than his buddies," Andy muttered as he shook his head and kept walking down the street.

Because of the killings in Tampa, every gay and lesbian person had to be more aware of his or her surroundings.

"Yeah," yelled the tall skinny man, "he's one of them."

Andy gave a quick look back in the direction of the truck and saw the pick-up speed up to the curb and screech to a halt about thirty yards away. The two men in the bed of the truck grabbed something from the floor and jumped over the side onto the street.

"Time for a game of *Smear the Queer*," the smaller man yelled. He held a baseball bat in his hand high above his head and then cheered, "Yahoo!"

The tall skinny one held a foot-long chunk of wood in his hand. It looked like part of a broken fence post. The driver bounded out of his door with a tire iron in his hand.

Andy's eyes widened as he froze.

The smaller man spoke again, "Let's get him and *straighten* him out." Then he giggled hysterically. All three of the men took off running toward Andy.

There was no thinking or guessing about the situation now. Andy kicked into gear and ran. His heart pounded as if it would burst out of his chest and he ran toward the corner. At the end of the street, he wheeled the corner with arms stretched out on either side for balance, like a high-wire walker at a circus. Still holding tight to the bags, they violently swung into one another. He almost fell as his feet pivoted to make the turn, seeking traction to move forward. His feet seemed to spin in place, resembling a stationary cartoon character with whirling feet.

Then his feet propelled him forward. Seconds later, he reached the front of the gallery and raced up the stairs taking them two at a time. At the top, the door flung open inches from his face and Andy jolted to a stop, almost falling backward. The bags swung back and forth in his hands.

Saffron and Claire stepped out looking startled.

"You're in a hurry," Saffron said.

They didn't notice Andy's pursuers who were now crossing the street in a fast walk.

Andy looked back panting and saw the three thugs walking toward a boarded-up building. Reaching the building, they leaned against the weather-worn wall, slid their weapons behind their legs, and glared at him.

Andy turned back to Saffron and Claire who were staring at him with puzzled looks.

"Oh, you know me," Andy said. He paused and gasped for breath. "I'm always in a rush. Don't like to leave things to the last minute."

He didn't want to alarm them and upset things with the opening only a few hours away. This night had taken months of planning. No ill-bred degenerates were going to disrupt the night's festivities if he had anything to do with it. "What are you doing here so early?" Trying to be nonchalant.

"Saffron's going to play during the preview," Claire answered.

Claire and Saffron had been together for almost six years. They were so different outwardly, but internally, their beliefs were in harmony. When Saffron met Claire, they hit it off instantaneously and a whirlwind romance began. That is if you could call it a romance. Saffron never would show her soft side, not even to Claire. Nevertheless, they were as devoted to each other as other couples who had been married for thirty years. Their serene devotion was an unspoken private connection to each other.

"You're wearing your usual uniform," Andy mocked as he looked at Saffron. "Nice to see you dressed up for the party."

Saffron was a stereotypical image of a lesbian. Rough and butch. She sported a blue jean jacket that looked as if it had gone through a street fight. She never went anywhere without it. It was like a second skin.

"What's wrong with this? It's clean. I like it—besides my fans haven't complained yet. They still come to hear me sing and buy my music."

Safforn's argument had value. Her popularity in the Bay area was unmatched from other local singers. Last month she released her fifth CD and she was the favorite topic on the radio with the disc jockeys comparing her to Melissa Etheridge.

"You look fine," Claire said, putting a comforting hand on her shoulder. "Andy's taste is more sophisticated, that's all."

"All I meant was that maybe you could wear a dress occasionally," Andy said. "Lavender or yellow with your jet-black hair draping on your shoulders—how exotic would that be?"

Andy was right about her looks being dramatic. Saffron's "look" was as popular as her music. She wore her hair straight, parted on the side, and tucked behind one ear, where a sole earring hung—a brown-speckled feather earring with a turquoise bead. Saffron's fans recognized it as her personal signature. Her photographer suggested her fifth CD have a photo of just the earring sitting on a plain white background and the title, *Sincerely from Saffron,* scripted. Saffron loved the idea. All the other covers had featured Saffron with her guitar.

Saffron was delighted because she hated posing for pictures. Hated anything that fussed over her, what was important to her was her music . . . and Claire

"Dresses are not for me," Saffron said as she blinked her coffee-colored eyes to hide her upset. "So get over it because it's not going to happen."

Claire jumped in, changing the subject. "We're on our way to get a drink over at the Green Iguana."

"No!" Andy shouted. He quickly glanced behind him. The three men were still across the street. Then Andy turned back to the women.

Saffron and Claire looked surprised. Saffron raised one eyebrow, "No?"

"I mean . . . I need your help," Andy said as he placed his arms around the two women turning them around toward the door, gently pushing and herding ahead. Appealing to their good hearts would probably be the best way to stop them from leaving alone. Saffron and Claire would never turn their backs on a friend in need.

Andy and Saffron had been friends for several years. Except for Claire, Andy knew Saffron better than anyone did. Despite

Saffron's tough exterior, she had the heart of Mother Teresa. Andy often joked that Saffron was like a S' more—hard and crumbly on the outside, and soft and mushy on the inside. Saffron had endless compassion and warmth for her friends. Hence, Andy knew how to handle her. Claire wasn't as big of a pushover; however, her loyalty for friends had the strength of steel.

"I need your help; besides I brought wine." Andy gave another quick look across the street. "We can have a glass before the guests arrive."

"Okay, okay," the two women said in unison.

"You don't have to push," Saffron added. "We'll stay and help you. Even without a glass of wine."

Before going inside, Andy looked over his shoulder once more. The man in black with a silver cross around his neck pointed his finger, put his thumb straight up, closed one eye as if aiming and jerked his hand back as a reaction from shooting an imaginary gun at Andy.

Andy felt a rush of fear. He pushed his friends through the outer doors of the building to safety inside.

Rainbow Colors for Life

Amber got to the gallery by seven-fifteen and found it already packed. On entering, she saw a sandy blond-haired young woman seated at a check-in table. Her badge displayed the name, Claire Reed. "May I see your invitation?" she asked.

"Oh dear, I didn't bring it with me."

"That's quite all right. I can check for your name on my list."

A few feet away in the crowd stood a Latin-looking man. He turned and looked toward the table as Amber gave her name. He headed toward them squeezing through the crowd as Claire scanned a long list of names on a pad. After thumbing through a box, she pulled out a nametag and handed it to Amber. "Yes, I found your name on our list. Here is your badge. I hope you enjoy the evening, Miss Moon."

Amber took the badge and clipped it on the collar of her outfit.

"You will find wine and champagne on the tables with the gold tablecloths," Claire said. "Soft beverages are on the silver cloth ones. Servers are going around with appetizers."

Amber thanked the woman and turned just as the slender Latin man reached the table. He looked artsy with a neatly trimmed goatee and slicked-back hair. "Amber Moon, welcome." He extended his hand, "Andy . . . Andy Martinez. Did you have any trouble getting a parking place?"

"No, but I think I got the last spot around back in the lot across the street." She looked around the room. "There's a good crowd here."

Andy shook her hand with one of those two-handed, confident but friendly shakes that linger while the conversation continues. "Yes, it's great, isn't it? The night should be a wonderful success for the Awareness."

He stopped shaking Amber's hand but kept hold as he placed her hand around his arm, turning and leading her forward into the crowd. "Let me show you around."

Amber hesitated only slightly as she looked at him sideways. *Strange guy.* She allowed him to escort her through the mass of people. *Seems harmless enough.*

They moved through the crowd as he chattered away. She wondered if this quirky man was one of the artists.

Maybe a runway model, she thought.

Amber always enjoyed playing the "what's his profession," game in her mind. She eliminated magazine model immediately. Her image of a male magazine model was bronze, un-naturally muscle-bound with not a hint of intelligence in his eyes. Andy appeared smart to her as he spoke, if not brilliant but definitely, a lightweight in the brawn division. *No, he's not a photo model.*

No matter how far she could stretch her imagination she could not see any muscles beneath his silky shirt. What she could imagine was, him swaying down a catwalk of a fashion show. He fit that role perfectly. Dressed in charcoal-colored European-cut fitted pants and a stunning purple shirt.

Andy told her he worked in the sales division of a large computer company downtown. His office was in one of the high-rise buildings. He admitted he loved art but didn't have a creative bone in his body, and couldn't even draw a stick figure. Amber knew now he was not one of the artists, which intrigued her more about this charismatic man. Amber weighed the possibilities as Andy chatted away and pointed out some of the exhibiting artwork. *He must be one of the gay supporters. Definitely not one of the "regular" guests.*

They meandered toward the back of the room. "Saffron is singing over there," Andy said nodding his chin toward the left side of the room. "She sings a little bit of everything, but I love her blues the best. She's very talented. Are you familiar with her?"

"No." Amber held back a snicker. She felt somewhat like Alice being led by the Mad Hatter to the tea party. Andy was a little friendlier than most but seemed pleasant enough and sincere. A unique personality.

"Let's get you a glass of something," Andy said. "Then I'll introduce you to some of the artists. Matt is somewhere in this crowd. He'll be around soon. He always makes his way to all his guests."

A man in a black sports coat waved and called out. "Hi, Andy."

Another guest commented, "Andy, the food is great

As Amber and Andy moved through the crowd of people, an attractive woman in a green dress turned and said, "Andy you were right about the wine, I do like this red."

Does everybody know him?

Normally, Amber would not have allowed someone she just met to be so controlling, leading her around the room like a timid female. But Andy's non-threatening personality must've come through to her. The friendly display from the guests reflected they liked and admired him, which made Amber more comfortable. Besides, it was obvious to Amber that she, or any woman for that matter, was not his type. His mannerisms gave Amber confidence that she would not have to fight off a pass from him. However, he did fit the role of a perfect host for such an event with his keen sense for detail and sensitivity toward the guests' needs.

Before Andy could offer her a drink at the gold beverage table, a server hurried over calling frantically. "Andy, Andy." The man stopped in front of them, paused to gasp for breath, and started to fan himself. He blinked nervously as he spoke without stopping between thoughts. "Ken can't find where the boxes are with the bottles of Syrah wine. And the back table is down to the last two bottles. And we looked everywhere. And—"

"Okay, okay. We have plenty. Calm down. I'll be there in a minute."

The man sighed, rolled his eyes, turned, and hastily disappeared into the crowd.

"Forgive us, Amber," Andy said. "Bennie can be such an airhead at times, Ken too, but especially Bennie. I'm afraid I'll have to go to help them. It's apparent; that they've worked themselves into a tizzy. They'll never find the Syrah in the state of mind they're in, but first, let me get you a glass of wine." Andy hesitated and then asked, "You do drink, don't you?"

"Yes, actually I love Syrah but usually only merlots are served at these functions."

"Great. Then I have a real treat for you. There's still a bottle of Syrah on this table." He grabbed a glass and poured the deep red liquid into the glass. "It's a South African and has wonderful peppery and spicy tannins."

As he turned back to Amber, his face lit up when he glanced over her shoulder. "Vic. Great to see you."

Amber turned and saw a man moving toward them dressed in black jeans and a crisp, white, dress shirt with French cuffs. He was a flip version of Andy's petite soft look. The man walking toward them was tall, probably close to six feet. Amber noticed immediately that although he had a debonair look, much like a suave James Bond, his broad shoulders gave a more brawny appearance. His shirtsleeves hinted a snug fit, but not a muscle-bound look of bulging biceps. Amber detested Hulk-like muscles.

"I want you to meet Amber Moon," Andy said as the man joined them.

"Hello, Amber Moon," he said in a deep velvety voice. He had salt and pepper hair and his five o'clock shadow added to his rugged good looks. Angelic dimples appeared when he smiled, contradicting the devilish twinkle in his aqua-blue eyes. An escaping lock of hair flopped down over one eyebrow suggesting a hint of unruliness.

"Amber Moon, may I introduce Vic Richardson," Andy said. "Vic is here with my favorite artist, Phillip Brooks. Phillip does big, dramatic, tropical paintings with vivid colors." Andy handed Amber the wine glass and added, "Vic you need to show them to Amber."

"How do you do, Mr. Richardson," Amber said.

"Amber is an interior designer," Andy continued. "I've seen pictures of her work. She does spectacular work."

A frown came over Andy's face as he looked toward the back of the room. "I need to go find some boxes of wine." He moved forward passed Vic, but then paused, and turned back. "Vic, would you entertain Amber?"

"No problem, Andy," Vic said.

Andy moved through the crowd, stopped, turned back, and called out over the noise of the crowd. "Amber, don't walk to your car alone. We don't want any of the guests walking unescorted to their cars." He looked serious and said firmly, "Vic, make sure she doesn't leave alone. Walk her to her car please."

"Yes, sir," Vic said. He glanced at Amber and smiled with his dimples reappearing.

"I just have to go help those boys find that wine," Andy added and then hurried off, squeezing through the crowd, disappearing out of sight.

Amber smiled and looked down taking another sip of her wine. She felt a slow warmth flow over her but the peppery wine had nothing to do with the heat she felt.

Vic shook his head and chuckled. He turned to face Amber. "Well, Miss Moon, have you seen any of the paintings, yet?"

"No, Andy nabbed me as soon as I walked in, but please call me Amber."

"Only if you call me Vic."

Amber had inherited her mother's love for art. In Florida, there were outside art shows and festivals almost every weekend in the months that had bearable temperatures. Amber attended most and even traveled to Mount Dora and Winter Park for those shows. She thought she was acquainted with the artists in the immediate area. Tonight surprised her though. She didn't recognize any of the artwork.

Amber and Vic moved toward the left side of the gallery where Phillip Brook's work hung. Phillip's talent was remarkable. Andy's description didn't begin to describe the beauty. The huge canvases gave a sense of looking through a magical window into an actual rainforest.

"Phillip's work is amazing. I'm impressed with all the artists," Amber said to Vic. She realized that she had missed some remarkable talent in her own backyard. "I see I need to start working with some of the Tampa artists, although, I use more glass pieces and sculpture for my design jobs. However, I prefer to use more pottery than anything else."

Behind Amber, she heard a familiar voice. "You're talking to one of the best potters in the state." Amber turned around to see Matt Connelly walking up to them with a champagne flute in hand and a gleaming smile on his face. "Good to see you, Amber. Have you been here long?"

"A little while, but Vic and Andy Martinez took good care of me. Andy greeted me at the door." She turned back to Vic, "You didn't tell me you were one of the artists here."

Vic furrowed his eyebrows then smiled and answered, "I'm not one of the artists. I'm only here because Phillip dragged me."

"I've been telling Vic he needs to do some gallery exhibits," Matt said. "He's committing a crime by not letting the world see his work. It's great. He builds his pots on the wheel and then Raku fires them. Gets the best colors because of the mixes of paints he uses. He gets some of the most breathtaking explosions of colors I've ever seen. Even without gallery shows he's built a cult following."

"Oh really. Raku pieces are my weakness," Amber said. "If I didn't own a small bungalow with very little display room, you could mean trouble for me."

Matt was aware that Amber's current clients were redoing their condominium at Tierra Verde on the Gulf of Mexico, so he seized the opportunity. "Vic's work is a must for the condo you're doing. It just might attract another magazine spread for you. With Vic's work and your Midas touch in design, it should be a shoo-in for another article."

Matt persisted until the two of them set an appointment. Amber agreed to visit Vic's studio the following Wednesday.

Later in the evening, Vic introduced Amber to Phillip. She automatically liked him. Phillip was funny and told entertaining stories. He graciously included everyone in the conversation and was not one of those self-absorbed, talented "artist-type" with an over-inflated ego. Phillip humbly turned the spotlight on each person in the circle, encouraging him or her to talk. Everyone spoke comfortably. Except when Phillip tried to get Vic to talk about his work and he declined to speak. Vic politely stated that everyone was there to see Phillip and the other exhibiting artists. They didn't need to listen to some guy who threw clay. His only purpose tonight was to give Phillip moral support, he added.

Amber enjoyed the conversation and the people she met. What started as just another social business commitment, turned out to be a very memorable night. She stayed longer than she expected and it was very late when she left the gallery but as promised to Andy, Vic walked her to the parking lot. When they got there, he unlocked her car door, said he looked forward to their appointment next week, and said goodnight.

Amber turned the ignition and pulled out of the lot as Vic stood watching to make sure she was on her way safely before leaving to return to the gallery where Phillip waited. While she drove home, she couldn't help smiling as she thought about the evening. Oddly, she felt the same tightness and jittery feeling inside that she experienced when she saw Vic for the first time. Her stomach fluttered again when she pictured his blue eyes and that run-away lock of hair. It was as if she just left a charming romantic date and she couldn't stop thinking about the handsome man who "threw clay pots."

Mentally replaying everything Vic said that evening, her heartbeat intensified and she thought about his smile, his dimples, and that *lock of hair* hanging over his eyebrow. Quick-changing emotions overwhelmed her the same way they had when she was a confused teenager with racing hormones. One thing was different though, she wasn't a teenager anymore.

"Amber, what are you doing?" she said, scolding herself. "He's not for you. Vic was there with Phillip, for goodness sake!"

She drove a little further. A smile crept back to her face. Her mind drifted back to the handsome man dressed in the white shirt with cufflinks and black jeans. *What's wrong with me? How can I have these feelings?* She smiled and muttered. "He sure was handsome, though."

Church Offering

The sounds of Detective Edward Harrison's car speeding through downtown Tampa cut through the quiet of the Sunday morning air. A dispatcher woke him less than twenty minutes earlier with the news about the dead body. Up, dressed and behind the wheel within six minutes and back in action. Operating on three short hours of sleep was Harrison's "normal" ever since he had been assigned to head the task force to apprehend the killer in town.

"Damn! The friggin' murders are getting closer together," Harrison muttered through clenched teeth. "We've got to get his guy."

He headed north toward the Tampa Heights neighborhood and made two sharp turns then squealed to a stop in front of the barricades blocking the street. The red brick church wouldn't have Sunday worship today. It was not a church any longer; it was now a crime scene.

Harrison jumped out of the car and grabbed his tact vest. He moved quickly as he mentally reviewed the details of the unsolved murders. Inside the crime scene tape, the bomb squad men crowded near the truck packing up gear. Two uniformed officers leaned against a Tampa Police cruiser parked outside of wooden barricades. One cop shifted his weight back and forth, looking very ill at ease—had the green look of a rookie.

The other cop Harrison knew well. He went by the name of 'Smitty,' and he was a tough old bird. He had been Harrison's first partner and almost his last. Harrison quit the force after six months on the job—for a whole five hours. The sole reason Harrison came back was due to Smitty's actions back then.

Harrison had graduated from the police academy. His first partner was Norman D. Smith, aka, Smitty. That first day on the job, eager to start on the right foot, Harrison went up and offered his hand to his partner to shake.

The senior officer just stared at him.

"I know who you are." Smitty shook his head and gave a disgruntled shrug. "Don't think you know everything there is to know because you made it this far. The learning starts now. Keep your eyes open and be alert."

Harrison pulled his hand back and tried to break the ice with his stone-faced partner. "Hear you've put in over ten years. Guess I can learn a lot from you."

"This ain't the classroom. I'm your partner," Smitty snapped back. "Not your boss—or your teacher. You learn from the streets. I won't take any excuses just because you're a newbie. No room for errors."

Then he turned and got in their cruiser, leaving Harrison looking dumbfounded.

That first year was rougher than most for Harrison. He'd trained hard at the academy, finished top in his class. On the gun range, he scored better than most—even beat the veteran cops. Still, he didn't think he'd ever need to draw his weapon on the streets—most cops don't. However, Harrison never fit into the norm.

Six months, three days, and four hours after graduating from the academy, Harrison was on patrol with Smitty. They attempted to pull a driver over who had rolled through a stop sign. What they didn't know was that the twenty-eight-year-old male had his girlfriend's lifeless body in the trunk. He had stabbed her thirty-two times before cutting her throat in his final fury to make sure she was dead.

Forty minutes later, after a high-speed chase, the twenty-eight-year-old man lay dead in the street. Harrison's bullet took the perpetrator down but not until the guy had shot two cops. One officer died on the way to Tampa General Hospital and the other survived after six hours in surgery to remove the bullet lodged in his heart.

Rattled beyond reason, Harrison turned in his badge. He said the job wasn't for him and went home with a bottle of scotch.

Hours later, Smitty showed up at Harrison's door. "Kid, open this door," he yelled. "Just because you pulled your piece and killed a man doesn't give you a pass to quit. We're not losing another good cop. Not today—now open up, dammit."

Young Harrison and Smitty were partners until Harrison's promotion to detective in the homicide department. Smitty remained a beat cop

Harrison, now in his fifteenth year on the job, walked up to the uniformed officers near the crime scene. His old friend looked up. "What 'ya doing here, Harry?"

Smitty tagged Harrison with the shortened version of his last name years earlier when they were partners and it stuck. Most cops on the force didn't even know that it wasn't his real name. Most thought his parents had a warped sense of humor naming him Harry Harrison.

"Thought you were heading up some special task force," Smitty said.

"Yeah, I am, but the bomb squad called. Said they had something that needed my attention."

"Oh yeah? The stiff connected to your case?"

"Maybe," Harrison answered.

"Hear tell you got a real serial killer on the loose."

"No serial on our streets!" Harrison snapped back at his old partner. Smitty frowned at him.

Harrison looked down and scuffled his feet a little. He respected his old partner. Smitty had an instinct that couldn't be taught. Harrison lifted his head, looked at the veteran cop and grimaced. "No serial killer loose *officially*, but off the record . . ." Harrison took a deep breath and let out a weary sigh. "It looks like it. Hope to lock him up before the press makes the connections to all the murders."

A dark-skinned man in a bomb squad t-shirt approached and motioned for Harrison to join him. A badge hung on the side of his belt, which displayed the name 'Sanchez.'

Sanchez looked at the uniformed officers and said, "We're good here men. Close enough to the end of your shift to head in, downtown needs your reports ASAP."

Sanchez and Harrison ducked under a yellow crime tape, which served to preserve the area for evidence gathering. They moved toward a team of people wearing latex gloves, who were methodically moving around a lifeless body on the steps of the church, like a well-orchestrated symphony but no one carried musical instruments with them. Each person did a specific job; some strategically placed number markers down, others bagged objects, while others twisted puffed brushes blackened with powder on various surfaces, obviously hoping to pick up fingerprints. Another person snapped pictures.

"Smitty and his partner answered the call," Sanchez said. He handed a bag to Harrison as he spoke, "The box, there," he pointed, "had a Bible in it and a note. We bagged them for you and your team. CSI signed off already on it." A small box sat in the location that Sanchez pointed to, one step above where the female body lay on the church steps.

"Wording on the note is like the others, according to our bulletin. Bible quotes, a lot of talk about sinners, and threats about redemption."

Harrison rubbed his forehead and raked his hand down his face then pulled the note out of the evidence bag. It was printed in pencil on plain white paper with scratched-out warnings about the devil, sinners, and Hell.

"Man, I feel this guy is just getting started." Harrison shook his head. He looked down at the body. The victim's long hair was draped across an ashen neck, which showed a half-inch wide purplish-red line on the exposed skin. In the center of the discoloration, a thin line cut into the tissue, apparently from some kind of rope or thick wire.

"She strangled?"

"Yeah. Nylon rope. It's been bagged."

"Church people find her?" Harrison asked.

"Nope, it's not a regular church. I mean, they don't have regular Sunday hours. They won't be here until after four p.m."

Harrison frowned and looked at Sanchez.

"The church is some new-fangled religion," Sanchez explained. "They put the word out on the streets that anyone was welcome . . . as in homos. They had a lot of static from neighbors. Folks weren't happy with the congregation. To settle things down, the church moved services to later in the afternoon. Guess that satisfied the neighbors since they didn't have to pass the faggots and lesbos on their way to their church in the morning. Go figure."

"Yeah, go figure," Harrison said. "So, who called it in?"

"An old couple on the way to the Columbia Restaurant for brunch. Saw her lying on the steps and thought she was a drunk. Smitty didn't have to get close to see that she was a stiff. He thought the box looked suspicious. So we came."

Harrison crouched down to examine the body.

"My men are done here," Sanchez said, "we're going to take off. The box is there at the top of the steps. That's where we found it but it's not released. They want to take it back to the lab."

Harrison stooped down, squinted at the body, and called back to Sanchez. "What's this on the back of her hand?"

Sanchez stopped and turned. "Looks like a stamp-like you get at the clubs in Ybor."

"Oh boy."

"Does that mean something?"

"Yeah." Harrison let out a deep sigh and stood up, shaking his head.

"Could it be your guy?" Sanchez asked.

"Sure looks like it."

Fire

Amber pulled into Vic Richardson's driveway next to a red Toyota pickup. The house was a decent size but not one of those massive, cookie-cutter homes that were popping up everywhere. This house had a personality to it and showed a style that suggested the artistry of a custom builder. There were carved double front doors painted a deep Indian red color and adjacent to them sat a Pygmy Date Palm tree in a clay pot.

The landscape reflected the softness of a tropical oasis with a lush green yard, which possessed a charm. Flowerbeds cushioned the perimeter of the lawn with Crotons, Hibiscus, and other tropical foliage. Matt told Amber that Vic owned two oversized lots with the house centered on the land and a building located at the rear of the property that served as his workshop for the pottery. Even with Matt's description, the proportions of the house and land caught her by surprise.

That must be the workshop, Amber thought as she looked to the right of the house in the backyard. Behind the freestanding building was more open grass area, then two large oak trees and a wooden fence a few feet beyond that.

Matt had not exaggerated when he said Vic hit a gold mine when he purchased the property. Deep oversized lots in Tampa were hard to find and to top it off; it was only forty-five minutes north of the center of town.

"The property must now be worth three times what Vic paid for it," Matt had said, "even without the workshop. He bought it eight years ago at a price that was a virtual steal. Vic didn't use all his money he had allotted for the purchase, so he took the leftover cash and built the workshop. He installed plumbing and extra lighting so it could easily be converted into a mother-in-law house to attract buyers whenever he decides to sell. He's very smart, plus very handy, can do just about anything. A real Renaissance man."

Earlier this morning, Amber had called Vic about their appointment for her to come out to see this pottery. They were to meet at three o'clock but there was a glitch. That morning Amber's clients had called to change their appointment time. She had scheduled it early and had planned to go directly to Vic's place immediately afterward. They lived in St. Petersburg Beach, but with the change, she would hit afternoon traffic coming back over the bridge and probably would be later than 3:00.

"I can't guarantee what time I can make it Vic, perhaps we should reschedule," Amber told Vic on the phone.

"No problem," Vic said. "We don't need to stick with any particular time. Come whenever you get finished. My work schedule is light this week. I had nothing scheduled this morning and only two stops to make in the afternoon after our appointment. I'll just move them to tomorrow and take today off. I'll stick around here, take advantage of the time, and do some firing needed for some orders I have. If you don't mind seeing me dirty from the smoke, that is."

"Oh no, that's all right." She had read about the raku process and understood about the smoke.

"It works out good," Vic said. "I'm a great procrastinator. I should've fired those pieces weeks ago. I'm already late for shipping the order. Don't worry about not knowing what time you'll be here, I can be more creative when I'm not clock-watching. I'll work until you get here."

What Amber had read was that raku was a two-step process. In the first step, the pots were fired in a kiln. Next, they were removed hot and placed in a contained area, like a pit or barrel with combustible materials, like sawdust, pine needles—anything that would ignite. The flames bring out the colors from the glazes painted on the clay. If left clean of paint the raw clay would turn blackish color from the smoke. Raku pieces are unique and never can be exactly duplicated because of the unpredictability of the firing process. Raku started in Japan in the sixteenth century and the age-old history added to Amber's love and passion for collecting it.

"Raku pieces speak to your soul," she often told her clients. She loved introducing the ancient art form to people who knew nothing about it.

Amber was glad Vic insisted she come, no matter if she would be late. It would be a rare opportunity to witness the physical connection between the potter and his creation. Also, it would be exciting to see the red-hot clay pots carried to the pits and engulfed in flames only to emerge later, reborn into a unique art form.

It turned out that Amber breezed through her St. Pete appointment, crossed the bridge, and even arrived a half-hour earlier than she expected at Vic's house. She stepped out of her car and saw Phillip coming around the side of the house from the backyard.

"Hi, Amber, Vic said you were coming by today," Phillip said cheerfully.

"Yes, I had an appointment in St. Pete and thought I would be later than this. Is Vic still firing pots?"

"Yup, he's around back." Phillip pulled his keys from his pocket as he spoke. "You can go around. There's a clearing behind the main house, that's where Vic has the firing pits. He's pulling the pots from the kilns and putting them into one of the pits right now . . . Have you ever seen the process?"

"No. I have books on raku with pictures but never actually saw it done."

"It's awesome to see. There's a chair out there, you can sit and watch. Let me warn you, he won't notice you while he's working. When Vic is moving his pots, he's in the zone and nothing else exists. I'm on my way out. Good seeing you again."

"Yes, good to see you too, Phillip. I'll go back quietly. Thanks."

Phillip got in the pick-up and backed out as Amber headed around the side of the house. In the backyard, Vic was in front of one of the kilns. He wore heavy gloves and held onto long tongs lifting a glowing pot. Amber slipped unnoticed into the chair under the nearby tree.

Vic's skin glistened with perspiration. The muscles in his arms flexed with the weight of the load and his runaway lock of hair dipped down past his left eyebrow. She watched him work systematically, gingerly moving pot-after-pot into a pit in the ground, for thirty minutes or more. After each pot had been placed perfectly, Vic threw some material, which looked like wood shavings, in over the top of the pieces. The shavings then burst into flames. Next, he pulled a heavy tarp-like cover over top, smothering the flames—the final step in the process.

Vic moved back to another kiln and started the process again. It was then that Amber realized the lure of her attention was not directed at the raku process going on in front of her. Instead, she had been fixated on the man who was orchestrating the fire pits. Totally preoccupied with Vic's physique, she had completely lost interest in the inanimate pottery. Amber continued to stare shamelessly at Vic's bronze body, focusing on a more interesting live subject.

Once the last pit was covered, Vic stepped back away and took off his gloves, mask, and goggles. He swiped his forehead, and as he turned Amber's eyes settled on his shirtless torso. The black hair on his chest held small beads of sweat, her eyes glided across the contour of his body up to his broad shoulders. A sooty smudge marked his left shoulder. As he raised his head, his blue eyes met Amber's watching eyes.

First, a look of surprise came over his face and then a dimpled smile followed.

"Amber," he called out. "I didn't see you walk back here." He started toward her, stopping momentarily to pick up his shirt from where it lay draped on top of a bush.

"Have you been here long?"

"A little bit. I got here as Phillip was leaving."

Vic asked her to come back to the workshop and look around while he washed up. Inside the building, she saw two potter's wheels, clay pots drying on shelves, and a deep shop sink on the back wall. Vic excused himself. Amber thought it was cute how embarrassed he seemed to be that she saw him dirty and shirtless.

Thank goodness he can't read my mind. Women weren't supposed to think such things that were whirling in her mind. *It's okay.* She disputed secretly. *Thinking is not doing.*

She walked into the adjacent room where shelves lined all four walls. A display table with stepped shelves stood in the center holding finished raku containers of varying sizes, shapes, and designs. The clean and orderly organization of both the work area and display area gave an interesting contradiction to the grime and sooty side she had just witnessed.

Amber turned around to see Vic as he walked into the room buttoning the last button on his shirt. "Like what you see?" Vic asked.

"Wh . . . what?"

"I divided the shop into two rooms, can't keep finished pieces in the work area—too much dust. What do you think?"

"Oh, that. Yeah, it looks good." She took a step over to the shelves on the wall. "Matt was right. Your pieces have a wonderful unique look to them. The colors are magnificent."

"Thanks," Vic said.

68

"I just love that larger piece over there." Amber moved to a large pitcher-like container, which had first caught her eye when she had walked into the room. *Time to come back to reality, after all this is a business appointment.*

"Yes, those larger pieces are more difficult but when they come out like that one, it is worth it."

"The way you sculpted the seahorse's tail and the seaweed forming the handle is beautiful," Amber said. "I've never seen a handle built that way before."

Vic smiled proudly. "It's part of my Vessels of the Sea series."

"It would be perfect for the condo I'm redoing on St. Pete Beach. The owner, Marcy Jacobson, would love it. She wanted the feel of the water but hates how people decorate with shells everywhere. She said she wanted beach elegance with subtle ocean influences."

Amber pushed back the thoughts dancing in her mind about Vic and tried to focus her attention on the pottery. "There are several I'm sure she'll love. Marcy never even knew what raku was until I explained it to her. When I show her your work, she'll be a collector for life."

Amber picked a half dozen pieces to take on loan for a presentation to Marcy and her husband. She even indulged in buying one pot for herself.

Amber watched as Vic wrapped the pots and secured them in boxes. *Just because he's good-looking, that doesn't mean we can't work together. I'm a professional. Besides, he's gay.*

Vic packed the vessel with the seahorse handle and smiled with his dimples tempting Amber. "Okay that's all of them," he said.

"Great. Marcy's so excited. She said she wants to commission you for more pieces if she likes these, and I can't see how she wouldn't love them. Both the Jacobsons said they want me to bring you out to meet them."

"Wonderful. Sounds like we'll be working together." Vic lifted the box, his biceps tightened; he turned and headed out of the room. "If you'll unlock your trunk, I'll carry this box to your car and then, come back for the rest."

"Okay," Amber answered. She watched Vic walk ahead as she thought about working closely with him. *No problem.* Visions of Vic, hot and sweaty, rushed back into Amber's mind and she felt a sudden rush of heat. *As long as he keeps his shirt on, it'll be okay–probably.*

Chemical Reaction

The Jacobsons loved Vic's pottery. They decided to keep all the pieces Amber brought. After hearing about Phillip's paintings, particularly his exotic bird series, they decided they wanted to purchase one. Amber set an appointment to return the following week on Wednesday with a projector to show the four images from Phillip's collection onto the living room wall.

On Wednesday, the Jacobsons picked the painting titled *Tropical Feathers of Blue*. Amber thought any one of the paintings would've been perfect for the area. While Amber was packing the projector, Marcy commented, "I can't wait to see the real painting on the wall. I think it will be perfect."

"The one you picked would've been my first pick for you," Amber said.

Marcy seemed pleased with the confirmation that she made the right choice. "Can you deliver the painting and our large raku piece this Friday?"

"That shouldn't be a problem. I'll need to make arrangements with a delivery company since I won't be able to deliver it by myself. A floor vase that size will be very heavy."

The Jacobsons had given a deposit for a large floor vase from Vic. It would sit next to the door in the foyer. It had to be hand-built, tall and narrow with a broad enough base and a substantial amount of bottom weight to ensure it would not tip over easily when people entered or exited the front door. Large pieces are more complex to build. Many potters never achieve the skill level to accomplish it. Vic had a knack for them.

"After the delivery of the painting and vase everything will be complete," Amber said. She gathered her things up and looked around the room, "Everything looks great. You made some excellent choices."

The Jacobsons' project had stretched over three months and Amber was anxious to conclude the job. When she returned to her home, she called Vic to get a time he would be available for the delivery company to pick up the floor vase she had seen in his studio. Vic made his living as a field supervisor for a roofing company; therefore, she needed to coordinate around his job schedule. Matt once told Amber that Vic had a dynamite business as a potter but the irregularity of purchases from collectors made it essential he remained employed. His supervisor position wasn't the typical eight-to-five job but it was perfect for juggling the duties between the roofing company and his pottery business.

I hope he'll be able to arrange to be home on Friday, Amber thought.

Seeing Vic so many times to iron out the details for every new piece became more emotionally difficult for Amber than she had anticipated. It didn't help that Marcy wanted her to pick up every piece upon its completion and deliver each one at a time. Marcy paid extra for this luxury, so Amber couldn't evade the requests without making it awkward. Because of the frequent pick-ups, Amber learned of Vic's flexible schedule. Whenever she needed to stop by, he had always been very accommodating to her. However, he had limitations because of the contractual deadlines of the roofing company.

With each visit to Vic's workshop, Amber hoped her attraction to him would cool. On the contrary, each meeting produced more sparks between the two of them from an unexplainable chemistry that seemed to exist. She dismissed it as an attraction to a forbidden person or something taboo. Still, she yearned to give in to her feelings, no matter how much she forbade herself. She told herself that once the Jacobson's job was over, Vic would be out of her life.

Amber waited for Vic to answer the phone as she heard endless ringing. *Vic,* ***please*** *answer and be available Friday. I want to finish this job finished.* Even now with an end in sight, it seemed that hopes for a quick finish to her internal fight of temptation wouldn't happen. She was about to hang up, when on the sixth ring, Vic answered with his slow-easy-going deep voice.

"Vic, I need to make arrangements to pick up the vase for the Jacobsons. I would like to combine the delivery of Phillip's painting and your vase this Friday. Can you arrange to be at home if I schedule a delivery company to stop by to pick it up? I know it's short notice but I can meet them there with the painting from the gallery. I plan to follow them to the Jacobson's."

"Friday I have one inspection scheduled to do in the early morning. I can be finished before ten," Vic said. "But wait a minute."

There was a brief pause before he spoke again. "Don't hire a delivery company. They'll charge you an arm and a leg. We can go together, in my van, and make the delivery. The job site I need to go to is near Matt's gallery, so once I'm finished with the inspection, I can swing by and pick up Phillip's painting then head home. We can meet at my place at around eleven. It will save you a trip to the gallery, and the delivery company's fee."

"Well, if you don't mind." It did sound reasonable and if Vic got the painting, it would save me a lot of time. "But I'll have the delivery service come to your place. I don't expect you to deliver the vase all the way to St. Pete Beach."

"Amber come on, it's only fair. Phillip's painting will fit in your vehicle. I'm not going to let you pay for a service to deliver my raku. I don't mind. Besides I want to make sure the dimensions are right to fit in the corner properly. I wouldn't want my masterpiece destroyed by a wayward hip passing by."

"All right," Amber said weakly. Once again forced into a corner she couldn't easily escape.

"No problem then," Vic said and then he paused. "Uh, maybe after we're finished at the condo, perhaps we can get a bite to eat? An early dinner, you know. Somewhere on the beach, to celebrate the completion of our first job together."

Amber didn't know how to turn him down without it sounding strange. Shakespeare's quote came to mind, "The lady doth protest too much, methinks." If she adamantly resisted, then her attraction might be obvious—how embarrassing would that be? For both of them.

Over the last months of working side-by-side with Vic, she sensed there had been something stirring with him, too. A sort of heat. Now he was asking her out for a celebration. But it wasn't a date she rationalized. *What harm is there in celebrating the end of a job?*

Amber dismissed her feelings and said yes, attributing her emotions as the result of an overactive libido caused by too long of a time between boyfriends and exhaustion from overwork. She told herself, she was overreacting. It was nothing. Still, questions nagged at her ever since that first day when she watched Vic work the fire pits in his backyard. Afterward, when he approached her, his aroma had an earthy manly smell—not distasteful—but arousing. Pheromones? Did a man produce pheromones automatically, even if there was no attraction felt by him? In addition, there was the conversation Amber had with her mother the day after she met Vic at the gala. Suzanne instinctively noticed Amber's attraction to Vic.

Suzanne had phoned for their ritual morning chat over coffee. "How was the art show? Meet any interesting people?" she had asked.

Amber remembered going on about how impressed she was with the artists and then she mentioned something about Vic. Just like a mother, Suzanne picked up on it right away and needled her asking if the dark mystery man was handsome.

"Mom, the exhibit was a fundraiser for AIDS Awareness. It wasn't exactly a place to cruise for men. Besides, Vic was there with his *friend*, Phillip Brooks," Amber said.

"Amber Moon Rosenbaugh, I am listening to your words but I hear what you're not saying." Then Suzanne's words of warning streamed in. "If this guy is gay then be careful. It's not an illness that you can cure. And don't think you're going to convert him either."

Now Amber had worked with Vic for months and the attraction to Vic that she denied to her mother was stronger than ever. If only she had listened to her mother's warnings. Now Amber questioned whether the attraction was mutual. She stood beside the desk where she had set the phone down.

Why did I agree to the celebration dinner? I can't go out with him.

It had been difficult enough having contact with Vic through the Jacobson's job. How she could have let herself get aroused when she knew about Phillip? Even if what she sensed was true, and Vic had been attracted to her—maybe he was bisexual—she couldn't let go any farther. She just wouldn't. She had to remember Phillip.

After Friday's delivery, the job will be over. Once the celebration dinner is finished that will be it. End of story!

Pink Palace

Vic finished hanging the painting and packed his tools.

"Mr. and Mrs. Jacobson I am very happy you like my work. It is a pleasure to have my pottery displayed in your beautiful home," Vic said as he shook hands with Marcy, and then, her husband. Picking up his toolbox, he turned to Amber, "Amber, I know you have some business to wrap up. I'll wait for you on the terrace."

He paused and looked at Mrs. Jacobson. "If that's all right with you, Mrs. Jacobson? I would like to take one last look at your wonderful view."

"Yes, of course. Enjoy," Marcy Jacobson said. "The sunsets are the reason we bought here."

The sun was low in the sky and warmed the air. The clear sky displayed an explosion of color. Earlier in the day, Marcy and her husband had insisted Amber and Vic stay for lunch, now the night was fast approaching. Vic had whispered to Amber they could change their afternoon plans to an evening dinner.

Vic walked out to the balcony, leaned on the wrought iron railing and gazed at the Florida sky. Amber watched Vic as he looked out with the fiery sunset outlining his body. The sky glowed with warm violets, rich yellows, and burning oranges. Vic wore a black shirt and khaki pants, his silhouette against the sky looked like he belonged on the cover of a romance novel.

"You two make a lovely couple," Marcy whispered to Amber.

Amber pulled her attention away from the view on the balcony. "Oh, we're not a couple. We just worked together."

Marcy stared at Amber for a minute with a broad smile on her face before she commented. "I bet that doesn't stay that way for long." She nudged Amber and then nodded toward the balcony. "I saw how he looks at you."

Amber's stomach felt that familiar weird feeling again. The same feeling she had when a friend in the past had tried to set her up with a blind date. *I just need to get through this evening.*

"Really Marcy," Amber insisted firmly. "Vic's a nice guy, but it's strictly business." *I'll make sure after tonight, never to get caught in a situation like this again.*

"Ah-uh, I see," Marcy said and placed her hand over her mouth smothering a small chuckle.

Amber pressed her lips together to maintain control of her temper. Marcy Jacobson had just given her a sizeable check, and she was a very nice person, it would not be good form to tell off a good-paying client.

I swear that if I ever sell any of his pottery again, I'll hire a delivery company. No matter what! I'm not going through this again. That's for sure.

After Amber agreed to the celebration dinner, Vic had made reservations at the restaurant inside the Don Caesar, St. Petersburg's famous pink hotel on the beach. Today, sometime after lunch, Vic slipped outside and called to change the reservation time to seven forty-five. There would be no problem making it on time since the condo was just a short drive away.

Amber and Vic arrived by seven-thirty and checked in at the door of the dining room. Vic asked the maître d' if they could hold their table so they could take a minute to walk out to the pool area overlooking the Gulf.

"That would be fine, sir," the maître d' replied graciously. "It would be a crime to come to *'The Don'* without seeing the sunset, especially when accompanied by a beautiful woman."

Great. Just what I need another sunset view. Amber thought as she managed to squeeze out a small smile. *Why can't we get through this as quickly as possible?*

They walked out to the pool, which overlooked the beach. The sunlight danced on the water for a few minutes as the sun sank into the horizon. The setting was perfect, made to order that is, for a couple on a romantic date.

When they returned to the dining room, Vic ordered a bottle of wine. The evening filled with laughter, candlelight, and good food.

Amber relaxed as her tension disappeared halfway through her second glass of wine. Talking to Vic seemed so natural and comfortable. She couldn't help reacting to him, evening flirting with him, as any woman would do while out with a handsome man.

A few hours later, they pulled away from The Don Caesar and were on the way home, Amber's thoughts to hurry the night toward a finish had almost disappeared. Amber thanked Vic and said his choice of the restaurant was very nice. They both agreed the wine was exquisite and the perfect complement to a delicious meal. Soon they eased into a tranquil quietness as they drove across the bridge toward Tampa. Amber looked across the water and gazed at the glow of car lights on a faraway bridge.

I need to remember Phillip. Vic was at the show with Phillip. Remember. The moonlight sparkled across the bay as it ebbed with flickering specks as if glitter had been sprinkled on top of the water's surface. Amber had mixed feelings. A small remaining conviction weakly yearned for the evening to end, but stronger was her feeling of giddiness and excitement mixed with anticipation of what would happen next. *Dinner at a beautiful restaurant with a setting right out of a movie doesn't change anything.* She fought back her emotions. *This isn't a date.*

Vic pulled into the small driveway in front of Amber's bungalow and got out, going around to her side. He opened the van door and offered his hand to help her down. The seat was high, and feeling the results of the wine, she slid down and lost her balance falling forward into Vic's arms.

"Sorry," she said and moved quickly back, composing herself.

"No problem," Vic said in a deep, smooth voice.

They made their way up the walk to the front door. Amber turned to Vic and said, "Dinner was good, thank you."

She looked down. Then back to the street, to the parked van, and then back to Vic. "I'm glad the condo is finished. The Jacobsons were nice, but they were a little demanding of my attention." She paused. "The money was good though. You did well. They really loved your pottery."

It was so awkward for Amber. She never had been on a date with a gay man before. But then, this wasn't truly a date, even if it felt like one.

"I think it helped that I had the sea series made," Vic said. "It seemed to trigger their interest."

They both stood in silence.

"You certainly transformed the place," Vic said.

"Thanks."

"I've enjoyed working with you," Vic said. "I hope we'll be able to see each other again, maybe next time in a more *personal* setting."

He leaned in and brought his hand up to Amber's cheek. The size of his palm covered the whole side of her face.

Feeling his caress, Amber took in a deep breath. His hand moved to her chin, tilting her face up to meet his kiss. Vic's hand moved gently to the back of her neck while he kissed her. His arms slid down her back wrapping around her, drawing her into his embrace.

Every passionate thought, all the heated feelings, the chemistry between them ignited and Amber felt as if she was going to explode with desire. She held him tight, wrapping her arms around his neck, and kissed him back. The world around them didn't exist, there was only the two of them.

Stop! Amber stop. A voice inside screamed at her. *Remember Phillip.*

She pulled her arms down to Vic's chest and tried to push him away. He held her, not letting go of his embrace. She turned her face away. His face was inches from hers. She whimpered, "No. I can't."

He remained motionless, still holding her in his arms. "What's the matter?" he whispered. "You said you weren't seeing anyone. I thought that I felt something between us. What's wrong?"

"Phillip. We have to think of Phillip. If he knew you were kissing me, he . . . he . . . we can't. We just can't."

"Phillip? I don't need to ask for my brother's approval."

"Brother. Yeah, right. Look, I don't care that you two are a couple, but I won't be part of hurting him. He's a sweet guy."

Vic released his arms from around Amber's waist and stepped back.

"You think I'm . . . *gay?*"

"Well, you were at the art show with Phillip. You said you were there supporting him and the benefit. *The AIDS Awareness Benefit.*"

"Yeah, because he's my brother!"

"Vic Richardson and Phillip Brooks? Oh, yeah. I'm buying that."

"My *half*-brother," Vic said in an irritated tone. He took a step back, crossed his arms in front of him, and leaned against the side of the house. "Let me explain. I'll talk slowly so you can understand. My dad had a bad heart. He went through a couple of surgeries and hospital stays. When he died, I was three. Charlie, Charlie Brooks, that is, worked at the hospital as a family liaison between the insurance companies and the patients, or the patient's families. Mom and Charlie got to know each other over Dad's two years in and out of the hospital."

"What?"

"A while after Dad's funeral, Mom and Charlie went out. As friends at first. Two years later, they got married. A year later—surprise! I had a baby brother—Phillip.

"Your stepfather's name is Brooks?"

"Yes." Vic's voice had a defiant edge to it. Then he asked again. "You thought I was gay?"

"You and Phillip do have different last names."

"My brother is gay, not me. Phillip announced it to Mom and me a year and a half ago. Nobody in the family knew. We didn't even have a clue. I didn't handle it so well. Then six months ago, Mom's next-door neighbor up and died of AIDS."

Vic raked his fingers threw his hair and stood silent for a moment before he continued talking. "He was a nice man, kept to himself except at Christmas. When we were little kids, he used to give Phillip and me Christmas presents every year. His death changed my thinking. I realized it didn't matter if Phillip was gay or not. He's my brother."

"Of course, it doesn't change who he is, not in his heart."

"I didn't want to say goodbye to my brother just because of my hang-ups. So, I've been trying to be there for him. Understand and support him whenever I can. That's why I was at the gallery exhibit."

"You're right, you should support him," Amber said, touching Vic's arm tenderly. She looked into his eyes. "You're *really* brothers?"

"Yeah, that's what I've been saying." Vic pulled his arm away from her touch. "Just because we are brothers, it doesn't mean I'm gay, too. And hanging out with his friends doesn't change my sexual preference, either. Being a homosexual isn't something that rubs off on others, you know."

A very long minute passed without either of them talking. Then Vic broke the silence.

"Do I act gay?"

"No . . . you don't."

Wonderful, he's not gay, but now he may never forgive me for thinking he was. How can I back up to when he was kissing me?

Amber and Vic stood there in silence, avoiding eye contact. Amber fidgeted with her purse, not wanting to take out her keys. Then she thought of something.

"Do you think Phillip acts gay?"

Vic looked at her contemplating her question for a minute before he answered. "Well, no. That's why it was such a shock when he told us."

"I didn't think he acted gay either," Amber said softly. "But he was at the gala. Andy, and the others, were there and they are . . .. I'm sorry. I didn't know what to think. And when I felt, uh, things between us, I was confused."

Vic looked down at Amber and smiled. His eyes changed; they weren't wide with anger anymore. He took a step forward, moving closer to Amber, and looked intensely into her eyes. "Let's start over," he said in a low voice. His tone was no longer sharp with anger and his eyes changed as an amorous look took over his expression.

He pulled her closer and kissed her again. There was not anything holding her back now. No more worrying about Phillip. A few intense kisses later, Vic moved his lips to her neck, kissing her neck below her ear, moving down to the depression near her collarbone.

Amber breathed deep, letting out a small almost inaudible moan, and he returned to her lips. She felt on fire and now nothing was in their way, nothing to keep them apart.

They kissed over, and over again. Then Vic stopped and gazed into her eyes. Seconds passed. He moved closer, brushing her cheek with his, and whispered in her ear. "I don't want to let you go. Will you come home with me tonight?"

Morning

Amber felt the sunlight on her face. Opening her eyes, she saw the cream color verticals that hung on Vic's bedroom window. The sun's rays pierced the weave of the fabric. Thoughts of last night wrapped around her. *I wasn't dreaming. Going home with Vic– after the first date? He must have put a spell on me.*

Even though Amber was comfortable in the skin of a twenty-first-century single woman, she never went home with a man after the first date. That had been the hippie generation of her parents' time . . . free love with no hang-ups. Although her parents' hippie days were not all wild and reckless. Amber's mother, Suzanne was seventeen when she and Jimmy ran off together but first, they got married at the courthouse before heading on their cross-country adventure. Amber's parents were more strait-laced than they wanted to admit to and somehow that conservativeness rubbed off on her.

Of course, Amber was not ready for a convent. She had experienced some steamy romances, which she didn't hide from her mother. Amber never felt a need to make excuses when one of her dinner dates lasted until breakfast. After all, she was a thirty-two-year-old adult. Suzanne and Amber had an open, comfortable relationship and shared everything–more like girlfriends than mother and daughter. However, the speed of the events of last night gave her an uncomfortable feeling about talking to Suzanne without explaining.

Don't get me wrong about Suzanne or Amber; they had rigid rules and didn't bend them haphazardly. They believed in true love and the sanctity of marriage. I'd hear Suzanne occasionally say something typically motherly like, "It's not good to wait too long before getting married." Amber's favorite "mother line" was, "There's no such thing as test-driving love." Therefore, there was no need for whispers of redemption. I guess you would say they had a modern-day strong moral fiber.

Amber felt Vic turn over next to her. He snuggled close and wrapped his arms around her body. "Good morning. Did you sleep okay?"

"Yes," Amber answered. She grabbed Vic's hand, wiggled her fingers between his, and pulled their hands into a joined embrace. *I'll think about Mom later.*

"I like waking up with you here," Vic said. "Do you drink coffee?"

"Uh-huh," Amber replied.

Vic kissed the nape of her neck then withdrew his hand and slid out of bed. "I'll make coffee. I can take you home whenever you say," he said as he slipped on a pair of jeans, "but I was hoping you would stay and hang out for the day. I don't want to say goodbye to you yet."

"That would be nice." Amber felt a warmth flow over her and everything seemed—right.

"Two coffees coming right up," Vic said. "You can stay in bed and relax, or if you want, meet me in the living room. There's a bathroom over there," he said and motioned to the side of the room, "and if you want something comfortable to wear to hang out then grab one of my shirts out of the closet."

Amber slipped into the bathroom and washed. After she chose one of Vic's shirts to wear, she went to the living room and sat on the couch. "I probably ought to get home by early afternoon," Amber said. "I told your brother I would call him about how the painting looked in the condo, and I know my mom will be calling me today."

"No problem," Vic said as he got two coffee cups out of the cabinet. "How do you take your coffee?"

"Black."

"Me, too. See we do have a lot of things in common," Vic said with a smile. "Why don't you turn on the morning news? News on Channel Eight is starting now."

Amber turned on the news as the local newscaster said, "Another body has been found in Ybor City. Police aren't releasing any information."

"How awful," Amber muttered. She picked up the remote, turned up the volume, and called out to the kitchen where Vic was pouring the coffee. "Vic, they found another body."

He came into the room and handed Amber a coffee mug. "I hope they caught the sick bastard this time."

They listened to the news anchor's report. "All we have right now is the male victim worked in Ybor City as a bartender at a night club called the *Cowboys*. The club is a known gathering place for the gay community. Their ads state '*they are gay owned and gay operated but all are welcomed.*' The authorities are withholding the name of the bartender until the family can be notified. The police wouldn't comment; however, our sources told us that the evidence gathered indicates that this is another Rainbow killing. We'll be back after this commercial break."

Amber turned off the television. "I can't stand listening to this. It seems they find a victim every two or three days. When are they going to catch this guy?"

Vic sat down next to her and shook his head, "Don't know, but they need to stop wasting time. Phillip is talking about taking some kind of martial arts class because he feels so defenseless. Quite frankly, I don't blame him. All of Phillip's friends are scared to death."

"I'm sure the police are doing everything they can, but you're right, they need to catch the killer."

Vic gulped some coffee, swallowed, and then said, "I read the victims were all drugged. The new theory is that the victims knew the killer since he could get close enough to slip the drug into their drinks. The newspaper even said the killer may be a regular at the gay bars. Now, this bartender shows up dead."

"It's just awful to be a target of some deranged person just because of who you love," Amber said before sipping her coffee.

"My mother is worried sick about Phillip. She worries about Phillip contracting AIDS, and now there's this for her to be scared for my brother."

Amber touched Vic's arm, "Phillip will be okay. The police will catch the guy."

Vic gave a skeptical look at Amber, "Gay murders? It's probably not high on their priority list. It's not that important to the general voting population."

Amber's purse sitting on the kitchen counter sounded a catchy samba song. She jumped up and headed to the counter as she called back to Vic, "That's probably my usual morning caller."

Amber dug out her phone and looked at the caller ID window. "Yup, it's my mom. If I don't answer it, she'll think my car is in a ditch somewhere."

"Well, you better answer then," Vic said smiling, dimples and all.

"Hello—hi, Mom—no, everything's okay. I finished the condominium and everything went fine. I'm at Vic's house. We came here after dinner last night."

Vic's eyes opened wide with surprise as he stared at Amber.

Amber turned one hand, palm up in the air, and shrugged. Amber knew it probably sounded weird to blurt out something like that to your mother, but not for her. After all, Suzanne was her best friend, besides being her mother.

"Amber, what happened? I thought he was gay," Suzanne asked. Before Amber could answer, she continued talking. "Don't answer that, I don't want to know what happened. Honey, this is not something you want to start. Remember my friend, Patti? It didn't work for her and now Kevin is happy with David. It's been ten years but Patti is still seeing a therapist."

"I remember Patti," Amber said. "But this house is a totally different style. I had it wrong about the house the last time I spoke to you. It's not like the one Patti had."

Amber and Suzanne had their secret code, a way of speaking, that only they could understand the hidden meaning in a conversation whenever someone else might be listening.

"Oh, he's sitting there."

"Yeah, that's right Mom."

"He's not gay? Are you sure, what about Phillip?"

"No, and yes, I'm sure this is the right style house for Kelly. She doesn't have to *convert* anything. I'll tell you about it Tuesday when we meet for lunch at the Columbia Restaurant. Is two o'clock still okay for you?"

"Honey, wild horses couldn't keep me away," Suzanne said. She had no problem following the code. "You better get back to your fella. Oh, and Amber I'm glad you were wrong about *Kelly's house*. Bye."

"Bye Mom."

Amber turned to Vic, "Now that Mom has called, the rest of my day is free."

"Great, but I want to get you home before dark, safe and sound, behind locked doors. I don't care if that creep is only killing gay men, with you living by yourself, I don't want to take any chances."

Amber smiled, "You and my mom are going to get along great. You're both mother hens."

Devil or Dream Boat

Vic kissed Amber at her door.

"We're giving my neighbors a real show," Amber said and giggled. "I'm seen leaving yesterday and coming home today and then I'm seen kissing a mysterious man on my doorstep. I'll be the gossip of the neighborhood."

"You can refer your nosey neighbors to me if they give you a hard time," Vic said, not budging an inch as he held tight his embrace.

"Good night . . . er . . . I mean goodbye, Mister Richardson," Amber said as she pushed him away. "I had a wonderful time but it's time for you to go home and me to go into my house."

"Okay," he said. He gave her one more kiss and then turned away heading back to his van to leave.

Amber went inside and watched Vic's van disappear down the street until the phone rang. She answered and heard her mother's voice. "Amber, good you're home."

Two calls in one day? That was not usual, especially when her mom knew Amber was sharing the day with a man. Suzanne respected her daughter's space and followed a self-inflicted rule not to interrupt Amber's romances. Besides, she told her earlier that she would wait for her to call back.

"Mom, is something wrong?"

"No. I wanted to know if you have seen the news. They found another body."

"I know, the bartender from Ybor City. Vic and I saw it on the morning news."

"No. Not the bartender. There has been another one. Your father and I heard it on the six o'clock news. A woman. They found her on the steps of a church near downtown. The news said they believe she is another victim of The Rainbow Killer and the police just won't admit it. They said if that is so, then homosexuals are not the only people in danger now. Amber, the woman found wasn't gay. She had a husband and children."

"That poor family."

"Try to catch the eleven o'clock news. All hell is breaking loose in town," Suzanne said. "The Mayor and the Police Chief were furious accusing the news of sensationalizing and instigating public panic. The Channel 13 Station Manager called a news conference and claimed the police couldn't protect the public. He said it was his duty as head of the station to have his staff inform people about a serial killer."

"Why would the police want to hide something like that, Mom? They have to be mistaken."

"Well, I don't know about that, but I'm glad you were safe with Vic last night. Make sure you lock your doors."

"I always do, Mom."

"Okay, honey I'll talk to you tomorrow."

Amber went over, locked the front door, and then returned the phone to the desk. *I'm glad I answered Mom's call this morning or she would've been sure I was dead somewhere.* She walked back to the front of the house and looked out the window. It was dusk; the neighbor across the street was turning off his sprinkler. She looked down the street and noticed a blue pick-up disappearing out of sight. It would be completely dark in a few minutes. She closed the blinds and went to the bedroom to change and get ready to settle in for the night.

After she was comfortable, she headed back into the living room to read until the eleven o 'clock news. As she read, her mind drifted off, thinking about how wonderful Vic had been last night. She felt tingly and like a teenager in love. That worried her. In high school and even the two years she spent at college; she had a history of bad relationships. It seemed like she had a talent for picking the wrong kind of guys. Either they were selfish, thinking only of their selves, or they were on the wrong side of the law. Amber figured she had outgrown her attraction to the "Bad Guy" image. *I'm smarter now. No more giving up my independence for a man.*

Besides, she figured last night probably was not love but just a case of plain old lust. She decided to distance herself from Vic to find out, which it was. If she was away from his charm, she could think clearly and reasonably.

The phone rang. "Who can that be?" she said. "Mom wouldn't call again tonight."

Grabbing the phone, she answered and heard Vic's deep sexy voice on the other end. "Hi, it's Vic. I know I just left you . . . but I, uh, I wanted to tell you how much I enjoyed our dinner last night. I'm glad we straightened out what you thought about me and my brother."

"Yes, I'm glad too." Amber tried to keep her tone casual. "It was a lovely dinner. Thank you for calling."

"Wait," Vic said quickly. "I would like to see you again."

Amber smiled and relaxed her grip on the phone. "Me too." *Great, I sound like an idiot . . . "Me too."* Determined to stick to her plan of a cooling-off time away from Vic, she would make herself unavailable. "I'm going to be very busy this week."

One week would allow her enough time to find out if she was making decisions with her head or with her emotions. She remembered mentioning to Vic at dinner, somewhere after her second glass of wine, that she didn't have any other design jobs on the horizon. She needed to think of an excuse. "I've been putting things off that I need to do, like some things with my mother," she babbled. "Like . . . going through some family pictures . . . and . . . other things." Frantically thinking she added, "I need to use all this week to take care of that business." *Why am I telling him my schedule? –I'm an idiot, that's why!*

"Yeah, I have three jobs ending down in Apollo Beach," Vic said. "I'll be on the road a lot next week. I also need to go way north for another inspection near Homosassa Springs."

"Oh, I understand." Amber held her breath and blinked a couple of times to push back tears of disappointment.

He was just being nice. Probably, he thinks it's bad form to dump me after last night's roll in the hay.

Amber took a slow, deep breath. "It was nice of you to call," she said. She felt like she had just been hit in the stomach. Why had she worried about holding him back, it was obvious last night was just a pleasant one-night stand. But it didn't feel that way to her. It had been much more for her and now she needed to hang up fast before he heard the upset tone in her voice.

"Well, dinner was nice. I'll call you if I have any other clients for pottery. Thanks."

"Amber, wait. What do you mean you understand? I don't *think* so."

"It's okay. We got a little carried away. We need to stay in a business relationship. Thank you for calling. I have to go now."

She hung up without waiting for him to say goodbye. She stood for a second and then started to pace around the living room. A minute later she hurried to the kitchen and grabbed a rag and a can of polish. Returning to the living room, she started feverishly dusting the fireplace mantle and then she moved over to the desk in the corner. Anytime she struggled with a problem, she would sit at that desk and muddle over her thoughts. But she didn't want to sit now. She didn't want to think things over. If she did, she would cry.

Why did I go home with him on the first date? Only a stupid person does that.

The phone rang making her jump. Frozen, she stared at the phone. "It's probably Mom calling to remind to turn the television on so I don't miss the news," she said looking at the

92

phone. "I don't want to talk to Mom now. She can always tell when I'm upset."

It kept ringing. The phone was on its fifth ring when it occurred to her that it may be Vic again. She gingerly picked the phone up.

"Hello."

No answer.

"Hello."

She heard breathing then a low whispered voice spoke.

"Jezebel."

"What? Vic is that you?"

"Repent. Evil is around you."

"Who is this?"

There was no answer. Amber heard more breathing on the other end. Then a click, then silence. Amber slammed the phone down and covered her mouth with her hand staring at the phone. She sat down at the desk, feeling a heaviness in her chest. Her throat tightened as she unconsciously held her breath for a few seconds before exhaling.

The phone rang again. She grabbed it. "Who *is* this!"

"Uh, Vic. What's the matter?"

"Oh, Vic. Nothing's the matter. Did you just call me?"

"No. I mean not since you hung up on me. Why?"

"Someone just called, but I couldn't hear them. I thought maybe it was you?"

"Not me. Look we need to talk. I think you misunderstood me."

"About what?"

The other caller had Amber scared. It was just a crank call. Silly to be so rattled. She had them before, a couple of years back. Some man would call every night at two a.m. The police told her crank callers were usually men who were afraid to meet women face to face. 'Harmless,' they said. Still, those kinds of calls scared every woman she knew who had received them.

She heard Vic speaking. Something about not being a "love-them and leave-them" kind of guy. She tried to pull her attention away from the nuisance caller and back to Vic.

"I didn't think it was a fling for you," he said. "And it definitely wasn't for me. I would like to call you."

His words seem distant as if she was listening to him speak from another room. "I'm sorry. What did you say?"

"I said, how about I call you after work tomorrow? We can talk on the phone at night this week. You concentrate on what you need to do during the day. Spend time with your mother, I'll button up things at work, and maybe, Friday or Saturday, we can get together."

Amber's mind was still on the heavy breather when she realized Vic had stopped talking and was waiting for her to answer him.

"How's that sound to you?" he prompted.

"Good. It . . . it sounds good."

"Okay, then no problem here?" Vic asked. Amber imagined him smiling on the other end of the phone, waiting for her confirmation that everything was fine. She couldn't feel any tender or romantic feelings—not now—she was still distraught from the other caller. Sure, everything was okay with Vic. She had agreed to see him again.

Is Vic really a nice guy? Or am I just another conquest? Amber wondered if she was rusty playing in the dating game. Did Vic just score as in, "Chalk one up for him?" Could there be a man this nice out there for her?

94

Eye Opener

The tall skinny man stumbled out of the bedroom scratching his head as he yawned. His overstayed houseguest sat on the thread-worn, brown couch in the living room. The man slammed the phone down on the coffee table in front of him.

"What's up, Samuel?" the skinny man said. His eyes widened and eyebrows rose as he asked, "You mad at your sister again?"

"No. I wasn't calling her." Samuel paused and then added curtly, "You finally decided to get up."

The sleepy man glared at him with an irritated scowl and headed to the kitchen without speaking. In the kitchen, a stack of mail sat on a table among dirty dishes and piles of empty, crushed beer cans. He walked over to the stack of mail, picked up the top envelope and tossed it aside, systemically going through each. He stopped at the envelope with the return address from TECO, Tampa Electric Company. Ominous blue paper peeked through the plastic window revealing the man's name, Leroy Carpenter. "Damn it!"

Leroy knew even without opening it what blue paper meant, "Final notice." His paycheck always seemed to run out two days before the deadline date of final notices. Last time he took off work early to race down to the payment center on Florida Avenue before the five o'clock closing time to pay the bill, only to get home to find out they had turned off his power at three-thirty. The next day, the old bitty, at the electric company said if it happened again, they would require a two-hundred-dollar deposit. To make matters worse, they charged him fifty dollars to turn the electricity back on—called it a *reconnect fee*.

"I better pay this." Leroy frowned and rubbed his forehead. "Wonder if Pete has any money I can borrow," he mumbled as he thumbed through the rest of the mail. Before heading back to the living room, he went to the refrigerator, got a beer, popped the tab and took a big gulp.

The man on the couch looked up when he returned and said, "If you and that idiot friend of yours didn't drink all night you wouldn't need beer in the morning to get rid of the shakes."

"I'm not a drunk, Samuel. I don't get the shakes. It just helps clear my head. I work hard all week, there's nothing wrong with unwinding on Friday and Saturday nights."

"Whatever you say, Leroy. I'm just a guest here. You don't have to answer to me. The only one you have to answer to is our maker, the good Lord."

Samuel stood up and looked around. "Where are the keys to the truck? I need to go round up something."

Leroy pointed to a bookcase by the door with shelves crammed full of *Popular Mechanics* magazines and where papers were spilling off the edges in a jumbled, disorganized mess. On the top of the bookcase, lay a heap of keys on a ring attached to a long chain and a metal skull with red stone eyes. "You're not dressed up as usual— more casual. How come?"

Samuel always wore a buttoned-up dress shirt and good jeans. Leroy's good jeans even had holes mended or patches on them. Leroy's houseguest outdressed him no matter what. Today, Samuel had on a black t-shirt, his usual color, even for the button-up shirts. However, his jeans were older, worn, and he had on a brown twill jacket with a corduroy collar.

"Going hunting," Samuel answered.

"Hunting? This time of year?"

"Don't worry. I don't need a hunting license. It's not that kind of hunting. No shooting involved; my catch will be live." Samuel narrowed his eyes, looking directly at Leroy. "The Bible tells about the people who spoke against God and Moses. The Lord sent fiery serpents among the people and many died . . . the people of Israel. People came to Moses; said they have sinned and Moses prayed for them."

Samuel stopped and his look softened with a concerned expression. "You read your Bible, son. Listen to me. You can still go the way of the Lord. My job is to open the eyes of the lost ones, the sinners who still have time. Sinners must repent and seek God." Samuel grabbed the keys lying on the bookcase and paused by the door. "I'll be back in a while." Then he turned and walked out the front door.

Leroy listened as his truck engine started up and then the whine of the motor faded into the distance. Leroy still had six payments left to make to *Ugly Duckling Used Cars.* Since Samuel had moved in, Leroy rarely used his own truck. "Damn Preacher, he's got to go," Leroy muttered. "He gives me the willies. He's bad news."

I found out from Leroy's Soul Follower that Leroy didn't know much about his houseguest, Samuel. They met at the *Watering Hole* one night and started to talk. Samuel commented that he had hitchhiked into town and did not know where he was going to sleep for the night. He seemed like an okay guy to Leroy because his clothes were good and he spoke intelligently, Leroy told Samuel he could crash at his place. Two months later and Samuel was still there. A prime example that bad decisions are made, while under the influence of alcohol. Leroy unwittingly placed himself between the proverbial "rock and a hard place." Samuel borrowed *his* truck all the time and never offered to pay for gas, which was what got under Leroy's skin most of all. What made matters worse was Samuel always had money in his pocket and never looked for work. He would take Leroy's truck, drive it, come back and hand him the keys, and say, "Your truck needs gas. You better put some in it before you go to work tomorrow."

Leroy held his tongue, though. Because living under the same roof with Samuel, he had witnessed his volatile preaching outburst. Leroy was afraid of the Bible-thumper, as he called him. He thought Samuel was dangerous and maybe just plain crazy.

Leroy took the last gulp of beer, crushed the can, and hurled it into the kitchen. It hit the open garbage can but ricocheted out and bounced across the floor. "Crap!" he bellowed. Outside, the loud sound of a muffler rumbled, diverting his attention from the missed target. Then he heard Pete's voice outside, thanking someone for the lift. A minute later, the front door opened and in walked Pete.

"What's up? See your truck is gone again." Pete walked past Leroy and into the kitchen. "Where's Samuel?"

I found out more about Leroy and his childhood friend a while back. Pete had been Leroy's shadow since they were young boys. They were both oddly devoted to each other. Leroy acted like a big brother to Pete, and Pete seemed to look up to Leroy, trusting in him completely. Pete was an unlikely sidekick to Leroy.

Pete had a cruel side. Despite his scrawny physique, he had become a bully, learning from masters who had bullied him as a child. Pete was abusive to his wives, girlfriends, and anyone he held an advantage over.

Leroy, on the other hand, was somewhat of a "lady's man" with a more tender side. However, he disliked people who were "different," as he referred to homosexuals. Sometimes, this dislike resulted in him weakening, allowing a meaner side to surface, to participate in the occasional gay-bashing excursions.

Despite his unproductive life, Leroy had above-average intelligence. Once he tried college and made it through two semesters before his dirt-poor background and abusive, alcoholic family played havoc on his confidence. He felt defeated, lost his drive to better himself, quit, and accepted life at the bottom of mankind's existence.

Pete opened the refrigerator and grabbed a Budweiser. "Need a beer?"

"Yeah, thanks," Leroy answered. "Samuel needed to go get something. Look, Pete, I need to talk to you before he comes back. We need to figure out a way to get him out of here."

"Why? He's not so bad," Pete said. Pete popped the can and handed it to Leroy.

"There's something not right about him," Leroy continued. "He's going to get us in trouble. I can just feel it. And I'm not going back to jail. Three months was long enough for me to decide, I'm *never* going back."

Besides his self-welfare, Leroy knew if Samuel did something, it would not only implicate him, but Pete would go down too. There was no way Pete would survive in jail. He had to protect his friend and himself.

"Well, you better not kick him out," Pete said. "He would get even if you did that. He's mean. Remember, he used to play with snakes when he was a kid."

"Nah, I told you, Pete. That was his dad. The church his father preached at used snakes in their Sunday services."

Pete made a face and said, "Weird people up in those mountains."

Slow Burn

Ybor City.

The thick wooden entrance doors to the Columbia Restaurant opened. The glow of the Florida sun outlined a curvy female figure with flowing hair. As she entered, the doors closed but a soft glimmer remained highlighting and lingering about her, very similar to the way a red-hot sparkler leaves a line drawn in the night after waving it about. Amber's mother, Suzanne, had an inner beauty, which stemmed from a good and pure heart. Even the sun's intensity seemed to wane in her present.

"Sorry, I'm late. I can't believe I got caught in traffic," Suzanne said.

"Hi, Mom. You look great, as usual."

The hostess led them to a table in the Patio Room. Over the last week, Amber spoke often about her mom to Vic in their phone conversations. Suzanne played a big part in Amber's life because she was her best friend, as well as, her mother.

Suzanne's youthful appearance made most people ask if they were sisters whenever they were out on one of their shopping excursions or luncheons. That was evident today, as they walked through the adjacent dining room and every male head turned toward Suzanne.

Amber nudged her mom at the table before taking a seat. She leaned in and said, "Mom, you got more looks today than me."

They both took delight in keeping a running tally of who got more looks from men whenever they were out together.

"I'm not sure, Amber," Suzanne said. "That one man in the corner looked like he was going to need a chiropractor if he twisted any more around when you passed him."

The waitress gave them menus and said she would return in a few minutes. She was barely gone when Suzanne, unable to wait any longer, asked, "Well, has Vic called today?"

Suzanne knew about Amber's decision to stay away from Vic for a week for a cooling-off time. Today was Friday and the week was over. Suzanne thought her daughter's plan was ridiculous. Her reply to Amber's plan when she heard it was, "Why? Chemistry is chemistry. You don't have to test it. If it's there, a week apart won't change it."

Vic had agreed; therefore, it didn't matter what Amber's mother thought, which ended any further discussion. Cooling off time had run its course now and Vic was no longer a taboo subject.

"Are you two going out tonight?" Suzanne asked.

"Mom, I think you're more excited about me going out with Vic than I am."

"Oh, I don't think that's possible, honey," Suzanne said. She knew her daughter and understood even the things Amber kept to herself.

Amber stared in silence at her mom with wide eyes. Then she broke her stare and picked the menu up. "You're scary Mom. How do you do that? I mean . . . know how I feel even before I do."

Suzanne knew that under her daughter's strong independent façade lay a frightened woman, unwilling to give up control. That was what Amber's "cooling off time" was all about and not whether Vic's commitment was sincere.

"I'm a mom. Moms know things. It comes with the territory." Suzanne understood her daughter's secret hopes to find a soul mate, although she resisted most commitments. Amber had always said if she could find a love like the one Suzanne and Jimmy had, she would be truly happy. However, Amber's insecurities, invariability seemed to block anyone who came close to her.

What Suzanne didn't understand was why her daughter fought marriage as if it meant she had to give up her personal identity. By finding the right man, a woman's independence does not get smashed instead, it is reinforced. The love affair ignited doesn't need to smother either; Suzanne knew this from her marriage. Still, her daughter clung to solitude.

Amber looked at her mother's fixated gaze and put the menu down. "Really, mother, you're like a dog with a bone. If you must know, Miss Nosey, I'm glad this week is over."

"You missed him?"

"Yeah, I guess I did. Only talking to him on the phone made the anticipation of seeing him again almost unbearable. This week I just about went crazy thinking about him—*but then*—you already knew that, didn't you?" Amber said glaring at her mom.

Then Amber smiled. "He's calling me at five-thirty, I don't know if we'll go out tonight or tomorrow."

"Maybe you'll see him tonight *through* tomorrow. Maybe he'll take you back to the Don Cesar for an overnight stay."

Amber rolled her eyes and picked up her menu again. "What are you going to eat for lunch—*Mother*."

Suzanne hoped Amber would not keep Vic at bay like she tried to do with Frank. Four years ago, her daughter's stubbornness pushed Frank Pellow away.

Frank asked Amber to marry him but her reaction mirrored a scared little girl. Amber sniffled through tears when she told Suzanne she loved Frank but wasn't ready to settle down. Suzanne remembered Amber's words from the past. "Mom, I can't see coming home to Frank every night to be the dutiful wife. He gave me an ultimatum. He said it was simple. I either love him and we get married, or not. It's over. He's gone."

Now Suzanne glanced at her daughter across the table. She appeared happy. It was a different kind of happiness than she had first displayed with Frank. This time she was glowing. Being too independent can hurt and lead to a lonely life. Suzanne hoped Amber would listen to her heart this time.

The waitress brought their lunch and a bottle of wine that Suzanne had ordered to celebrate the conclusion of "Iceberg Week."

"The scary thing is, Mom," Amber said between bites of salad, "This week Vic and I talked every night. I found myself watching the clock, waiting for his call. I've never done that before. We talked about everything. He told me about playing Tarzan in the woods when he was a little boy, and how he felt when his father died. All kinds of things."

"Sounds like you got to know him well."

"I guess."

"What's the problem then?" Suzanne asked.

"Nothing, but I don't want to lean on him too much. After all, we've only been out on one date."

"I don't think you're leaning on him by having phone conversations."

"No, not by talking on the phone."

Suzanne looked puzzled. "What then?"

"Mom, remember when I had that crank phone caller a while back? I've been getting calls again. They started right after I met Vic and this week, I got so scared, I wanted to ask Vic to come over and stay with me. That's what I'm talking about. I didn't ask him to come to the rescue but it was hard not to."

"Did you need a rescuer? What did the caller say that was so frightening? Did he threaten you?"

"Not really, but I don't want the calls to influence my decisions with Vic. I mean, I don't want him to be a convenience. Anyway, it's Friday. Cooling-down time is over—and I'm not cooled off."

Lace and Deep Breathing

After lunch, Suzanne and Amber went shopping in Hyde Park. After entering a small boutique shop, Suzanne thumbed through some satin pajamas hanging near the front door. Amber moved toward the back to look at some lingerie on a table.

"Mom," Amber said, turning toward her mother. Holding up a sexy midnight blue nightie with a black lace bodice she asked, "Do you think this would be proper attire for *The Don?*"

Suzanne giggled, "It's perfect, but Honey, don't give a preview fashion show at home. If you do, you won't get to The Don CeSar."

"That's what I like about you Mom, you give outstanding advice."

Amber arrived home by four-thirty. She had time to gather her thoughts before Vic's call. After unpacking her shopping bags, she poured a glass of a South African Syrah, the one Andy introduced her to, and headed to the chair at her desk. She sat and admired the deep mahogany wood. *I still love this desk.*

It was her favorite piece of furniture. She had come across it on vacation in a little shop outside of Charleston. A bit oversized for her little bungalow but it still tucked nicely in the left corner of the living room. The small Tiffany-style lamp on top gave warmth to the area that she called her "tranquil place."

Amber remembered the old man who sold her the desk—Mr. Sweeney. She had been on vacation and stopped at his antique store. When she saw the desk, she knew she had to have it. Her taste was eclectic, decorating with items like a contemporary Warhol original from her mother, and mixing it with a Victoria couch. She had thought that the formal Queen Anne desk would give an elegant blend to the room. There were two drawers on both ends, separated by a long center drawer with carved beading along the perimeter edge at the top. The sides bore detailed leaf carvings flowing downward from the top of each leg that ended in a ball-and-claw foot.

Mr. Sweeney had argued that the shipping would be too expensive for her purchase but Amber insisted stating she would make the arrangements and pay for the shipping cost.

The conversation between the two of them went something like, "Pretty thing like you should have your husband handle things like that," Sweeney stated.

"I am not married."

"No husband?"

"No, but I'm perfectly capable of buying and shipping furniture by myself."

"You girls today think you don't need a man. It's not natural. Women need men to handle important things. You girls should stick to raising babies like God intended for you."

Men like Sweeney reinforced Amber's independent ways and her stubbornness to remain single. Whenever Amber thought of Sweeney, I could feel her anger surface. However, even remembering his words didn't put her in a bad mood today.

Amber's mind drifted to Vic. *Vic is a nice guy. So different, not like Frank. Not Controlling.*

Amber understood Vic was different from Frank. Frank would've never backed off for a week. With Frank, there had been only his way or the wrong way, and it was all about him winning.

The phone rang. Amber picked it up before the second ring.

"Hi, I was just thinking about you," Amber said. She waited. No response. "Are you there?"

There was dead silence followed by a click.

"Strange. Maybe it was my deep breather."

Her nuisance caller didn't always preach the Bible to her; sometimes he would just breathe heavily into the phone for a minute before hanging up.

"Guess he ran out of evil things to warn me about," Amber said with a shrug.

The phone rang again.

Amber sat for a minute looking at the phone. On the fifth ring, she picked it up. "Hello?"

"Hi Amber, it's Vic. How did lunch go with your mom?"

She let out a held breath with relief, and then, took a sip of wine. "Great. We did some shopping afterward. I got home a few minutes ago."

They talked for a while. Soon the topic of the weekend came up.

"What do you say I pick you up on Saturday? We can go to Tarpon Springs, walk around the antique shops, and then head over to the sponge docks in the evening," Vic said. "Do you have plans for Saturday night? I really want to see you again. This week has been the longest week. I couldn't get you out of my mind."

Amber smiled. "Me too."

She bit the side of her lip, took in a deep breath, and blurted out, "I have plans for Saturday." It was a lie but she was worried about letting Vic know how important he had become after a one-night stay with him. Plus, she didn't want to sound too easy.

"Oh . . . I know it's late notice and you need your space," Vic said. After a long pause, he added, "It's just that I've missed you this week."

He sounded so . . . wounded and felt horrible. *What am I doing? I'm being just like Frank, controlling. I'm going to drive him away. He has been patient but there is a limit.*

"What I meant to say, was I'll be finished by two o'clock. Tarpons Springs sounds like a great idea."

"That's terrific." His voice picked up speed with excitement as he talked. "I can pick you up by three-thirty. Would that be too early?"

"No, that's not too early. Tarpon Springs is one of my favorite places."

"Mine too." He paused and added in a slower more seductive voice, "But sunsets at The Don will always hold special memories."

"You better be careful, you'll spoil me. It's only our second date. It doesn't have to be anything special. We could rent a movie and stay home—unless you're afraid you will find yourself bored with me."

"No problem there, I'll never get bored with you."

The Box

They shall take up serpents; and if they drink any deadly thing, it shall not hurt them; they shall lay hands on the sick, and they shall recover. **Mark 16 American King James Version**

* * *

The old Chevy pulled up in front of the dilapidated, frame house and two men hopped out. "Thanks for the ride, buddy," Leroy said to the driver before he closed the door. "Yeah, thanks," Pete added as he walked around to Leroy's side. The two men turned and headed up the front sidewalk as the car drove away.

"What the Hell. . . ." Leroy said when he spotted Samuel crawling out from under the house.

"Weird," Pete said in a low voice. "Why's he under your house?"

"Don't know. I told you, he's just not right," Leroy answered. As they approached, Samuel straightened up and brushed the dirt off his pants.

"Hey Samuel, what's the matter?" Leroy asked.

"Nothing's wrong." Samuel looked more threatening than usual still dressed in the brown hunting jacket from that morning, but now, he also had on black rubber wading boots. "Just needed to store something in a dark, cool place. Under the house is perfect. That's where we use to keep the . . . uh . . . I mean, it's a good place to store things."

"You stored things under the houses in the mountains?" Pete said with a confused look on his face.

"You never mind, Pete," Samuel said sternly, "and Leroy, don't you be bothering that box under there. It wouldn't be wise."

108

Leroy frowned. "Sure thing, Samuel"

"I'm going to head in and get a shower and then I'm going to hit the sack. I was up late last night." Samuel plunged his hand into his pants pocket, dug out keys, and tossed them to Leroy.

"Here are your keys to the truck. Needs gas."

Kidnapped

Amber and Vic had dated for three months but still, their eyes possessed that "newly-in-love" look. Amber didn't care about her changed behavior. She was happy, truly happy. It was a new experience for her, that dating utopia where couples shared secret glances, while in the company of others, and processed hidden giddy feelings inside. She never had that with Frank. Their relationship was more of a mature compatibility. With Vic, she yearned to be with him when they were apart, and it had nothing to do with enjoying romantic dates at Tarpons Springs or the sunsets at the Don Caesar. She told herself that any influence of romantic settings would have worn off by now. Besides, she was content to spend time with Vic quietly at her or his house, sipping wine, listening to music, and talking. Of course, they never talked for very long.

Although things relaxed and grew comfortable between them, it was never tiresome. Amber loved that Vic and she seemed to move in sync. The passionate fire between them still burned red-hot. That was another difference between her and Vic and the relationship she had experienced with Frank.

Life was perfect. Amber had her house and her freedom. She did what she wished during the day, while Vic worked. In the evening, most nights, Vic would come over for a few hours and then return to his house. After he would leave, and only then, the troublesome calls began. Weekends were different because Vic and she usually spent the entire time together at his place. Those times the calls stopped.

The only thing that spoiled Amber's idyllic life was the persistent and disturbing calls. Most of the time the caller would just breathe into the phone and not speak as Amber asked, "Hello . . . is anyone there?" When it seemed he was bored with that, he started to talk in a low and threatening voice. Soon his calls changed to increased enthusiasm, laced with disgust, and demanded for Amber's retribution. His raspy warnings about sinners were more unsettling than the sounds of his dreadful heavy breathing.

Amber was positive the calls would stop, once the caller realized he did *not* scare her. That is one reason she didn't want to tell Vic because his overreaction to protect would make her apprehension grow. She was determined not to panic and have a crank caller win by turning her into a quivering female.

This morning, after her ritual phone chat with Suzanne, Amber headed to the bedroom to change into workout clothes. She had finished a small remodel job last week and now there were no future contracts on the horizon. It was the law of the land in the design industry. An occupational hazard, one might say, it was either feast or famine. Famine usually meant months between design jobs. Amber wanted to stay busy and with empty hours to fill, she joined a gym and went every morning around 10:00 a.m.

As she dressed, the phone next to the bed rang. She stood holding her shorts in mid-step—one foot in a pant-leg, one out—frozen—mid-air.

Who can that be? It had become routine to think every unexpected caller was her heavy breather and preacher of righteousness. The thought brought every nerve in her body to the surface.

Matt didn't call until late afternoon on weekdays. Today was Thursday and Vic usually worked late on Thursdays, in order to leave early on Friday to start the weekend with her. He wouldn't call until after dinner.

Ring . . .

It can't be creepo. Amber stood still.

111

Ring . . .

But . . . he only calls at night after Vic's leaves. She pulled her cotton workout pants up and then sat on the edge of the bed staring at the phone as if she could will it to stop ringing.

Last night Amber woke to the phone ringing at three-thirty in the morning. Drowsily she grabbed the phone in the dark and heard his voice—that evil methodical voice—drone out hateful things. Spewing accusations about sinners, when he started with vivid warnings of hell and damnation, his voice surged with a frightening zest.

Ring.

Amber snatched the phone up and shrieked into it. "Why are you calling me?"

"Because . . . because your sins don't go unnoticed. You're going to burn for them unless you repent," the throaty voice whispered.

"Stop calling me, you creep." She slammed the phone down.

Last night she paid for her outburst. After screaming into the phone, he kept calling and calling. Drawn at first to answer the ringing phone, Amber answered it. He continued from where he left off when she had hung up on him. He spoke about sinners and said that through God, her soul could be saved. Amber resorted to picking up the phone and immediately placing it down, hanging up on him. That seemed only to encourage him to redial continually. It had gone on for over three hours. Relief only came after Amber unplugged the phone but by then she was so shaken and felt completely vulnerable. Every time she would drift off, she would wake suddenly believing she felt his heavy breath exhaling on her neck and darting up fearing he was in her bed.

The phone rang again.

Ring . . . ring . . .

Amber stared at the phone. With fingertips, she gingerly picked it up; afraid it was the monster again. He wouldn't stop. He would never stop.

She listened.

Silence.

"Hello?" she said timidly.

"Just wanted to let you know early—"

"Vic."

"Yeah. You disappointed?"

"No . . . I . . . uh, never mind. Why are you calling?"

"Tell Suzanne, she won't hear from you this weekend. I'm kidnapping you."

"What?"

Vic gave a mischievous laugh.

Amber relaxed. "Oh, you are. So, where are you taking me?"

"I'm not telling. Pack some comfortable clothes and plan to stay at my place Friday night. We will be leaving before the sun's up. So call your mom and tell her not to expect your daily check-in call."

"That's all you're going to tell me?"

"Yup. Don't forget, I don't want her to send out the Cavalry when she cannot reach you."

Saturday morning.

The alarm clock buzzed early. Vic pushed the off button. "Time to wake up," he said as he slipped out of bed.

A few minutes later, Amber heard him banging around the kitchen and looked at the clock. It glowed 4:30 am. She groaned. "Man, he wasn't kidding about waking up before the sun."

Amber and Vic had grown accustomed to sleeping in at either her place or his and eating breakfast in bed. Sometimes they stayed there until dinner.

Vic entered the bedroom and flipped on the light. Amber's hand flew up covering her eyes.

"Sorry," Vic said sheepishly. "I have coffee brewing. We need to be at our appointed destination by daybreak."

Amber squinted, and pulled herself up resting on her elbows, blinking at the brightness. Vic stood at the end of the bed, buttoning his shirt, smiling with his dimples appearing as his smile grew wider. He winked at her.

"It's so early," she moaned. "No hint to where we're going?"

"Okay, but just one hint. It's connected to when we met at the gallery for the *Rainbow Colors for Life* exhibit and the silent auction. You have to come with me. Call today a celebration of the night we met."

"You're so mysterious."

"Hurry up. Get dressed," Vic said. Calling back as he walked out of the room, "We can't be late."

Amber needed this diversion—to go somewhere—and not think. Not about murders in town or serial killers. No worrying about Phillip, or the others in the group. A day of no phone calls with whispered warnings or heavy breathing from the other end of a phone line. An escape with no thoughts of anything bad. It was exactly what she needed.

"Do I need to throw you under a cold shower?" Vic called from the other room. "Come on chop-chop!"

"Okay, I'm up. A shower sounds good but not cold." Amber hurried toward the bathroom. "I am jumping in the shower to wake up, I'll be quick," she shouted. "I promise."

In the safety of Vic's shower, warm water ran over her face, thoughts about late-night calls crept back. She had kept it a secret that the calls had started again. She had finally convinced her mother and Vic to stop worrying. After nearly two weeks without any threatening calls, they figured the caller was some weirdo prompted by the murders in town to frighten women over the phone. They assumed he had gotten tired of his game and that was why the calls stopped.

Then, four days ago, on Wednesday morning, at 3:40 a.m., his calls started again. The phone rang and Amber heard him.

"Ammberr . . ." A barely audible voice spoke. "You haven't listened. Heed my warning. Sinners must pay." She lay shaking alone in her bed with the covers pulled tight around her neck for an hour without moving. Once out of the paralyzed state she went through the house, turned every light on, and waited for sunrise when Suzanne would call for their morning coffee chat.

She decided not to give in to her fear. She would go this round of calls by herself. She had to have some control of her life. She wasn't a child. Adults handled their own problems.

Amber stood in Vic's shower with the water flowing over her. *I'm not going to think about it. He's just a weirdo who gets his kicks scaring women over the phone.*

Daybreak

Dew-covered streets glowed as the sun broke through the predawn fog. As Vic drove, Amber looked over at him and smiled. "You look like the cat that swallowed the canary."

"Amber you ought to know by now that I'm a very passive man," Vic said. He looked at her with his runaway lock of hair brushing the top of his eyebrow. "I detest violence. I couldn't hurt an innocent little canary, even if I were a cat."

"Very funny," she said and playfully slapped his shoulder.

They drove a few minutes down the road then she spoke again. "You know I must get home Sunday night early. Mom and I have plans at the Safety Harbor Spa on Monday morning. Remember, it's my present to her for her birthday. If we're catching a flight out of town . . . I'm not sure—"

"No problem, we're not catching a plane. I don't know why you insisted on driving your car to my house last night. You can stop worrying about tomorrow. You can go home early tomorrow night," he said. "I don't know why you wouldn't let me pick you up. I said I'd get you home by seven on Sunday night. Don't you trust me?"

"Yes. It's me that I don't trust. If I have my car, I'll leave early. When I have you drive me home, I tend to stall and put off leaving you. It's silly but if I need to drive myself, I'll stick to a schedule. It's my way of being a grown-up."

"Amber, believe me, you're all grown-up," Vic said with a devilish laugh.

"Stop that!" she blushed. "I want to get home early Sunday and get in bed so I'm not tired for the spa with Mom."

"Getting you in bed hasn't been a problem for me," he said chuckling.

Amber blushed again.

They drove for thirty minutes then Vic pulled off the road and followed a dirt path with deep ruts leading into an open field. A small group of people stood near a big wicker-like basket in the middle of the field. On the ground lay a multi-color cloth draped out across the grass. A pick-up truck was a few feet away with a magnetic sign on the door, which read, "Up, Up and Away Hot Air Balloon Rides."

Amber squealed and a big smile stretched across her face. "You were the one who beat me out of the winning bid at the auction."

"Yup. I figure that if I didn't want you to hold a grudge against me, I'd better share. I didn't even know why I put a bid on it. Something just made me. I never even thought about going on a hot air balloon ride before, but I guess destiny moved the pen in my hand."

"It's wonderful." Amber threw her arms around Vic's neck, giving him a big hug.

"Well, come on," he said. "We don't want to miss the champagne toast. It's tradition, as well as, lift off at dawn."

In another part of Tampa.

Andy Martinez slid out of the bed and put his slippers on trying not to wake the man beside him. The sleeping man had tossed and turned most of the night before finally falling asleep. Weeks of restless nights for Andy's partner had become normal. Andy knew he must be stressed to near exhaustion. Normally he was the first up to go into the kitchen and brew the coffee. He would be reading the morning paper and on his second cup of coffee by the time Andy woke.

The ever presence of danger from the maniac on a gay killing rampage would cause any homosexual man stress. But not Andy's partner, he denied any stressful worry. His efforts were futile because Andy saw through him to the truth recognizing the denials as a made-up façade of strength to camouflage his fear. After thirteen years being together, he couldn't hide his fear from Andy.

Before closing the bedroom door, Andy looked back at the bed in frustration. "I love you," he whispered. "You don't have to pretend to be macho with me. Why can't you understand that?"

Andy got the morning paper outside and headed back into the kitchen. He opened the cupboard, grabbed two mugs and then filled the coffee pot with water. He took the coffee out of the cupboard and paused. He couldn't remember how many teaspoons of coffee grounds were needed. Frustrated and worried about his partner, he leaned his elbows on the counter and put his head in his hands. *Man, he's going to kill himself holding things in like this.*

Andy straightened up and went back to measuring the coffee grounds into the basket, put it in place, poured the water in and pushed the brew button. He grabbed the phone, headed to the stool at the breakfast nook and called Saffron's number.

"Hi, it's Andy. I wanted to call and tell you I met that David with the Pink Pistols organization."

"Why are you whispering? I can barely hear you." Saffron asked.

"Sorry. He's not up yet. Can you hear me now?"

"Yeah."

"I don't know if I can take it anymore, Saf," Andy said. "It's my fault, I encouraged him to keep the secret about us being a couple to people, except for you and our group, but I'm sick of this charade."

"Then tell him."

"It's too late for that now," Andy said. "Coming out now is not an option. The whole town thinks he's a happy heterosexual male. Announcing anything different would be disastrous for him."

"Andy, I know you had your reasons to encourage him to stay in the closet, but you know what I think, the price is too high. It's like Claire and me, if people don't like it then too bad. Screw them all."

"Well, there was a lot at stake for him when we met. I still think it was the right decision to keep us private."

"Maybe . . . who knows?"

Andy let out a heavy sigh. "But Saffron, now he's keeping his worries private from me. Bottling everything up and not sharing with me. I can't stand it! And pretending every time we're out in public to only casually know each other—I don't know if I can do it anymore."

"Andy you have to tell him to come out. If he doesn't, it's going to break the two of you up."

"No! I can't. Not after all these years. I got what I asked for; besides, you remember what happened when I told my dad. At least I had my mother and my sister's support, I was lucky. Not everyone is so lucky. I couldn't stand it if I was to blame for him losing his girl and everything else."

Andy had spoken from experience. His Soul Follower's heart nearly broke apart when it happened—when Andy, at eighteen, announced to his family that he was gay. That day struck Andy down with such venomous hurt that it left him scarred forever.

Andy had thought it would be easy because he figured everyone could tell. He wasn't a flamer, per se, but he had the walk, and when he talked, he couldn't help waving his delicate hands about. No matter how hard he tried, he couldn't macho-up his natural body language. There just was not *anything* masculine about him, so who would be surprised?

What Andy hadn't realized was that some relatives wanted to remain blind to his preference. As long as it wasn't talked about, they didn't have to face it. That was how Andy's father was—being forced to see his son's homosexuality had resulted in a display of pure rage. He stormed out of the house, vowing never to speak to any of them again. "Anyone who accepts that little deviant is no better than he is," Andy's father yelled. "You are all going to Hell."

Weeks later, divorce papers came to the house for Andy's mother. His father never stepped foot in the house again.

Another blow came to Andy a few years later, around his twentieth birthday. Andy ran into his father. The incident took place at The Center for the Performing Arts. Andy's friends bought him theatre tickets to the *Phantom of the Opera*. During the intermission, Andy looked across the lobby and saw his father standing with a blond woman.

Andy decided to go over to say hello. After all, it had been two years. Time enough for his father to come to grips with the idea his son was gay. Anyway, he figured his dad always realized the truth because he used to refer to him as "soft." Complaining often, saying, "Why don't you toughen up?" Asking Andy, "Why don't you want to play football or join the wrestling team like 'normal' boys?"

Andy made his way through the crowd and stopped beside his father. "Hi, Dad."

His father turned around, with a look of shock, and blurted out, "What? Dad!" Waving his hand and almost pushing at Andy as he raised his voice and demanded, "Go away."

He turned back to the women and said in a louder voice, "He must be crazy. I don't have a son. Damn queen, they're all sickos. They think any man might be their father. He's probably drunk."

After that, Andy claimed he always hated his father, therefore, he didn't care what he thought or did. Said he was glad his father was out of his life. That was Andy's lie that he would live with and keep to himself.

"Anyway Saffron, I didn't call to cry on your shoulder," Andy said. "I just wanted to let you know I'll bring the info from David about the Pink Pistols to the book club meeting."

Saffron and Andy said goodbye and hung up.

I can't believe Saffron asked me to get the information about a gun club. Andy smiled as he remembered a day last summer when they met at Saffron's house for a book club meeting.

There were about six or seven at the meeting. They were all sitting on Saffron's back lanai. She had her white Himalayan cat in her lap. All of sudden the cat stood up, stiffened, and gave a deep throaty growl staring straight ahead. Everyone stopped talking and looked at Snowball. The cat's tail twitched left, right and then she leapt off Saffron's lap. The furry cat scrambled with nails digging into the outdoor carpet tearing toward the screen after something. Saffron let out a scream and jumped out of her chair after her cat. Plunging down on her knees, chasing Snowball, crawling behind potted plants screaming, "No, Snowball. No."

Finally, she caught hold of the cat and climbed to her feet, Saffron held the cat tightly. Snowball wiggled like a runaway fire hose in her hands trying to get away but not letting go of the lizard dangling in her mouth. Saffron shook the cat until Snowball lost her grip of the small green thing. The lizard dropped and made its escape.

"Well, thanks a lot for helping," Saffron said. She was almost in tears as her face flushed a bright red color. The group roared with laughter.

Saffron became furious. "You guys were going to just sit there and watch her eat the poor little thing? Even if it's small, it's still one of God's creatures. Laugh if you want but I'm the one who will sleep at night with a clear conscious."

Andy gave a quiet little chuckle from the image in his mind of Saffron's face that day. "Yeah, Saffron you're going to learn how to protect yourself with a gun," Andy said. "Like you could ever shoot someone. No matter how butch you are that will never happen."

Andy opened the newspaper. The headlines read; *The Rainbow Killer could be a Cowboy Club Regular.*

Articles speculating that evidence indicated the killer moved freely among the homosexual community only fed to every gay person's fear. Some experts theorized the killer could be a homosexual himself. Theory was he could be psychologically unbalanced from something that happened in his childhood and be lashing out at other gays. Some experts went as far to suggest that his actions could be a subconscious act of killing himself. Andy and the group did not buy that theory.

Andy started to read. The paper said police were questioning the staff of the Cowboy Club, and wanted to interview more people in the homosexual community.

Andy heard the creak of the bedroom door open. In the doorway stood the muscular, Matt Connelly stretching. He had on the black velvet robe Andy got him for Christmas last year. He walked into the kitchen to where Andy sat.

"Good morning," Andy said. "I made the coffee. Your cup is on the counter by the pot."

"Thanks, I didn't sleep well . . . uh . . . the owls were hooting all night and kept me awake."

Last Call

Leroy and Pete had to work overtime on Saturday and they weren't happy about it. Traditionally, Leroy slept in on Saturday mornings, did nothing all day until afternoon when he'd drive over to pick up Pete and head to the bar. They usually got there around two or three in the afternoon, would shoot some pool, drink and stay until closing. Considering Leroy's financial situation of dodging bill collectors, one would think he'd be happy for the overtime pay, but Saturdays were reserved for drinking. The way he reasoned, he worked all week, therefore, he deserved Saturday to sleep and drink. Sundays were for doing nothing and nursing a headache.

This Saturday, overtime day, was supposed to be only a few hours. Three hours—four tops, but it turned out to be a full day. Leroy dropped Pete off at his house at five-thirty and told him he was going home to get some "shuteye," as he said. He told Pete he'd return in a few hours and they would go to the Watering Hole then. They could shoot some pool and salvage the rest of their Saturday.

Leroy turned down his street and he pulled the pick-up into his front yard and went inside the house. He put his keys down and looked around the living room. The lights he thought he had turned off before leaving for work were still lit.

"Samuel . . . Samuel, you here?" *Wonder where he went off to*, he thought.

Leroy kicked his shoes off in the middle of the floor and shuffled into the bedroom. He collapsed on the bed in his dirty work clothes and was asleep within minutes.

123

Eight hours later, he woke up and looked at the clock beside his bed. "Shit!" Bounding out of bed, "We'll barely make it for last call."

Leroy rushed out into the living room to the front window. "Good. Truck's still here. Guess Samuel didn't come back," he said grabbing the phone to call Pete. He answered on the third ring. "Hey, be over to get you in about five minutes."

"What happen to you? It's after midnight."

"Overslept. Damn work."

Seedy side of Town, the neighborhood hangout.

A beat-up, blue pick-up truck pulled to the curb in front of graffiti marked building. The truck door squeaked open and Leroy stepped out from behind the wheel. On the passenger side, the door pushed open and Pete jumped down from the high seat to the sidewalk. Overhead a red and blue neon sign hung above the building entrance that read, "The Watering Hole." The letter "O" flickered on and off with an ominous warning that any minute it might go out for good leaving a blank space between the "H" and the "le." The dreadful building matched perfectly with all the rest of the buildings on the street.

Leroy, still in his work cloths, opened the bar door and stepped inside. Pete in a graying white t-shirt and jeans with holes in the knees followed.

The room was one huge space but it gave a distinction of two separate rooms. To the left, four pool tables sat with shop lights above each. There were no plastic covers, which left the exposed fluorescent bulbs. The result was a harsh white light that shown down on the felt tabletops. The light spilled over, somewhat, into the adjacent darkness on the right side of the room. A bar sat in the cave like area. A dozen or so, t-shirt clad men were bellied-up to the bar clasping half-empty beer bottles in their hands. Above the bar top was a light bulb hanging from the end of a long cord, there were three in a row running down the length of the bar to provide barely enough light to see what the men were drinking.

The tattooed crowd turned and squinted with bloodshot eyes to see who entered and then turned back to their beer and pool games. No one seemed to care about the new arrivals. A bearded man at one pool table had stopped talking to look toward the door and then he turned back to finish talking and a roar of laugher followed—evidence of a punch line delivery.

A man wearing an apron around his hips stood behind the counter with a rag in hand, wiping the bar top as he puffed on a nub of a cigar wedged in the corner of his mouth. His muscle t-shirt had narrow straps exposing portly arms covered with black hair resembling a French poodle. The center of his shirt stretched tightly across a round protruding gut.

The rest of the area on the right side faded into a cave-like darkness. A foggy haze of cigarette smoke hung thick in the air and only added to the difficulty to adjust vision when entering from outside. At about the same time as any newcomer's eyes focused, a foul smell of whiskey, smoke, and lingering vomit odor would hit his senses. The bar's permanent stench lingered because someone usually would be sick in a corner at least once a day. Harley, who was nicknamed from his biker days, was the bartender and the owner of the place. He would pay an old rummy to clean-up the joint in exchange for ten bucks and a bottle of watered down liquor. However, he only did that, every two days—after last call when the place would be empty.

Leroy and Pete shuffled past a silhouette dressed in black sitting with a bottle of beer in the shadows of a darkened booth to the right between the front door and the bar. Neither Leroy nor Pete noticed the glow of his a cigarette as they passed by.

"What's up Harley?" called Leroy. Without waiting for a response he said, "Give me a boiler maker."

"I was wonderin' if you two would come in tonight." Harley put a dirt-spotted glass under the beer spigot, pulling the handle and out poured a foamy brew. "Regina was in looking for you Leroy," he said and puffed smoke as the glass filled. He slammed down the beer mug and a shot of whiskey. He turned and looked at Pete. "Just a beer for you?"

"What do you think asshole?" Pete answered.

With his two middle fingers of his right hand, Harley grabbed his cigar butt out of his mouth and pointed his index finger and cigar nub in Pete's face. "Hey," he yelled. "You aren't startin' anything tonight. Cause if you do, I'll kick the both of you out on your asses. The cops are getting pissed off about coming out here to stop fights. I'm telling you, I 'aint gonna have any trouble. Last time they came out, they threatened to get the beverage inspectors out for an unannounced visit and those fellas are just dying to shut me down."

"Okay, okay Harley," Leroy said putting up both hands in defense. "You know Pete didn't mean it."

"All right then," Harley said. He put the soggy cigar back in his mouth but stared hard at Pete for a full minute. Then he added. "But I'm warning you two."

Leroy grabbed the shot of whiskey in front of him and slugged it back then gulped the beer and wiped his mouth with the back of his hand.

Harley smirked, leaned in and gave a little nod. "Regina looked hot-to-trot. You coulda' got lucky if you'd come in earlier."

"Leroy always gets lucky," Pete pouted. "Women like him for some reason."

Harley laughed and moved back to rinsing glasses off. He dipped a glass into a sink filled with liquid that resembled the color of dirty skim milk and then dipped it in an adjoining sink with what appeared to be brownish rinse water.

"That's because I treat them special," Leroy said. "I don't get kicks out of knocking them around, like you do, Pete."

"Bitches need to get knocked around every now and then to keep them in line," Pete spat in defense.

"Yeah, well you keep it up and your wife will kick your butt out in the street."

"Ah you two fight like my old lady and her mom," Harley said. He rinsed two more glasses and then dried his hands. "I expected you in earlier, it's almost last call. Why so late?"

"He fell asleep," Pete said point a thumb in Leroy's direction. "And tonight, of all nights, The Preacher didn't take his wheels like he usually does. It's like Leroy don't even own a truck, the way Samuel takes it whenever he wants." Pete looked at Harley and snickered. "Leroy's scared of him."

"I am not scared," Leroy snarled.

Harley chuckled. "I think Samuel knows a couple of clowns when he sees them."

"Leroy's afraid God's going to get him cause he's one them sinners that The Preacher's always talking about." Pete said. "Afraid you're gonna burn in hell, Leroy?" Pete laughed, grabbed his glass and took a big gulp of beer. He started coughing and gasping then spit a mouthful of beer out on the floor.

"I hope you choke to death, you moron," Leroy hissed. "I ain't afraid of The Preacher. The next time he tells me to hand over my keys, I might just tell him, go to Hell!"

"Shhh." Harley shook his head and nodded to a darken booth. "He's over there. I don't want any trouble." Harley leaned in and whispered. "He knows how to handle that big hunting knife he carries. He cut a man's finger off last week, just cause he made fun at his snake tattoo."

Leroy and Pete turned toward the booth. The outline of a figure mashed-out the red glow of a cigarette and a small silver object flickered from his torso as traces of fluorescent light caught hold of it.

"You two idiots get over here." The raspy voice called out from the darkness.

The Preacher

Leroy and Pete walked over to the booth where The Preacher sat. Pete gave a nervous laugh.

"Hi Samuel," Leroy said. His thin lips parted and formed a crooked half smile. "We didn't see you sitting here." Leroy watched the man dressed in black and waited for him to speak. Around his neck hung a two-inch hammered silver cross on a leather cord.

Leroy had met Samuel the first night he rolled into town. After a brief conversation with the stranger in black, Leroy learned he didn't have a place to stay, so he told him he could crash at his place. That night in the bar, Samuel spoke like a preacher speaking of Hell and Damnation. It didn't bother Leroy. He had seen his kind before, called people like him "Bible Thumpers," always thought of them as soft and out of touch with the world, never seeing real life. He wasn't shaken by the fiery warnings

Leroy had a strong Catholic upbringing and he was taught to show respect to someone speaking the Gospel.

He had stopped going to church years before. His Soul Follower told me he could feel Leroy's uneasiness about the absence. Deep inside there was a desperation to do good deeds because of his fear of the consequences of his lack of religious devotion. Secretly he worried he wouldn't be permitted entrance into heaven. Lending a helping hand to a stranger with no place to stay would shine well on him. However, it wasn't long before Leroy learned that Samuel was not a soft Bible Thumper and Hell was not the only thing to fear.

One night while Samuel spoke about brothers in need of guidance, Leroy saw his darker side. Leroy made the mistake and called Samuel "Preacher," that slip-of-tongue resulted with Leroy at the end of The Preacher's powerful chokehold. After that, Leroy swore he would never make that mistake again.

Tonight, Samuel might have heard him utter the name once again. Leroy and Pete stood next to the booth in silence waiting like two children in front of the school principal. They fidgeted.

Samuel did nothing.

Pete put his hand to his mouth to hold back an uncontrollable laugh. His shoulders jiggled and a muffled nervous giggle escaped. Leroy glared at him and slapped him on the side of his head, "Shut-up dip shit."

"Sit down Leroy," The Preacher said without looking up. "You too, Pete."

Pete slid into the booth across the table from The Preacher and stopped mid-way. Leroy motioned with his eyes for Pete to move over, but Pete just chuckled and said, "Leroy, you gonna sit down?"

"Yeah, give me a chance." Leroy narrowed his eyes at Pete and slid in next to The Preacher. Leroy and Pete sat motionless and waited.

The Preacher took a slow drink of his beer. He put the bottle down, took a white monogrammed handkerchief out of his pocket and wiped his mouth.

"Leroy," he said, pausing while he folded the handkerchief slowly. Then he put it back in his pocket as the two men squirmed. "Do you have a problem with loaning me your truck?"

"Nah, I was just horsing around. Got no problem." Leroy shifted his body weight and dug the keys out of his pocket. He placed them on the table in front of The Preacher. "Use it anytime you want, there's no problem. Really."

"Good." In one quick motion, The Preacher reached past the keys and grabbed Leroy's hand, twisted it in an impossible and unnatural position. Leroy winced in pain. The Preacher moved forward stopping an inch from Leroy face and held a fixed stare.

Leroy's eyes widened and tears formed. He froze, barely breathing, while every muscle tightened. His eyes desperate.

The Preacher's cold black eyes held fixed and unyielding. His eyes resembled the same look of the opossums he described that he'd trap and kill deep in the mountains as a child. He spoke once, about his childhood to Leroy, said back home the opossums would get into the hen house and his father appointed him the job to get rid of the vermin—he was only ten-years-old.

Samuel's stare burned into Leroy as he spoke, "You don't want to speak of selfish thoughts. The Bible says, *'But if you have bitter envying and strife in your hearts, glory not, and lie not against the truth.'*"

The Preacher held tight Leroy's twisted arm. He raised his voice and projected out as if he were giving a sermon, *"Cain* was envious and jealous of his brother Able. *Cain* had a selfish heart. *Cain* was a sinner. We learned this from the Bible.

Genesis reads, *'And if you do not do well, sin is crouching at the door; and its desire is for you, but you must master it. But Cain struck down his brother.'*"

The Preacher pulled his head away from Leroy's face, but he kept his grip of Leroy's twisted arm. He looked up and raised his other hand into the air and said,

'And it came about when they were in the field, that Cain rose up against Abel his brother and killed him.'

Then the LORD said to Cain,

'Where is Abel your brother?'

And he said,

'I do not know. Am I my brother's keeper?'

The LORD said,

'What have you done? The voice of your brother's blood is crying to me from the ground.

Now you are cursed from the ground, which has opened its mouth to receive your brother's blood from your hand.'"

131

The Preacher lowered his hand and turned back to Leroy. "You see my son; you must not shame yourself in the eyes of the Lord with selfish thoughts and an unkind heart. We *are* our brother's keeper."

He released Leroy's hand.

Leroy grabbed his hand and moaned. "You broke my hand."

The Preacher grinned and looked from the corner of his eye to Leroy and said, "It isn't broken. I didn't hear a snap."

Finding the Note

10:00 pm. Sunday night.

Amber sat shaking, waiting for Vic to finish talking to Office Young outside.

The hot-air balloon ride Vic had planned was a wonderful surprise and the day had been perfect. Now all that seemed eons ago to Amber. Everything came to a terrifying stop when she arrived home and found the note on the floor. Somehow, the euphoria of being in love had made Amber feel untouched by the evils of the world, like the murders that gripped the town with fear. But the note she found tonight changed everything. The reality was that bad things can happen to good people.

Since Officer Young insisted they see Detective Harrison, it seemed obvious that he felt the note could be from The Rainbow Killer. And her crank caller? Maybe it wasn't just a crank. Maybe, his warnings weren't just idle words spoken in the middle of the night. Forced now, she had to face it. He had targeted her. She had to face that she *was* in danger.

"Why?" Amber whimpered to herself.

The killer's focus was on the gay community, and obviously, he had been watching the group. His deranged mind saw Amber's soul as damaged, purely by association. She couldn't understand that reasoning. Amber only saw logic.

Amber shuddered. Her childhood friends would say, "Someone just walked over your grave," whenever someone shuddered for no reason. At the age of six or seven, it would always bring on laughter but tonight the thought of the childhood saying only brought fear that perhaps it could be an omen of her fate.

Amber didn't know what frightened her more, the thought that a killer might be watching her, or that someone in the group might be next. Phillip, Andy or Saffron, or maybe she could be the next person to die.

She had thought the group's fear had been a byproduct of emotional homosexuals over-reacting to the hyped-up news. Now she felt differently. They weren't paranoid, not even Bennie. The danger was real—and it included her.

The television news leaked about the notes last week and all Hell broke loose between the police chief and the media. The local news anchor said the notes said the killer claimed he was an instrument of God, ridding the world of sinners.

Today may have been like a romantic love scene fresh out of the movies but tonight turned into a scene from Blair Witch, where a no-face stalker lurked and watched her every move. Now, Vic was outside talking to the police because some faceless person had been at her bedroom window.

"I'm so stupid. Why couldn't I be a victim? Like I'm some princess that's protected from harm?"

The door opened and Amber let out a scream.

"Amber it's me," Vic said. "It's okay." He rushed to her and wrapped his arms around her. Amber's whole body was shaking. He kissed her forehead and leaned back on the couch pulling her with him. "He's gone now. Probably just a Peeping Tom."

Amber pulled away and sat forward, staring at the door. "Vic, you didn't lock the door."

"Okay, I'll lock it. You have to calm down," Vic said as he went and locked the door. He returned and took her back in his arms. "I'm not going to leave you. I'll stay tonight. I'll take tomorrow off and we'll go together to see Detective Harrison. This guy tonight probably isn't connected to . . ." Vic stopped. He couldn't lie. There were too many similar details reported in the news about the killer's

134

notes and the one Amber found tonight. Vic kissed her forehead again. "Don't worry."

"But Vic, if the person tonight is connected to the murders, then he has killed men. He could overpower you. Sometimes being big and strong isn't enough. I mean, even cops get killed."

"Rarely," Vic said. "Besides, the bad guys get people when they're not paying attention. They catch them off guard. I don't get caught off guard." He brushed her hair back and looked at her intently. "Tomorrow after we finish talking to the detective, we'll get an alarm system installed here. I'll stay with you every night, as long as you want. Until you feel safe and kick me out. I'll even buy you a big, mean dog."

"No dog."

"A big gun?"

"Absolutely not!" Amber said. "I hate guns."

"Well then, I guess I'll have to be your Superman."

Amber laughed. The scared feeling she had before was disappearing. In fact, she felt she had overreacted—a little bit like hysterical and melodramatic Bennie.

"Guess Bennie better move over, Amber the 'Drama Queen' is here," she said.

Vic pushed back away from her and looked her in the eye, frowning. "Please, don't put that image in my mind. This Superman doesn't want to put his arms around Bennie or even think about that. He's a good guy but he still kind of creeps me out."

Amber laughed. "He's not that bad."

"Are we talking about the same Bennie?"

"He's no different than Phillip, he's just. . . " Amber stopped and sighed. "Different."

"Yeah, different. Definitely different than my brother. But then . . . I guess, not so different."

Amber reached up to Vic's cheek and caressed it in her palm. "You're a good man, Vic Richardson. Phillip is lucky to have you as a brother." Vic bent over and kissed her softly on the lips and then they leaned back on the couch together, Amber safely in his arms. Amber put her head on his chest.

After a minute, she sighed and said, "Let's turn the lights out and go to bed. I think I can sleep now that I have my Superman with me."

Death Threat

In the morning, Vic woke and slipped out of bed quietly. He wanted to let Amber sleep a little longer. She woke up countless times throughout the night reaching for him, checking to see if he was next to her. Finally, sometime after four a.m., she seemed to settle into a deep sleep.

Last night, Officer Young had told Vic that Harrison's task force was working at the sheriff station house in Ybor City since most of the bodies had been found in or near that community. The department gave the task force one of the vacant offices for Harrison to set-up his unit.

When Amber and Vic arrived by ten o'clock, they were escorted into an empty interview room. Vic sat holding Amber's hand as she fidgeted in her seat. The door opened and in walked a man who looked to be in his mid-thirties.

"Sorry to keep you waiting. I'm Detective Harrison." Vic noticed he kept pulling on his already loose necktie while they shook hands. It seemed strange to Vic that the detective seemed totally at ease with the gun holster around his hefty shoulders but uncomfortable with a tie.

"I read the note Officer Young turned in," Harrison said as they all sat down around a long table. "I would like to tell you it is just a prank and not connected to our guy, but I don't think so. We stopped the news teams from reporting any more details about the notes, but in this case, it was lucky you heard what had leaked out."

Harrison opened a file folder and flipped paper after paper over until he came to some crime scene photos. The first one was a body with a rope wrapped around the victim's neck and a note pinned to the dead body's clothing. Harrison looked up to find

Vic's eyes locked onto the photos and he quickly flipped the stacks of pictures over.

Harrison cleared his throat and Vic looked up at him. The detective continued, "Not every aspect of the notes found on the murder victims, like the Bible references or exact wording, got out to the general public. Miss Moon, the note found at your residence was consistent with many identifying markers from, The Rainbow Killer. I'm going to move ahead with the assumption that your note was written by our guy."

Amber gasped and covered her mouth.

"Detective Harrison," Vic said, "Amber isn't gay, nor myself. Why would he target her? It doesn't make sense. All the victims were gay. The note did mention my brother, Phillip. My brother is gay. Maybe the warnings and threats are for my brother and the killer is using Amber as his conduit to pass on his threats to Phillip. Perhaps you need to provide protection to my brother. Do you really think Amber is in danger?"

"Amber definitely is in danger. The note was addressed to her. In the note, he explicitly threatened her, you, and Mr. Brooks. He's targeted all of you."

"Well, then what are you going to do?"

"We can't give police protection to all three of you. We don't have the manpower. What I am going to share with you must remain confidential. I don't want any more leaks to the press, but you need to know. There have been heterosexual victims, two women, and the same type of notes pinned to their bodies."

"That's right. Mom told me about one woman, she had a husband and children," Amber said softly with her head down. Then she looked up at Detective Harrison. "If I'm the target then are Vic and Phillip safe?"

"I didn't say that," Harrison answered. He needed to remember that he was talking to civilians—scared ones. He had to choose his words carefully. "What I am saying is he's not restricting himself to any particular group anymore. I'm going to tell you what we know so far. You need to stay alert and help us with anything you know."

Revealing some facts just might keep them alive. Harrison had been warned by his superiors not to let any more details about the victims leak out, but Harrison wasn't exactly accustomed to following orders.

"Our killer has crossed over the line," Harrison continued. "He doesn't fit a tight profile. He isn't adhering to any preferences now. It's going to be very hard to catch him. Without patterns to follow, there is no way to tell who will be his next victim. But we'll catch him. Mr. Richardson you need to call your brother and have him come down to talk to us. Maybe he will shed some light on who the killer could be and why he has picked you three to warn. He never has done that before."

"He didn't warn Vic and Phillip," Amber said. "The warning was to me, to repent and save myself. He said everyone else would perish." She hung her head and wept.

Triangle of Danger

Vic and Amber drove away in silence from the Sheriff's Operations Center building. They sat rigid like perfectly formed wooden toy soldiers positioned in the car seat. After five minutes Amber spoke, "You need to call Phillip and tell him to meet us immediately."

"He's at work."

"He has to be warned now. We can't wait."

Vic thought for a moment and then pulled his cell phone out of his pocket and punched in his brother's number.

Phillip agreed to meet them at *J Alexander's* on Dale Mabry in an hour. Alexander's was far enough away from Ybor for Amber's liking, Detective Harrison's voice saying all the bodies had been found in Ybor City or in a vicinity very near played in her mind.

The gallery was located in Ybor and Matt worked there every day except Sunday. Was he in danger too?

She wanted to tell Matt about the note and their talk to Harrison but he made them promised not to alert any of the others—just Phillip. The group was not a target, that is, not any more than any other gay person in Tampa.

This morning, they found out being gay was not the only way into The Rainbow Killer's exclusive target group. Straight people were on his private membership hit list, too. However, the general public was not privileged to this information, yet. Vic, Matt, or any of them could be in danger.

They arrived at *Alexander's* early and sat at the bar where they could watch the front door for Phillip. Eleven o'clock was a little early for a drink, but Amber needed and wanted one. She ordered a white wine. Vic had a seven and seven.

"Amber, we have an advantage knowing what we know." Vic said quietly and took a drink. He paused and jiggled the ice cubes around in the glass, deep in thought. "He, this man who is responsible for . . ." Vic paused and took a drink then said, "He must feel some compassion toward you to warn you. I mean, his notes and calls are not threatening to hurt you, he just wants to save your soul. He is obviously insane, or at the very least, very disturbed so we need to be very careful."

Amber leaned toward Vic as she kept an eye on the bartender at the opposite end of the bar and whispered. "What you're not saying is—if he wanted to kill me, he would have already done it?"

"No! That is *not* what I said. You're not in his target zone for now. Like Harrison said, maybe reaching out to you is his unconscious way to get someone to stop him. If the police do their job, they will catch him before he tries to hurt anyone else. What I need to do, is keep you safe until the police catch him."

"Okay." Amber noticed the sunlight stream into the restaurant's entranceway. "There's Phillip."

Vic got up to go meet his brother and reached him before he approached the hostess. Vic whispered to Phillip and pointed to Amber waiting in the lounge. There they could talk undisturbed.

Ten minutes later, at a small table in the corner Phillip sat with an ashen face staring at his ginger ale. "I need a real drink," he said.

"I'll get you one," Vic said. He got up but paused. "Phillip, everything is going to be all right. You're smart and strong. Guys like this bastard prey on the weak and careless. You're neither. But maybe, you should take a vacation. You haven't taken time off for two years."

"If he has been watching us then I need to be here to cover your back," Phillip said without any hesitation. "We both can keep Amber safe."

"You and me against the bad guys, like when we were kids," Vic said

141

"Something like that."

"Are you sure?"

"Absolutely."

"All right. I know when you've made your mind up. Thanks." Vic smiled, then turned, and walked over to the bar to order Phillip's drink.

Amber reached across the table and took Phillip's hand. "Maybe Vic's right about taking a vacation. Why should you put yourself in danger just to watch after me? Besides the killer hasn't threatened me, he wants me to be saved."

"No, if I'm out of the equation than he'll be more focused on you and Vic. You're not out of danger; you must remember that this guy is deranged. Like in the Wild West when everyone circles the wagons for protection, the three of us can protect each other."

Fire and Brimstone

The flames shot up from the floor. A delicate blond man started to cry. His eyes searched from side-to-side looking around the room, beside him another man cowered. There was no escape from the flames. Two other men stood within the circle of fire, defiantly straight and tall, exhibiting a united front.

A distance away, two women clung to each other. The dark-haired one stroked the flaxen haired woman's head. As she lovingly comforted her, she laid her head down on top of the smaller women's head and wrapped her arms around cradling her then started to rock back and forth.

I'm outside the fire ring watching them. The woman's coffee-brown eyes are fixated on me as if she is resolved to their fate. Her black hair covers her lover's face and her hair separates near her ear exposing a single feather earring as the strands drape across the other's forehead.

I feel nauseated and repulsed as she stares coldly at me, unyielding, refusing to show fear.

Flames are getting higher as I watch. I can feel the heat and hear a muffled crackling sound of the fire. The heat is intense.

"Yes, go ahead and stare. I want my eyes to be the last thing you see here on earth," I shout at them and laugh.

Flames soar higher and higher. There is no way out for the trapped sinners.

"Burn! This is what eternity holds for you. Burn Sinners."

The heat feels closer as the flames grow. Hotter, red-hot. Oranges and red flames flicker in front of me, burning white hot. I wipe the sweat beads from my forehead.

"You must pay for your sins," I shout again.

The heat is so tremendous. Hotter than I ever dreamt it would be—it feels like . . .

I look down at by side, to my arm. Flames have engulfed my arm. The fire is traveling up to my torso. It's hot! Burning. The pain. All I can see are orange-red fingers snapping in front of my face. Oh the pain!

"Dear God, help me! I'm burning."

The pain I feel is unbearable.

"No! I'm not a sinner."

I can't believe the pain.

"I'm only carrying out your will," I cry. I can feel my skin peeling off from my face. I am burning.

"Please no, God, help me."

Samuel shot straight up in bed; his eyes wide full with fear. The sheets were soaked and sweat beads ran down the side of his face.

"Dreams! He mumbled. "Damn dreams!" He threw back the sheets and climbed out of bed. "I won't sleep until I rid this town of the sinners. Perverts and deviants, all of them."

He walked out of the back bedroom into the darkened living room. Leroy lay on his stomach on top of a brown plaid tattered sofa. His one arm dangled off the side with fingertips brushing the floor.

Pete sat across in a black leather recliner snoring, his head back with his mouth open. Suddenly he gulped the air, sputtering followed by a loud snort after which his mouth fell open again and the snorting continued.

"Damn low life," Samuel muttered again. "If I didn't need a place to stay or need wheels to get around . . ." Samuel shook his head and walked into the kitchen. He looked around, dishes were piled on the counter, the sink filled to the rim, beer bottles everywhere and a half-eaten pizza slice sat on the countertop. A roach scurried across the front of the sink ledge.

Samuel headed to a drawer, opened it, rummaging through the clutter until he found a pencil and paper. He took a seat at the table.

"How can people live like this?" he said as he slid his arm across the top of the table sweeping the debris off onto the floor. The items fell causing a loud clashing sound as they hit

"What ... what's that," Pete said sitting up from the chair in the other room. He looked into the kitchen, "Oh it's you Samuel."

"Yeah, go back and sleep it off, Pete."

Pete waved his hand at him and said half under his breath, "The Preacher thinks he's better than us. He ain't no better." A fly flew by Pete's face and he shooed it away. The nuisance thing buzzed around for a second while Pete flapped at it then the fly flew away. Pete turned on his side in the chair. A few seconds later, the snoring returned.

In the kitchen, Samuel spoke to himself with disgust in his voice. "Our farm pigs were cleaner than these animals."

He grasped the pencil, knuckles white with conviction, and pressed down hard on the paper. He quickly wrote:

Sinner,

The Lord sent me to extinguish those who don't deserve to live. You must repent and pay for your sins.

California or Dead

Saffron filled the ice bucket and placed it on the counter next to the pitcher of ice tea Claire had made.

"Claire, what else do you want me to do?" she called out. "I got the ice and put out the glasses. Should I put the platter of sandwiches you made out?"

Claire came into the kitchen, putting on her watch. "No, let's put them out after the group gets here. Did you put our books on the porch?"

"Yes."

"When did you finish reading it?"

"Last night."

"This month's discussion should be a good. I loved the book." Claire grabbed a glass and poured some tea. "By the way, Andy called. He said he had the information you wanted him to get. He wouldn't tell me what it was, said he wanted to wait for our meeting. What's all the secrecy about?"

"Oh, you'll have to wait and see."

Claire and Saffron took their drinks to the porch to sit until time for the book club meeting and everyone's arrival. The group's size had shrunk considerably since the "Rainbow" killings had started. The monthly meeting used to be on Thursday nights but they had moved it to Saturday morning to avoid any one having to go out after dark.

The group stopped other outings too, like getting together with Amber and Vic to go out to restaurants, art openings and movies. It was too dangerous for homosexuals to travel the streets at night even if they were going to a straight establishment.

A self-inflicted six o'clock curfew gave the illusion that the streets were safe. No one wanted to go anywhere in the evening except for their usual appearance at the Cowboy Club on Saturday nights–they refused to give up all of their social life.

Of course, this meant that Saffron and Claire's straight friends like Amber and Vic were out of touch with the group. Saffron hadn't seen either of them for weeks. Saffron hated it. Amber had become Saffron's "straight" best friend. In addition, for some strange reason, Phillip had dropped out of sight about three weeks ago. Saffron felt it very odd about that whole situation.

The dwindled down book club meetings were hardly worth getting together because only Bennie, Ken and Andy came now. Seemed like their small, yet very personal world, had changed drastically. Even though the murders had stopped, everyone still kept the habit of exclusion. Saffron hoped that the information Andy would bring could change things and everyone would stop being so frightened.

Claire looked at Saffron after sitting in silence for a few minutes. "You look tired."

"I know, I fell asleep reading, but woke up around three and finished the book. I've missed the news for the third time in a row this week. I think the stress of the murders is wearing on everyone. I know they haven't found the guy, but maybe it's over now, there hasn't been any new murders reported for two weeks."

"Yeah, maybe he's moved on," Claire said. The doorbell chimed and she looked at her watch. "Right on time. I'll get it."

She let Andy in and noticed Ken and Bennie pulling up to the curb. Once everyone was inside and had gotten their drinks, all except for Bennie and Ken, they refused Saffron's offer of refreshments, everyone headed outside. On the lanai, Bennie stood leaning against the sliding glass door biting his fingernails. Ken said he and Bennie weren't staying long.

"Since Ken and Bennie need to leave early, we need to start quickly, because Andy has something to share afterwards," Saffron said. "What did you think of this month's book selection?"

Bennie blurted out, "Books! What about reality? They found another body last night. It was Duncan."

"No," Saffron gasped. "Not Duncan,"

"Yeah, Duncan. He won Miss Gaybor last year. Remember, even when Luscious LaMay called him a fat bitch, Duncan was still nice. Said Luscious was right and he probably didn't deserve to win the crown because he needed to lose weight."

"Everyone liked Duncan," Claire said adding, "except for Luscious, that is."

"Why did it have to be him? He wouldn't hurt a fly," Saffron said.

"Well, that didn't save him, did it?" Bennie said.

Ken put his arm around Bennie. "It'll be okay. Don't get yourself riled up; your blood pressure is already too high."

Bennie pushed away from Ken and looked at Saffron.

"Well, I'm not going to stay calm and wait to be murdered. If something isn't done, we'll all be dead."

Ken stepped forward, looking at the others. "What Bennie is trying to say is we've decided to leave Tampa. Bennie and I are moving to California."

"What!" Saffron and Claire said together.

"When did you decide this?" Andy asked. "Tampa is your home. You have friends here and your work, too."

"We can't take it anymore," Bennie said wildly. "We're all just like sitting ducks at a shooting gallery. The cops aren't going to catch him. After all, he's only killing fags! Stopping him is not a priority."

"Bennie that's not true," Saffron said. "Anyway, there are nuts everywhere. You can't just run scared."

"Yeah? Why not?"

"California has murders, too," Andy said calmly.

"But the Rainbow Murderer is *here!*" Ken said. "Bodies are stacking up. I agree with Bennie that the police don't give a shit. They just keep sitting with their thumbs up their asses."

"You ought to come with us, Saf," Bennie said.

Andy and Ken had started quietly talking to each other. Ken was telling Andy it was their only choice because Bennie was so frightened.

Bennie sat down next to Saffron and continued with his plead to her. "You could probably get more gigs out there than here. Maybe a big Hollywood music producer will discover you and you'll get internationally known."

"I can't move to California. I own this house—there's my cat . . . and I volunteer at the animal shelter three times a week. They don't have enough help there now. And I have performances booked for the next three months."

Claire sat in silence. She looked at Saffron with tears forming in her eyes. "Your cat . . . that's what's keeping you here?"

Andy and Ken stopped talking when they heard Claire's quivering voice. "Are they your only commitments?" Claire's face was flushed and she sat grasping her hands together in her lap.

Saffron whipped around to face Claire. "No. Not just my cats. A move involves both of us." She turned back to Bennie, "It's not possible, even if we wanted to move."

"Because of me, I guess you're pinned down here," Claire said.

Saffron turned back to look at Claire. "No, not pinned." She turned back to Bennie. "Claire's got a good job and is up for a promotion. We're not free to move like the two of you, besides we like it here. And there's my house." Saffron stopped and looked to Claire reaching over to touch her hand. "We have this house, the both of us. It's our home."

"Home is where the heart is . . . but the heart needs to be alive and beating," Bennie said in his usual melodramatic way. He had always been a drama queen, always over-reacting to any situation.

"Why do you two think it's so safe in California?" Saffron asked.

"Because we're accepted there. Gays—that is," Ken said. "Maybe after they catch the, *Rainbow Maniac,* we'll come back. There will always be bartending and servers jobs open. We like it here, really. But Bennie's scared. The both of us are."

Andy raised his right hand in protest, "Stop arguing. I think I may have a solution, so everyone won't be so scared."

"Yeah, all of us move to California," Bennie said.

"No, something Saffron suggested for me to check out and it doesn't involve moving," Andy said. "I called and met this guy about his club. It's called the Pink Pistols. It's a gun club. If we join, we can learn how to protect ourselves and everyone won't feel so afraid. And you and Ken won't have to go to California."

"Oh we're going to California, that's for sure," Bennie said shaking his head up and down like a bobble head doll.

"Oh shut-up you fairy," Saffron said. She turned to Andy, "Tell us about the Pink Pistols and where do they meet?"

In Hiding

Amber was unhappy about the plan to stop all contact with the group, but Detective Harrison insisted. She couldn't understand his reasoning behind demanding that she, Vic, and Phillip keep the secret that the killer had been, not only watching Amber, but also, the group. She was laden with guilt at the thought that her silence might put her friends in further danger. *How could it be wrong to alert them?* she thought.

When Amber quizzed Detective Harrison, he was unyielding. He insisted she keep silent and added, "civilians need to be ignorant of what goes on in the homicide department. My men are professionals and they will catch the killer if you let them." He convinced her that her friends' reaction to the situation would put them in more danger. Amber's involvement had not been a matter of her choice, but there was a choice about others' involvement.

Detective Harrison's perspective was from a cop's mind. Amber wondered if he saw murder victims as unfortunate spoils of war and not as real people. If another killing was necessary to make an arrest, did he accept it as part of the job, therefore—so be it? She hoped he couldn't be that cold-hearted, because if he was, one of her friends could be the next to die.

Visions of Matt or Saffron's picture displayed on the six o'clock news as another murder victim haunted her. Saffron kept calling Amber and leaving messages that she was worried about her. Saffron asked why Amber wouldn't return her calls. Amber needed to ignore Saffron's calls to be able to stay strong. One night Amber snapped after hearing another voice message. "I don't care what Detective Harrison says, I'm calling Saffron."

"Amber, you can't," Vic argued. "I don't like how Harrison is handling this but at least you're protected between Phillip and me.

The cops aren't making any progress. You and I know that. The others have to take care of themselves, Phillip and I can't watch after everyone in the group. As long as you keep checking in with me every hour, stay in the house during the day, and I'm here at night, we can get through this. Making contact with the group, or Saffron, could draw attention to them."

"How?"

"I don't know but it is safer if less people are involved."

"The squad car drives by my house," Amber said. "Plus, I have you and Phillip to protect me but our friends don't even know the killer has been watching them. They need to know."

"I hate to agree with Harrison. He's a jerk, but I think he's right about this. Even without being targeted, everyone in the group has been cautious. Can you imagine what Bennie might do if he thought the killer even knew he existed?"

Amber rolled her eyes and shook her head, "It's anyone's guess. He probably would go running and screaming down the street."

"And that wouldn't get the killer's attention?"

"You're right. Okay, but I'm only going along with this for so long before I call it quits."

Matt's calls were even harder to deal with for Amber. Ignoring them was virtually impossible because Amber and Matt both had been accustomed to weekly phone conversations. Matt was getting suspicious so last week Amber decided to lie. She said she was sick, but she could tell from his tone that he didn't believe her.

Amber stayed isolated in her house for weeks. Only Suzanne was allowed in the circle of knowledge. Even Harrison knew a mother couldn't be kept from her daughter. Especially a mother and daughter who were best friends and spoke to each other every day.

Suzanne was terrified for her daughter's safety and called Amber between Vic and Phillip's check-in calls.

Amber followed instructions for three weeks, letting others rule her life while she hold-up in the house like a recluse. The other Soul Followers and I were very proud of her patience. Amber didn't even step foot outside to get the mail.

There'd been no more bodies found. No leads, at least, none the task force was sharing knowledge about. Amber had not received any more notes or phone calls demanding penance. I felt her patience wearing thin. She began feeling claustrophobic, like the living room walls were closing in on her.

Amber sat in front of the television. The actress in the movie declared undying love to the leading man as she fell into his arms and soft music drifted in as the scene faded out.

Amber leaped off the couch and turned off the television. "Grrr! If . . . I . . . have to watch another gushy romance story—I'm going to scream. I'm going out!"

Amber grabbed her purse, reset the alarm and headed out the front door. In the car, she flipped her phone open and hit the speed dial number for Phillip.

"Phillip Brooks, may I help you."

"Phillip, it's Amber."

"What's the matter?"

"Nothing. I'm calling to let you know I'm going out. Maybe shopping, I don't know where yet. This whole thing about staying at home is ridiculous. It's been three weeks and nothing more has happened."

"Amber, call Vic. We agreed you weren't to go anywhere alone."

"No. He'll only want me to stay home and wait until tonight when he comes over to guard me. I feel like Peter Pumpkin Eater's wife. Remember him in the Mother Goose Nursery Rhythm? He kept his wife locked in their house."

"It's just temporary, Amber. Hang in there."

"No, I've had it. It's over. Detective Harrison doesn't think I'm in danger. He must not, because he doesn't even call anymore to check to see if I've gotten any more threats. I think the police figure the killer is not out there anymore. There have not been any new bodies found. The last time I spoke to the detective he said that he was told his task force was going to be dissolved and ordered to stop the investigation in a few days."

"Amber, that's not going to happen."

"I'm not making it up, Detective Harrison really said that."

"Amber stop. Listen to me. There's been another victim. They found a body last night. It was on the news."

"Who?" Amber asked shaking. "It wasn't someone we know."

"No, you don't know him. He wasn't in our group, but I knew of him—he was a drag queen."

"Oh." Amber's rage waned. "Well, I still want out from under yours and Vic's surveillance."

"I understand, Amber. My brother is watching me like a hawk, too. I've told him I'm careful and I want my normal life back. But Amber, the threats you've received are real and all of us need to take precautions."

"Vic was threatened too. He's only worrying about us. I can be responsible for myself. He is too focused on protecting me. He even wanted to teach me some judo moves."

"Amber, he's not wrong about that. You can't be passive about your safety. Taking action is needed to remain safe." Phillip paused and took in a deep breath. "Look, don't make a decision now. Go back home and wait until Vic gets there at five. You might feel differently by then."

"No, I won't."

"Okay, then." Phillip paused. "Go see Harrison and talk to him. Will you do that for me?"

"All right, but it won't change anything. I'm turning the car around. I'll go. You and Vic must realize though, I'm a big girl and no matter what Detective Harrison says, you two will have to back off. Call Vic and tell him where I am so he doesn't go ballistic when he calls the house and I don't answer."

Fifteen minutes later Amber pulled in a parking space at the station and walked to the room reserved for Harrison's team. When Amber told Harrison she was finished with hiding, his reaction surprised her. He didn't argue, actually he practically agreed with her about her decision. She wondered if he agreed because her reappearance on the streets could serve as bait for the killer, but she dismissed that thought almost immediately as very unlikely. Harrison said with the discovery of this new victim, it looked like the killer probably had forgotten about her and returned to his original MO.

Now armed with what Detective Harrison said she would tell Vic to go home tonight. She could handle her mother's paranoia but not Vic's constant watchful eye over her. The danger from the killer was over for her, even though he still was on the loose. Now the only barrier between her and the freedom to get her old life back was Vic.

Keepsakes

The man's gold badge clipped to his belt was barely visible underneath his overhanging stomach as he poured a mug of coffee. He watched across the room as Amber spoke to his boss, Harrison, and then she left the room.

Harrison walked back to the coffee pot where the other man stood.

"Are we done holding the broad's hand now, Harry?"

"Yeah," Harrison answered and poured a mug of coffee. "Let's get back to business." He walked across the room where another man sat with his feet propped up on a desk with bony arms folded on his chest and his eyes closed. A board to the left displayed a map with several pushpins clustered around Ybor City. Attached to each pin, a string led off to the side where numerous pictures hung. They ranged from things like, a rope, foot impressions, and lifeless bodies each with numbered square markers next them.

"Wake up," Harrison said as he pushed the man's feet off the corner of the desk. "Naptime's over. She's gone. Grab the box Smitty brought and we'll see what our guy sent us this time."

"Sure, boss. Just catching some shut eye until the girl left." He picked up a six-inch square box wrapped in plain brown paper and followed behind Harrison to a large table. Written on the outside of the box, printed in black ink was one word, "Sinners."

The six men gathered around the table. "The bomb squad says it's clean. I'm not bothering them anymore if we get other packages." Harrison peeled away the brown paper and opened the box. He picked up some long tweezers, removed a gold chain and placed it in an evidence bag.

"Stone, get that interview log," Harrison said to the bald man next to him. "I bet our perp has sent us a friggin' trophy. I

156

remember reading a statement about one of the victims always wearing a necklace that he never took off. The victim's partner said it was missing in the belongings that were returned to him."

A Night Out with The Group

Phillip had decided to let his brother cool off for a few days in hopes that Vic would stop blaming him for Amber's decision.

Three days earlier, Amber had put her foot down.

She called Vic and said that she wanted to resume her independent life, like it had been before finding the note on her living room floor. She'd stay at her house and Vic at his, except for the regular weekend sleepovers.

Vic was furious.

Amber explained that there would be no more of Vic's bodyguard efforts to keep her safe. After they hung up, Vic called Phillip and asked what he had said to Amber to prompt her change of attitude.

"Nothing, Vic. I said nothing to encourage her to stay alone." Phillip had never heard his brother so out-of-control and enraged.

"You told her to ask Harrison, that dickhead, for permission to send me home."

"No I didn't. I tried to get her to go home and wait for you so you two could talk it over. She wouldn't have any part of that. She was going shopping at the mall. I thought Harrison's office would be safer than a public place like the mall."

"Amber doesn't go to the mall," Vic said. Then he slammed the phone down.

Phillip called him back immediately but it took over an hour before Vic calmed down and realized no one could've changed Amber's mind. Phillip could still hear the fettered anger in his voice when Vic said goodbye.

Three days had passed since then. Phillip picked the phone up to dial Vic to tell him about Saffron's opening. Minutes before, Amber had called to say she was going to go hear Saffron sing.

"I don't mind meeting you there, Phillip," she said when he said he would be there, too. "But I'm going by myself."

Phillip didn't argue, but he got her to let him call and invite Vic to meet them there. However, he had to promise to talk to Vic and make him understand that he needed to ease up. Phillip pleaded his brother's case and reluctantly Amber agreed that if it made Vic happy, she'd allow him to follow her home and make sure she got in safely–but that would be it.

Phillip punched in Vic's number. He rubbed his forehead feeling tension build as the phone rang. He wanted to help Amber and Vic get back together. Even though they wouldn't admit it, they basically were not talking to each other and Phillip knew they were both miserable.

Vic answered.

"Vic, it's Phillip. Look I've got something to tell you. But you have to let me finish."

"Is Amber, okay? I've phoned her, but she's not answering my calls."

"That's because you're still calling her every hour, like before." Phillip heard a disgruntled grumble before his brother's quick response.

"Oh, I understand now. She's talking to you, but not me."

"Yes, we've talked," Phillip answered. "Just a few minutes ago, in fact, and before I hung up from her, I asked if I could call you to tell you what she called me about."

"Oh, so now, Amber is doling out her permission to my brother. Allowing him to call me."

"Vic you're letting this thing get totally out of hand. She feels smothered. Your reactions are making her take unnecessary chances. Instead of protecting her, it will make her be more determined to prove she's not in danger. And *that* is what will be dangerous. You need to cool it."

"Phillip, I'm telling you this Detective Harrison is not going to protect her."

"I know. We need to. We're all she's got."

Phillip knew Vic was right. Harrison apparently was top in his field but his focus was on the perpetrator. Harrison needed evidence for an arrest. If more deaths occurred as a result in waiting to get that evidence, then the good detective was probably willing to let that happen.

"How do we protect Amber when she's so stubborn," Vic said. "I can't keep her under house arrest."

"Well, that's what you were trying to do. It's important to cut her some slack, so she'll let us be around to watch out for her."

Vic let out a heavy sigh.

"She needs her independence, Vic. That's okay as long as we can stay close."

"I didn't realize how smart my baby brother was. Sounds like you have a plan."

"No plan, I'm not that cunning. I'm more like a diplomat."

"What did Amber call you about?"

"Saffron has a gig Friday night and everyone is invited. Amber wanted to call you but said she was tired of arguing with you. I got her to allow me to call and invite you"

"How generous of her."

"Do you want to hear what else I have to say?"

"Okay. Go ahead."

"Amber agreed for the three of us to meet, as long as you don't bring up anything about the threats or murders. I told her she was completely right but she needed to humor you. She needed to compromise and allow you to follow her home so she would not be going into an empty house late at night. You can make sure Amber is in the house safe and sound before you leave and *go home*."

"No problem. Did you convince her to get a gun since I'm not allowed to stay?"

"You've got to be kidding me. Don't push your luck."

Friday night.

Phillip met his brother outside the lounge at seven-thirty. He was glad to have Vic back talking to him. After Amber's decision he worried that Vic wouldn't forgive him for whatever part he'd played in it. Vic had come so far in accepting Phillip as gay, even getting to know his friends. He didn't want to lose that and feared that if Vic lost Amber, his brother would retreat into himself. He'd lose Vic forever.

Phillip had grown to love Amber like a sister and if something happened to her, he'd have to deal with the grief of losing both his brother and Amber.

"I think Saffron arranged for a table for the whole group to sit together," Phillip said as they entered the lounge. "If you would rather not sit with the group, we can make up a reason why we want a separate table."

"No problem. I told you your friends are my friends now." Vic leaned into Phillip and lowered his voice. "Bennie's a little, uh, much. I'm not sure if I'm ever going to get used to him."

Phillip laughed. "Bennie is in a class of his own. Well, you won't have to put up with him much longer. He and Ken are moving to California next week."

"California?"

"Yeah, they're scared to stick around here."

"Oh."

"You seem to have no problem with Andy? I don't get it, he's swishy too."

"Phillip, I'm shocked. Swishy? I would never use that term anymore."

"I know but that's how you see it, don't you. I suppose you're right. Anyone can spot him across a crowded room. So tell me, what is the difference between Bennie and Andy? Andy is not much different. Certainly not macho. I don't understand."

"You're right, Andy's definitely gay but he's a down-to-earth guy." Vic paused for a moment and then added, "He's not so emotional like Bennie. Guess I'm not perfect. But give me a break; you wouldn't like all the straight guys I know."

"Point taken" Phillip knew his brother had changed so much. A year ago, Bennie was Vic's only image of a gay person. Now the preconceived picture had faded into the background and Vic treated gay people as "regular everyday people." More than that, Phillip felt his brother was proud of him again, like before he announced he was gay.

Phillip and Vic stood inside the door as people pushed in like sardines behind them. The radio had been playing Saffron's music all day and it looked like half the population of Tampa had come. Saffron told Phillip earlier that the management started getting reservations on Tuesday for tonight's performance.

"Saffron is doing two sets, one at seven-thirty and another at nine-thirty," Phillip said raising his voice over the noise. "The manager pressed her to give up our table for one of the shows but Saffron said if her friends didn't have a table for both sets, she wouldn't sing. She's never been that brazen before. People usually push her around—really she's not as tough as she looks."

"Saffron is a pretty cool gal," Vic said. "Good for her for standing up for herself. They'll make plenty of money off her tonight."

The hostess squeezed through the crowd and asked Phillip how many in his party.

"We're guests of Saffron—Phillip Brooks and Vic Richardson."

"Saffron reserved a table two rows from the stage for your party, sir." The attractive brunette led them through the packed lounge to the reserved table at the left side of the room, a few feet from one of the bars.

As Vic took a seat and Phillip said, "Man it's packed. I'll go over and get us a drink at the bar. By the time the waitress gets around to our table, we'll be ready for seconds."

"Okay, I'll wait here for the rest of the gang," Vic said. "Get me a CC and Seven."

As Phillip left, he noticed Matt walking with Claire toward the table and Vic.

Phillip worked his way to the bar, ordered Vic's drink and a rum and coke for himself. While he waited, he heard a familiar voice call to him.

"Hey buddy, I thought that was you." Phillip turned around to see Derrick. It had been over a year since they'd talked, still he considered Derrick a close friend. Phillip had many loyal friends but somehow, Derrick was different from the rest. How or why, he wasn't quite sure. He did know one thing; he could count on Derrick's support anytime.

"Derrick, it's great to see you." Phillip extended his hand to shake. "Saffron invite you?"

Derrick was the one that helped him the most when he struggled about whether or not to "come-out" to his family. Derrick didn't force his opinion on him. He just listened with a patient ear. They talked for hours on end about worries, conflicts, and the repercussion of such an announcement. Maybe that added to the strength of the bond he felt with him.

"Yeah, she called me out of the blue last week," Derrick said. "I just got here. I was told at the front that Saffron reserved a table for everyone. The poor hostess was overwhelmed. I told her not to worry that I could find the table myself."

"Yes, it's over there." Phillip pointed to where Vic, Matt and Claire were sitting. Nearby, Andy Martinez was working his way through the crowd, toward the table.

"Sure, I see Matt," Derrick said. "Who's the hot new guy sitting next to him?"

"Change your tune. That's my brother, Vic. Remember I told you about him—my "straight" brother."

"Is that the same Vic who hooked up with Matt's friend, Amber?"

"One and the same."

"Hear tell the group thinks they are great match-makers now. When I spoke to Saffron, she told me about the two of them and acted like they were some fairytale couple."

Phillip laughed, "You know Saffron always believes in happily-ever-after."

With that, Bennie and Ken walked up to the bar. "Hi, Phillip." Ken put his arm around Bennie's shoulder. "Derrick, haven't seen you in a month of Sundays."

"Ken, move your arm off of Bennie," Phillip whispered through clenched teeth. "Are you crazy? You're in a straight club. Can't you ever be discreet? This is a prime example of why the public gets so upset with us. Besides, there's a psycho killing gays out there. Let's not make ourselves any more of a target than we already are."

Derrick and Phillip paid for their drinks and made their way back to the table. Phillip introduced Derrick to Vic. They seemed to hit it off okay. Everything was going okay until they heard a gruff voice bellow from behind Andy's chair.

"Well, if it isn't the hen club."

Vic turned to see a woman in non-regulation camouflage fatigues standing there. She looked about five foot two with *Eyes of Blue*, as in the lyrics of the old-time song. However, nothing about

164

her would conger-up any cute girly picture like the song reflected. A stripe of psychedelic blue hair spiked straight up perpendicular to her right eyebrow, which had three piercings. She looked like she probably could drop kick any man out of the place better than any seasoned bouncer.

"Hello, Terri. I guess they'll let anyone in here." Bennie said as he walked up to the table. Ken and some others muttered hellos.

"I should've guessed you *ladies* would be here for Saffron's opening." Without missing a beat, she sneered, "Girls must stick together."

"Unlike some people, who repel anything that breathes," Bennie snapped back.

"Good seeing you too, Bennie. Don't mind me, if I don't join you. I see an empty seat at the bar. Oh, by the way, I hear the bartender can put a cute little pink umbrella in your drinks if you ask him."

"Thanks. They have a drink special you should try. It's called arsenic on the rocks."

"Yeah, yeah, bite me."

She pushed through the crowd like a bull going down the streets of Pamplona. Bennie glared at her as she disappeared and the hole in the crowd closed up. He pressed his lips tight and shook his head. "I don't get her. She's so . . ."

"Hard," Ken said finishing Bennie's sentence.

"Yeah, that's it. Why do some people choose to be that way? She doesn't have to sign up for Miss America—but come on."

"Let's not judge," Phillip said. "Anyhow, look at Saffron, she's not much different. Only difference is, we like her."

"Oh, Saffron's different," Bennie said. "Saffron dresses like she does because of style choice. Terri dresses that way because she's one of those *in-your-face* lesbians."

The group sat sipping their drinks in silence. Vic looked toward the entrance of the lounge, scanning the crowd for Amber.

165

His eyes caught hold of her as she came to the edge of the crowd. The hostess pointed to the table as Vic started to wave. "There's Amber," Vic said with a relieved tone in his voice.

Amber squeezed through the crowd, stopping behind a man dressed in black with a silver cross on a leather cord dangling around his neck. She touched his arm, "Excuse me."

The man stepped aside, letting her go by. He watched her as she made her way to the table.

"Hello everyone," Amber said. "I haven't missed Saffron, have I?"

"No. she should be coming on in five minutes," Phillip said.

A few minutes passed and conversations began to form between sets of couples around the table. Derrick, Phillip, Vic and Amber talked together. Phillip explained he had known Derrick for a couple of years but hadn't seen him for a while.

"I met Phillip at a Chamber of Commerce meeting," Derrick said. He explained that they ran in different circles. Soon Vic and Derrick were talking about sports.

"Derrick's a sport freak. He couldn't live without ESPN," Phillip said to Amber.

Amber sipped her drink. Phillip watched Derrick and Vic as they compared football teams, challenging each other's opinion on who was the best player. Phillip knew enough about sports to carry on a conversation for about one minute.

Derrick paused, looked over to Phillip. "We're boring Phillip and Amber," he said touching Phillip's cheek. Then he quickly pulled his hand down, grabbed his glass and took a drink.

Vic raised his eyebrows and he gave a quick look over to Amber. Amber blushed as a small smile escaped. A look of recognition rolled across Vic's face as if he just received a note with a password to a secret club on it. He looked at Phillip and smiled.

"Yes, my baby brother never did have an interest in football," he said.

Phillip looked back at Derrick, who had changed the subject and was saying something about Saffron's singing. *Why haven't I stayed in touch with Derrick? I'll have to change that.*

Across the room, the man in black watched. His eyes narrowed into a defiant stare as he fingered the silver cross around his neck for a moment. He turned pushing through the crowd and stormed out of the club.

Evil Delivered

Things slowly eased back into a normal routine for Amber and Vic after Phillip had intervened. Amber stopped fighting with Vic and her mother. She knew they were right about being careful until the killer was arrested. And she knew Vic loved her.

Vic stayed at his place, reluctantly. However, he insisted she call him every time she left the house and then again, when she was in the car safe with the doors locked. Between her mother and Vic's calls, Amber figured that they could calculate down to the second where she was at all times.

Today had been one of those rare days when Amber and Suzanne went to an afternoon movie. Afterward they stopped for appetizers and some soup.

When they were finished and waiting for their checks, Suzanne mentioned she wanted to follow Amber home. Amber firmly said she didn't need an escort. A few minutes later, they were still in the midst of an angry discussion when the waitress came to clear the table. She looked uneasy, said she would return in a few minutes, and made a hasty retreat. Suzanne looked at Amber and stated curtly, "Fine, I guess you've made your mind up."

"Mom, please. Don't be upset. What's going to happen? It's still light out."

Amber yearned for her normal life back—before notes of warnings, dead bodies in town, and scary, late-night phone calls.

"It'll be dark by the time you get home or at best twilight. Twilight is a great time to conceal yourself in bushes and wait for someone to come home unescorted. But you know best. You always know best." Suzanne stood and excused herself, saying she needed to go the ladies room

"Mom, wait," Amber said as she grabbed her napkin from her lap. "I'll go with you, you're upset. We'll talk privately."

"No! I don't need an escort either. I'll be okay. We won't talk about it anymore. I'll be back in minute. Stay seated. I'll be fine."

Suzanne returned after a few minutes.

"I told the waitress we're ready for our check," Amber said.

"Well, I'm not ready to go. I think I'll have a cup of coffee. Maybe a dessert."

"Ooookay." Amber wasn't going to argue with her mother. If it was one thing she knew about Suzanne, when she got very angry, like she was now, no one had better mess with her.

Twenty minutes later, Suzanne took the last bite of a slice of vanilla bean cheesecake with raspberry topping and sipped her cappuccino. She waved for the waitress and said they were ready for the check. After paying, Amber and Suzanne headed to the door without speaking. Outside in the parking lot, a familiar van pulled in from the street and turned down the aisle where they were walking. Looking over her shoulder Suzanne said, "Amber isn't that Vic's car?"

Amber looked as the van drove up next to them. "Yes, Mom it is."

Vic rolled his window down.

"Hi, Vic. what a surprise," Suzanne said.

"Hello, ladies. I was heading home and decided to swing by your place, Amber," Vic said casually. "To see if you were home, yet. I thought you might've stopped here, since it's your favorite restaurant. Lucky I caught you."

"Lucky, right," Amber said.

"Are you coming, or going?"

"Cut the act, Vic." Amber turned to her mother, "Okay you win."

Amber hugged her mother goodbye. She called back over her shoulder as she started to walk to her car, "You can follow me home, Vic."

Amber turned the key to start her car. As she backed out, she heard Vic tell Suzanne he'd wait for her to get to her vehicle safety. Amber pulled out of the restaurant parking lot immediately and sped down the street. She hated having to follow "mother's orders." *Who do they think they're fooling?*

By the time Amber passed Kennedy Boulevard, a few blocks from her house, the sun had already gone down. The sky was in that "in-between" state but far past her mother's "lurking stranger twilight time." The sky had an eerie glow with hues of rose, navy, and purplish blues that didn't belong to twilight or night. It was more like a prerequisite to pitch dark.

Vic had almost caught up with Amber when she saw his headlights in her rearview mirror slow down to a stop at a traffic light. His lights vanished from her mirror as she continued driving.

Amber turned down the brick street that once felt like a safe haven, which led to her little bungalow. The tree lined street emitted dangerous shadows across every neighbor's yard. It seemed more like a haven for a sharpshooter to hide in waiting for an unprotected target for his kill site.

Amber pulled into her driveway; her car lights swept across the front yard. She turned off the engine, gripped the steering wheel, and waited for Vic like a good little girl. She looked across her front yard and saw nothing suspicious. There was no one hiding in the bushes. No one waiting for her. Weaved across the grass was the garden hose attached to a three-foot high circle sprinkler. The sprinkler that she spent way too much money for at an art show. The posters pictured one just like it with sparkling water drops spiraling out, cascading down on a luscious green lawn with a caption that read, *Watch the water dance spectacular as you keep your lawn green and beautiful.*

Even though she was furious, she had promised her mother. So she sat waiting. Her speeding tantrum from Vic had worked like a pressure cooker *Vic won't be long*, she thought as she released her steam of anger. Now she felt childish and remorseful for her action. *Mom must have been very upset to call Vic like that. It won't hurt to wait a minute or two.*

Amber looked across the yard again and then turned around to look down the street for Vic's van. Shadows from the oak trees cast across the already darken street. Down the road, she could see her neighbor's work van parked. A little farther into the darkness, a pickup sat on the other side of street, barely visible.

"Oh, this is ridiculous. He'll be here before I get to the front door," Amber said out loud. "I can walk to my door by myself."

She grabbed her purse and pulled the key out of the ignition, gave a quick look around the yard and glanced down the street again. She had promised not to go into the dark house alone and she wouldn't. She could unlock the door, by then Vic would be there. Flinging the car door open, Amber hopped out and hurried to the front steps of the house. As she stepped up on the first step, the bushes under the living room window rustle. She let out a scream and a black and white cat darted out. When she dropped her keys, the poor scared cat turned around and ran back to the safety of the shrubbery.

"Romeo! You scared me." She bent down and put her hand out. "Come here Romeo. I'm sorry. I guess I scared you, too." The cat hesitated, meowed and starting purring.

"Come on, Romeo. I'm not mad." Romeo came over to her hand just as sounds of a car screeched to the curb. Amber jumped and the cat ran. Feverishly Amber fumbled, feeling on the dark steps and ground for her keys as her heart pounded. Heavy sounding steps bounded up behind her.

"Amber! What are you doing?" The panicked baritone voice was Vic's.

Amber felt the metal of the keys, stood and turned around. She found herself face to face with Vic.

"I was unlocking the door and dropped my keys. I knew you were behind me, I figured you'd be here before I let myself in."

Vic looked at her. She could tell he was furious, his gorgeous blue eyes, which usually held an amorous look for her only glared back with anger and irritation. "Why did you race out of the parking lot like that? Are you crazy? Or do you just not care if you get hurt?"

"Come on, there was no Boogieman hiding in the bushes. Only Romeo. The Brown's cat from down the street. Besides I knew my big, strong guy was only minutes away," Amber poked at Vic's side and tried to tickle his anger out of him.

"Stop it, Amber! You know this guy has been watching you. Why do you fight us when we're trying to protect you?"

"All right! That's enough. I'm sorry. You know I don't like this anymore than you. And no, I don't have a death wish, if that's what you're thinking. I just wanted to come home, pet a cat and unlock my own door by myself. I'm tired of having bodyguards. Detective Harrison doesn't think I'm in danger anymore."

"Harrison is an ass!" Vic yelled. "There could've been someone waiting."

Amber started to cry. "I just want to get my life back."

Vic tenderly brushed back her hair. "I'm sorry. You mustn't let your guard down. Someone can't commit a crime without an opportunity. They need a defenseless person. Don't cry."

"I'm not crying—and I'm not defenseless."

"Okay, humor me and let me be the big strong guy. Give me the keys. I'll turn on the lights, and take a look around, then I'll go home. Promise. I'll be happy and you'll be happy. Okay?"

They made their way up the three brick steps, Vic unlocked the door and stepped inside. As Amber started in, her foot kicked something beside the doorway.

"What this?" she said. "Oh, it must be my jewelry tools I ordered."

Vic stopped and turned back. "What?"

"Mom's going to give me lessons. I wanted to start doing some jewelry pieces to sell on her web site." Amber bent down to pick up the box at her feet. "With the economy, design jobs are few and far between."

"Wait!" Vic shouted. "It might not be your tools. I'll get it."

Vic picked up the box carefully.

"It has some weight to it but not heavy enough for a lot of metal tools. Strange, the box is cool," Vic remarked. "Get the lights. I'll take it to the kitchen so I can get a better look before we do anything."

Amber paused and looked at Vic. "You think it's from him? He has only sent letters." She turned on the light switch inside the front door as Vic passed her heading to the kitchen.

"I don't know. There's no return address on it. Any company shipping something would put a return address on the box."

The box shifted in his hands as the weight of whatever was inside slid. Vic stopped and re-balanced the box and then walked on. "I'm not about to let you open this. I'm not taking any chances."

Neither Amber nor Vic noticed the small puncture holes on the one side of the box near the corner where Vic's fingertips griped the box.

In the kitchen, Amber turned on the lights, put her purse down and looked at Vic with concern. "Why would he send me a box? And what *would* he send?"

"Who knows what goes on in that sicko's mind? There's no telling what he might do." Vic examined the taped seams. "Get me a knife to cut this tape."

"Here." Amber handed him a small paring knife.

Vic slit the tape and slowly opened the two top flaps. Next, he lifted the flaps underneath.

"Holy shit!" he shouted as he jumped back. Vic grabbed a kitchen towel off the oven handle and threw it over the opening.

"Call that detective," Vic yelled as he flipped closed the flaps of the box. He snatched the whistle teapot off the stove and put it on top of the closed lid as a weight.

"What is it?"

"It's a snake. Call that damn detective and tell him to get over here now! He needs to catch this guy. That maniac just sent you a fucking rattle snake!"

The Pink Pistols

After receiving the box with the snake in it, Amber agreed she needed Vic's protection and she wanted it.

Detective Harrison said he didn't think the snake was from The Rainbow Killer—it didn't fit with the profile. The detective was empathic to Amber's situation but the delivery of the snake was not a matter for homicide *or* his task force. He insisted his team had to focus on the investigation, besides Amber hadn't received any more notes or calls prompting her to repent.

Harrison's attitude enraged Vic.

In the light of Detective Harrison's indifference, Amber agreed to let Vic come over in the evenings but insisted he go home by eleven o'clock. If anyone were watching, that would be long enough to discourage him. Amber would go about her day as normally as possible. She promised Vic and her mother that she wouldn't take any unnecessary chances.

One Week Later

On her way home from the gym, Amber stopped at a gourmet shop. She purchased her favorite cheddar cheese with small bits of chives in it and a wedge of a Spanish cheese for appetizers for her and Vic.

At home, after entering the house, Amber locked the dead bolt and reset the house alarm. As she had agreed to, she immediately called Vic. When they hung up Amber went to take a shower. She had started taking showers during the daylight ever since the delivery of the snake. Taking showers at night only brought to her mind violent movie shower scenes. She didn't dare confess her daytime shower schedule because of her fear to Vic. He would take it personal, as if she didn't think he could protect her long enough to go take a shower while he was there.

Amber returned to the living room after showering. The clock on the mantle showed four o'clock. Vic would be there in a half hour, which gave her enough time to prepare the plate of the cheeses, cover it and put it in the refrigerator for later.

Once she finished, she opened a bottle of white wine and poured a glass. There was still time to call her mother. They didn't get their usual chat this morning because Amber overslept and wanted to get to the gym before the crowd.

Keeping structure gave her a feel of normalcy. Talking to her mother helped her relax. It almost allowed her to forget about the killer who prowled the city.

Amber called Suzanne's number while sitting at the desk. She sipped her wine, thumbing through the mail as the phone rang.

Good, only junk mail. Nothing addressed to Resident Sinner.

Suzanne answered on the fourth ring

"Hi, Mom. Vic will be here soon, thought we could talk until then."

"Anything new?' Suzanne asked. New, nowadays meant, *did you hear from Detective Harrison? Or have there been any threatening deliveries?*

"No, nothing. Detective Harrison wouldn't call me even if there was anything. He thinks I am out of danger. Therefore, I'm out of the loop. I guess I'm old news."

"They don't think rattle snakes are dangerous?"

"Don't care mostly. It's not important to them unless it's about homicide."

"Well, I guess if they think you're not important then they must think you're not one of the killer's targets. I hope they're right. You know honey, I've been reading about crimes around the country and it is amazing how many unsolved murders are out there. Apparently, people commit crimes and just move away. The cases remain unsolved. Seems like unsolved cases are routine to the police."

"It's okay with me if this mess stops and whoever he is goes away. Things could get back to normal then," Amber said. "Matt says the crowds are picking up around the gallery like before. Although, the bars and nights clubs there never did notice a big drop in business."

"How's the construction going with the condos at Matt's building?"

"Great, the building is done but the parking garage got delayed. Something about the Historical Society. The developers are having a ribbon cutting and a party for new tenants. Matt is hosting it at the gallery. He says the place is almost sold out. Vic and I are going to attend the party."

"Are you sure it is safe?"

"I think so, everything considering, I'm not scared to go to Ybor anymore. I think Matt feels better too, but he's still a little cautious."

The sound of a car pulling in Amber's driveway diverted her attention. She looked out the window. "Mom, Vic's here. I have to go. Talk to you tomorrow."

Amber went to the door to find Vic coming up the steps, dressed in his black jeans and a Prussian blue short-sleeve shirt. The sleeves were rolled up farther to allow a comfort fit for his muscular bi-ceps. The dark shirt contrasted his ice blue eyes, which resembled the color of the Caribbean Ocean. Amber smiled, although she hated the thought of having a man protect her, if she needed protection Vic was a perfect choice.

"Hi, come on in."

Vic stepped in and gave her a kiss on the cheek.

"Sit down. I made a plate of cheese and crackers. I opened a bottle of wine. I'll get you a glass. We haven't tried this one yet."

Amber put her glass down on the table next to the sofa. "It's good, has a hint of pear, but with a crisp clean taste."

"Did you think of where you want to eat tonight?" Vic asked and took a seat on the couch.

"No, I thought we could discuss that over our wine." Amber returned from the kitchen with the wine glass, handed it to Vic, and put the cheese plate down. She headed to the desk. "I brought a flyer home for you to see. One of the women at the gym had picked it up at a café downtown."

Amber grabbed a pink paper off the desk, handed it to Vic and sat down next to him. The bold letters read:

GAYS AND LESBIANS
TAKE CHARGE OF YOUR SAFETY

- LEARN HOW TO SHOOT A GUN
- EXPLORE DIFFERENT KINDS OF PISTOLS AVAILABLE
- LEARN ABOUT REGISTERING A FIREARM.

INTERESTED PERSONS ARE WELCOME TO COME TO AN ORGANIZATIONAL MEETING FOR NEW MEMBERS OF THE PINK PISTOLS NEXT SUNDAY AFTERNOON AT THREE O'CLOCK.
STOP BEING SCARED. DON'T BE A VICTIM ANYMORE.
FOR DETAILS, CALL ANDY MARTINEZ...555-0258 EXT. 315

"Oh, he distributed them downtown too." Vic looked at the flyer.

"You knew about this?" Amber's voice rose an octave higher. "What is Andy thinking? Does he think walking around carrying a gun will make him safer? . . . Detective Harrison says—"

"Harrison doesn't know what he's talking about."

"Look it's not his fault if the killer has left Tampa. He's doing his job. Mom said there are a lot of unsolved cases."

"And why do you think that is? If police work is so damn good, then why are there a lot of unsolved cases. Shouldn't most of them be solved?"

Amber widened her eyes and raised her voice louder. "That's not what we are talking about here. You knew about this . . . this, Pink Pistols thing!"

"Oh, is that what we're doing? Talking? Sounds like you're telling me, Amber."

"Well, maybe I am. Guns aren't the answer. This isn't the Wild West, you know!"

"What do you want everyone to do? Hope the killer is bored here and has left town? Is that your answer for this? At least, Andy isn't putting his head in the sand."

"What! I'm not putting my head in the sand."

Vic looked at Amber. Her eyes were wild with rage. She had a short fuse. Vic thought about Phillip, how his levelheaded brother tamed her rage with patience. Patience wasn't Vic's strong suit but still he was not going to let himself get provoked into a fight.

He took a sip of wine and set the glass on the table. Before speaking, he took a slow, deep breath. "Andy came to me about a week ago and asked me what I thought. He met some people that belong to this gun group. They're not radicals or anything like that. They meet at a firing range to learn how to handle and shoot guns. They believe that armed gays stay safe."

"So, you're telling me Andy asked you about this?"

"Yes, honey, sometimes people have to be responsible for their own safety." Vic slid his arm around Amber but she jerked away and faced him.

"Don't honey me. You condone Andy and the others carrying guns?"

"Boy, how single-minded can you be? Your stubbornness is a real problem and it's going to get you killed. If you think you're going to talk me out of what I feel is right then plan on being disappointed. I'm not going to let my brother or anyone else I love get killed. It's right that Andy and the group are taking charge of their own safety. You're just wrong about this one Amber."

"Wrong? You think I'm *wrong*. You think I'm the one with the problem? I know what the problem is . . . Phillip doesn't fit into your world. He's not the person you thought he was and you wish he were more macho. Strapping on a gun is not the answer for your hang-ups about homosexuals."

"That's it." Vic stood up. "No more! Look, sure, I had a problem adjusting to my brother being gay, and maybe I'm still dealing with it. The real problem, as I see it, would be having to identify Phillip's body, or Andy's, or Claire and Saffron's, any of my friends. That's right—I have homosexual friends. Your problem is you're spoiled and you don't understand that you can't always be right."

"Well, you can't have it both ways." Amber was shaking with rage. "It's okay for Andy to take charge and be responsible for his safety but not me? You're playing this macho superman thing with me and I was stupid enough to go along with it. Like tonight, you're just here to make sure I know how to lock my front door. Well, I'm a big girl, and if I need someone to be *my Daddy*, it won't be you. I already have a father. I don't need you."

Vic stood there looking at her and clenching the pink paper in his hand. "Gay or not, people have a right to protect themselves. And they shouldn't have to walk around scared."

He threw the paper down, turned and charged for the door. Opening the door, Vic turned back to Amber, "I'm going home. Oh yeah, I won't tell you to lock the door behind me. I wouldn't want you to think I want to be your 'Daddy.' And as far you being in charge of your own safety, no problem, you're in charge. I'll stay away."

Vic walked out of the house and slammed the door.

"Good," Amber shouted at the closed door and then she burst into tears. She ran to the door and turned the dead bolt lock—the one that Vic installed for her the day after she received the threatening letter.

The Gift

Bruce Whitehouse exited the plane at the Tampa International Airport, walked down the ramp, and into the terminal. A chauffeur stood in a waiting crowd holding a sign that read, "Whitehouse."

The plane landed early and there would be plenty of time to get to the gallery by six-thirty as planned.

When Bruce proposed the Ybor project earlier this year, he hadn't considered the many delays that the Historical Society's involvement brought. So many unseen delays that continued for months caused failures to meet sales projections, like Bruce's first goal to have one fourth of the condominium units sold by the date Matt Connelly had his gala and opening party. That had been the first major miss for one of Bruce's investment projections. However, all the setbacks seemed behind them now, thanks to Matt's help. All the stores were leased in the building and the condominiums were eighty per cent sold out. Matt's stamp of approval had been all that was needed to get back on track.

Matt Connelly's contacts in the city were abundant. After one quick phone call to the local television station, they booked Matt for an interview, and that was the turning point for Bruce's project. Immediately people wanted to own one of chic luxury units of Casa de Ybor. It became the most popular place to live.

Tomorrow's ribbon cutting at four o'clock, and the cocktail party following was a celebration of the success. The project was the most profitable investment Whitehouse and Partners had ever done. It was due to a combination of Bruce's vision and his wisdom to realize the public persona of Matt Connelly and his power in the city.

Bruce called Matt's number, while in the car. "Matt, Bruce Whitehouse here. My plane got in eight minutes early. I'm on my way. I wanted to tell you again how glad we are that you chose to move your gallery to our building."

"Well, Bruce, you made me a very enticing offer. The space couldn't be any better for a gallery, not to mention you've been very kind with the rental arrangements."

"I feel a little guilty that you won't take our offer to buy into the project. As much as you have contributed to its success, it's only fair you should reap the rewards. You could make enough money to retire in three years. Buy an island or something."

Bruce wasn't exaggerating. Whitehouse and Partners timing was right on the money for the rebirth of Ybor City. The jealous, Blair Casey, didn't even put up a big fight when Bruce suggested offering Matt an option to buy into the project. It was just good business to keep Matt happy. If he ever decided to move or stop his support, it could be devastating.

"I don't need an island," Matt said. "I'm a small-town guy. I'm happy with my little gallery."

"Okay, but I don't get it," Bruce said.

"You don't have to, trust me, I'm happy—enough said. By the way, I thought we could walk over to the Columbia Restaurant for an authentic Spanish dinner tonight. You can get a feel for the local flavor. On Friday nights, they have the Flamenco dancers. I reserved a table right up front."

"Sounds great. See you in a few."

Bruce looked out of the window as the car exited from the highway and headed toward Seventh Avenue. He looked at his Rolex watch and then down at the box in his lap. Inside was a Submariner Rolex for Matt. *Small town guy. I hope he wants a Rolex, it's the least I can do for him.*

Bruce ran the figures two days earlier; this venture had already made all the board members over a million dollars each. Bruce liked buying expensive things, it made him feel secure. He called them his trinkets, a Lamborghini to replace the Mercedes, three houses, each bigger than the last one bought. It was his way to remember the promise he had made to himself that he would never be poor again. His need to spend money was the same as other people needed air, but he only bought things for himself—this time the Rolex was a gift.

He thought back to years before, when Chip walked into his office with a box in hand and said he wanted him to have a gift as a token of their friendship. That was Bruce's first Rolex.

"I've never gave a man an expensive gift, let alone jewelry," Chip had told him. "I only buy jewelry for my wife. I guess a Rolex falls in the class of jewelry, but Bruce, I respect you and wanted to give this to you. You're a remarkable person and I treasure your friendship."

Bruce touched the watch on his wrist; the one Chip gave him. It was the basic everyday variety, no diamonds but Bruce never replaced it with another. As a child, he never got gifts, not even at Christmas. Money had to go for food . . . or his father's drinking.

He thought about Matt Connelly, he was genuine, descent, and an honorable man. There were very few men like him around anymore. Charleston Black the third was the only other man of that caliber Bruce had ever met. He wanted to show his respect and appreciation to Matt like Charleston had to him. Bruce tapped the box as he thought. *I hope I don't insult the guy.*

Hope he doesn't think I'm trying to pay him off like hired help.

Casa de Ybor Ribbon Cutting

After the Ribbon Cutting

The gallery was full of people. Saffron, Claire, and the group were there, all except for Ken and Bennie, who now were in California. Amber and Vic made excuses for arriving separately. They awkwardly avoided each other.

The new condominium owners of the building received welcoming ruby colored bags filled with all kinds of goodies. That was Matt's idea. He orchestrated all the arrangements and made sure the media people were invited. The local television station's staff moved through the crowd waiting for the arrival of the mayor.

Guests mingled inside the gallery, while a large number overflowed out into the lobby and more wandered around the outside patio areas. Servers maneuvered through the flock of people with trays of assorted appetizers that were provided by the top catering company in town. The company's owner offered ample food and drinks for a crowd of three hundred in exchange for the acknowledgment in the welcome letter that was included in all the gift bags.

The mayor was expected, and once again, the eyes of Tampa Bay were upon Casa de Ybor.

Andy pushed through the crowd and approached Bruce and Matt with a reporter in tow. "I'm glad to find both of you together. The newspaper needs some pictures of you two."

The reporter snapped a half dozen pictures, thanked them and then left to take some shots outside. Andy stayed with the two men. "This is so exciting. Mr. Whitehouse you've put Ybor City on the map again." Andy looked around the room and added, "Everything looks great, doesn't it? Matt sure knows how to throw a party."

"Yes," Bruce answered without making eye contact as he glanced beyond, staring into the crowd as he spoke. "I think we have a success."

Andy waited for Bruce to turn back to him to continue their conversation. Bruce kept scanning the room.

An awkward silence passed and Andy said, "I understand you flew in from Atlanta?"

"Yes."

"Did you have a good flight?" Andy asked as he looked at the side of Bruce's head.

"Yes."

Andy stood, shuffled from one foot to the other and fidgeted with his hands. He glanced at Matt, who looked very uncomfortable witnessing Bruce's indifference toward Andy.

The apparent rudeness to Andy seemed based on nothing except for the standard reason experienced before, which was that Andy was unmistakably gay. He was use to receiving cold shoulders after meeting some people for the first time. *Poor Matt, too bad his new friend is such a jerk. How awful for him.* Andy paused for a few seconds more, then he cleared his throat and said, "Uh, I better go check with the bartenders to make sure they don't need anything. Would you excuse me?"

Bruce twisted back to look directly at Andy. "Of course, it was nice talking to you Mr. Martinez."

Andy left without another word.

"Matt," Bruce said. "There seems to be quite a lot of gays around—like that Martinez fellow. I noticed a few of them even are some of our condominium owners. I hope that doesn't present problems. We wouldn't want another protest demonstration like you had before your opening party."

"I think we're going to be all right," Matt said. "There is a good mix of people here. Besides, some important and influential people in town are homosexuals and they're here tonight, too."

"Oh, don't get me wrong, I was worried about the other people causing trouble, not the gays. By the way, Mr. Martinez was right, you did do a great job putting this together and I'm so glad you liked your watch."

"Oh yes, I do. Thank you. I never owned a Rolex before."

Two to be Hold

Bruce walked down the dark street toward Seventh Avenue. The sounds of the party echoed behind him. There had been no signs of the cluster of people back at the gallery leaving any time soon. That probably wouldn't happen until the free food and liquor ran out. After all, most of the remaining people were tenants and they only had to walk upstairs to get home. Bruce, on the other hand, had a flight to catch. When he called for a cab, he told them to pick him up at the corner of Seventh and Sixteenth, it would be easier than having a driver maneuvering down the narrow street where parked cars lined both sides of the road all the way to the gallery.

It's amazing, Matt was right about Ybor coming alive once night falls.

Bruce preferred to catch the taxi at the corner since weaving through narrow streets while sitting as passenger would be nerve racking to him. Once he caught the cab, they would precede to his hotel, pickup his suitcase then head straight to the airport. He would be back in Atlanta by midnight, if there weren't any flight delays.

The sounds of music drifted down the street from Seventh Avenue and became louder as he continued to walk. Beneath the laughter of partygoers and distant rhythmic sounds from the clubs, there was another sound. It nudged through the air unable to blend into the distant festive melodies. A muffled sound . . . more like a cry or a whimper.

Bruce frowned and turned his head to listen. He couldn't make out what it was but he knew there was something wrong. He walked on, listening. *Maybe a car hit a dog.*

Clouds moved across the half-moon making only a few feet ahead visible. *It's so dark.*

Parked cars were jammed, bumper-to-bumper lining both sides of the narrow brick street. Bruce walked down the middle of the side street avoiding the hazard of the occasional SUV pulled up over curb onto the sidewalk. He passed a parked Toyota and a Saturn, while listening for the sound again.

There it was again. This time, it seemed more like two distinctly different noises overlapping in unison—one, more like a laborious grunting, and the other, an obscure whimper or moan. As Bruce passed a blue pick-up, the clouds drifted in the sky and the moonlight shone down on a shadowy figure yards ahead. The silhouette hunched over something in the road.

What is that?

Bruce could not identify the man, however, the moonlight breaking through the clouds, flashed on the object dangling from his neck. It was a large cross swaying. At his feet, lay heaped a motionless bundle.

Bruce squinted as the clouds moved across the moon again. *Too big for it to be a dog.*

Bruce moved forward, walking faster—then he stopped.

It's a body!

"Hey! What are you doing?" Bruce yelled. The figure stood erect and turned facing him.

Double Entry

The phone rang in the station room where a baldheaded man stood at a bulletin board removing pushpins that held an assortment of papers and pictures of dead bodies. He stopped and walked to a nearby desk and answered the ringing phone.

"Task force, Detective Stone. Yeah, he's here . . . okay I'll send him down." He placed the phone back in its cradle and yelled across the room, "Hey, Harry, that was Smitty. He's downstairs. Needs to see you. He's got another package."

Harry looked up from his desk and said, "Stop packing men. Put everything back. If Smitty has something for me then our guy is still in town." He slammed his fist down on the desk. "Damn-it." Why can't we catch this guy?" He sprung out of his chair and stomped toward the door mumbling. "He's really pissin' me off."

Officer Smith had orders to go directly to the task force if he got any more packages. No need to waste the time of the bomb squad. Bombs were not the Rainbow's M.O. He only sent personal items taken off the victims and always sent them by way of Smitty. Boxes showed up mysteriously near his patrol car, marked with Harrison's name on it. Except for once, when a kid walked into the station and said some man gave him five dollars to deliver a box to an Officer Smith. The killer got more brazen as time dragged on. It was as if he was thumbing his nose at them.

The task force had considered the killer could be a cop because he had picked Smitty as his gopher. Harrison and Smitty's longstanding history and friendship was well known among the force, but evidence strongly indicated that the killer's choice of delivery was just an ironic coincidence.

Boxes had come in like clockwork after every killing, and then two weeks earlier, everything abruptly stopped. No new bodies. No deliveries—nothing. Headquarters believed Harrison's team might have gotten too close and the killer got nervous and fled Tampa.

Harrison came in carrying two small boxes. He put them down on his desk, put on protective gloves to avoid contaminating any fingerprints on the items inside, although there never were any, and then he cut the brown wrapping paper on the first box.

This delivery would cancel any shutdown orders from Harrison's superiors to pack up and dissolve the investigation. The delivery wasn't just one package this time but two. Perhaps The Rainbow Killer was trying to make-up for lost time.

Harrison opened the first box, inside lay a Rolex watch.

"Our perp is moving up in his world," Harrison said with a sarcastic tone. "This victim is rich enough to own a Rolex."

He opened the next box. "What the fuck." He picked up an army green camouflage piece of cloth. "What—he's going after military now?"

"It's a pocket," the bald man said. "There's something inside it. See. There something's sticking out from the edge."

Harrison pulled blue strands out in his hand. Pieces of blue slipped through his fingers and floated down to the desktop. "It's hair."

"Blue hair isn't army regulation, that's for sure," Stone said.

"Shit. We have two bodies out there to find," Harrison said. "He's escalated to killing two at a time now."

Identifying Bodies

The task force realized the killer had changed his pattern. They had two victims to look for, or so the trophies in boxes indicated. It didn't take long before a call came in to Harrison informing him that two uniformed officers answered a call in Ybor City that reported dead bodies were found—two of them.

Whitehouse's wallet was logged in as evidence, it had been found in the pocket on one of the bodies. The picture on the driver's license inside allowed for temporary identification. Three hundred dollars remained inside the wallet. Therefore, robbery was ruled out. Whitehouse had put up a fight by the looks of the bruising on his body. Even before the officers found the money, they had pegged it as another Rainbow killing. There weren't any notes pinned to the bodies, however, both victims had evidence of strangulation and a rope remained twisted around Whitehouse's neck. The twisted knot behind his head implied that the killer must have slipped it over Whitehouse's head from behind during the struggle.

It didn't take Harrison's team long to have a complete background on Whitehouse. He was high profile in the press. Shit was going to hit the fan by the time the six o'clock news aired. Whitehouse wasn't gay, but neither were three prior victims. Harrison had been able to keep the press from connecting the dots of the other heterosexual victims to the Rainbow murders, but fat chance he could keep Whitehouse's death a secret. This would blow the lid off the highly explosive Rainbow case for good. His men would have the screws put to them, not only from Harrison's supervisor but also all the way up to the mayor's office to make an arrest and stop the killings.

Four Hours after the Discovery of the Bodies

Harrison spoke to Whitehouse's business partner, Charleston Black III. He told Harrison that once Bruce's body was officially released, he would have it flown back to Atlanta for burial. Black said he would make all the arrangements. The last surviving relative of Bruce Whitehouse had been his father, and he had died some time ago. The only person Bruce was close to was Charleston. He explained he'd fly to Tampa if necessary to identify the body but suggested that Matt Connelly might be willing to do it.

Harrison thanked him and said he would call Connelly. He wanted to talk to him anyway since it appeared he might've been the last to speak to Whitehouse. The paper reported that there were over four hundred people at the ribbon cutting and cocktail party at the gallery.

"Stone, call and find out if they got a name for our blue-hair lady from her prints," Harrison said. "Who knows, maybe the female is straight and just dresses freaky."

"Got'cha. But if that girl isn't a dike, then I am Santa Claus."

Harrison picked up the receiver. "I'll call this Connelly guy. Maybe he might be able to shed new light on the case."

Andy looked at the caller ID. "Matt, caller ID says it's private, you better answer it."

"Okay, but it's probably a telemarketer . . . hello."

"Mr. Connelly, this is Detective Harrison. I have some bad news about Bruce Whitehouse."

At the Morgue

Matt followed the detective into a brightly lighted room. A steel gurney stood in front of him and a man in scrubs pulled back the sheet that covered a body.

"That's Bruce," Matt said nodding. The ghostly grey color of Whitehouse's once tanned skin assaulted Matt's memory of Bruce. Abrasions, bruises and a purplish-black line around his friend's neck were visible. It would be hard to erase the images of them from his mind. "I'm not feeling well. Is that all you need?"

"We're done here," Harrison said. He walked over to the door, opened it and stepped back holding it for Matt. As Matt passed by, Harrison said, "I need some additional information from you." Harrison moved out into the hallway, motioned, and said, "We can use an office down the hall.

The two men walked the narrow hallway. "I just talked to him at the party," Matt said in a monotone voice. His face was flushed a bright red. He felt clammy and began to sweat. The walls blurred and his head swirled as he muttered, "We ate at the Columbia Restaurant the day before . . . now he's dead."

Matt had never identified a body before. It wasn't as he had imagined. But then, he didn't know what he had imagined. What he did know was that it wasn't this. It seemed so surreal, as if he was moving about the scene but not really part of it.

They entered a small office. Matt took a seat and started talking. "I don't understand. Bruce was just in town for a few hours for the ribbon cutting. He didn't really know anyone." Matt's voice was almost inaudible. He looked at the Rolex on his wrist and squeezed his eyes shut. "Except for me."

"Mr. Connelly, we have reason to believe that Mr. Whitehouse was killed by the Rainbow Killer."

"What!" Matt's eyes flew open. "Why? He wasn't gay. There must be some mistake."

"Are you certain that he didn't have any homosexual contacts in Tampa?" Harrison asked. "If he had some connection to the gay community that could be why the killer targeted him."

"Can anyone be certain who is gay or not, Detective? I know a lot of people. Gallery patrons, apartment owners of Casa de Ybor, some are openly gay, some straight, but most are very private with their preferences. Do you expect me to start pointing a finger?" Matt looked at him with anger in his eyes. "What difference would it make if Bruce had been gay, would that justify his murder?"

"Of course not, Mr. Connelly. We're just trying to gather anything that might give us a lead."

Matt relaxed his stiffened posture. "Well then to give you an answer, I feel certain Bruce Whitehouse wasn't homosexual. The night of the party Bruce noticed many of the guests attending were obviously gay, and I assure you, his attitude wasn't kindhearted toward homosexuals."

"Was there a confrontation between him and another guest?"

"No. I didn't say that. He was just concerned about any bad press we might get, like the same kind we received when I hosted a fundraiser for AIDS Awareness. Bruce was a dear friend. He wasn't a bad person, just very business minded. His perception of things focused on how they would affect business."

Matt glared at the detective and stood. "Is that all you need? I need to get home."

"Yes, you're free to go. But before you leave, could you take a look at the other victim we found with Mr. Whitehouse?"

"Another victim?" Matt stood there unmoving. "Why? Is it someone I know?"

"Not that we are aware of, however, it's possible she may have been one of the guests."

Call for Help

Matt kept the gallery closed Saturday. The problem he now faced was that Andy had scheduled the first organizational meeting for the Pink Pistols at their house on Sunday. Twenty-five people were expected to show up. There would be more questions about Bruce's death and Matt did not want to deal with any more discussion about murders. Besides, the thought of seeing people made him want to run and hide. Andy offered to cancel the meeting but Matt declined his offer. There was a killer still loose out there and the information Andy had could help people.

It would be a long time before Matt would be able to erase the images of Bruce's lifeless body lying on the metal table at the morgue. Even though co-hosting the meeting was the last thing Matt wanted to do, there wasn't any time to waste. People had to protect themselves.

The gallery had been the last place Matt and Bruce spoke. Haunted by the memories of Bruce's smiling face at the ribbon-cutting event, Matt wondered if he could even go to the gallery to post a closed sign in the window on Monday.

What was a reasonable time to close for mourning the death of a colleague and friend? Matt shuddered at the thought. Perhaps Andy would go for him before the Pink Pistols meeting on Sunday.

Sunday morning

Vic decided to ride down to Apollo Beach to do a final inspection on an Italian restaurant his crew finished on Friday. The job had been a problem from the very start. To top it off, late Friday afternoon the field supervisor called to tell him he had fired two of the workers that day. He found them at lunchtime snorting cocaine on the jobsite.

Vic recognized the men's names. They were experienced roofers who had helpers under their supervision. Every inch of the roof needed a thorough inspection before Vic would be comfortable signing off on the job. He wanted to do that inspection in private.

It was six a.m. when Vic left his house. The inspection plus the two-hour round-trip drive would take all of the morning. It would be well after noon when he'd be back home. When he pulled into his driveway the clock on the dashboard glowed 2:00. It was too late to work with his pottery, besides his heart wasn't in it. All his thoughts were about Amber.

As he unlocked the front door, he got angry over again thinking about the fight they had a week and half ago. Her words still enraged him. *She's wrong and her opinion is going to get her hurt. Or maybe even . . ..* Vic shook his head, refusing to think about what could ultimately happen if the killer came after her. *Damn you, Amber!*

He went inside and headed to the kitchen to grab a cold beer out of the refrigerator. After picking up the morning paper off the counter, he headed back to the living room. He sat in the leather chair next to the couch where Amber and he used to curl up into each other's arms to watch movies on weekends. He unscrewed the bottle cap, took a drink, and opened the paper. Scanning the headlines for news about The Rainbow Killer, he came up empty. Thoughts that Harrison could be right went through his mind. Maybe Amber was out of danger.

Vic knew inevitably, her pig-headedness would make her take undue risk. If the killer was still out there, and without him there to protect her, it could be fatal.

Vic put the paper down. "I respected your viewpoint, Amber, why can't you respect mine?" Whenever Vic thought about their fight, it enraged him all over again. Furious that Amber wouldn't even consider he might be right.

She had been so quick to tell him she didn't need him; it cemented his opinion that Amber didn't want him in her life anymore. Bottom line was that she wanted to be single.

Vic supported Andy's involvement with the Pink Pistols. Although Vic was as strong and determined as Amber, she could manipulate him. But now, he was drawing the line. She wasn't going to tell him what he could and couldn't think. It seemed obvious to him, if he didn't think the same way she did, then Amber demanded that he hit the road.

"Respect goes both ways, Amber!" Vic shouted in the empty room.

It was done. She set the limits, and he was not going to call to apologize. He had survived breakups with girlfriends before and he could handle this. The only thing he couldn't handle was Amber's death because of her foolish stubbornness.

The phone rang. Vic hesitated . . . *maybe it is Amber.* He knew better, she was too sure she was right. She wouldn't call him.

He picked up the receiver.

"Vic? I'm sorry to call . . ." Then there was silence.

"Matt, is that you?"

"Yes. I didn't want to trouble you, but Phillip said I should call you."

"What's the matter, buddy?"

Matt's voice sounded strained. A million things swam through Vic's mind, and every scenario involved Amber. Matt was always upbeat. Even when everyone else was frantic about the murders in the news, Matt stayed cool, never sounded panicky. However, panic was exactly what Vic heard in his voice.

"We're all at my house for the Pink Pistols meeting but I forgot and left the paperwork I copied for Andy at the gallery."

"Is that all it is?"

"I'm really worried. I shouldn't have called you but Andy went to go get the papers and put a sign in the window for me."

"I'm not following you, Matt," Vic said. "What's the problem?"

"Andy left a couple of hours ago. Everyone is here and he's not back. The meeting was scheduled for one-thirty."

"He probably just got tied up in traffic," Vic said reassuringly.

"But Vic, I spoke to him at twelve-forty and he just opened the gallery. He wanted to know where to find the papers. He should've been back here by now."

"It's after two-thirty."

"That's why I'm worried."

"Do you want me to go over and see what's happened?"

"Could you?

"No problem."

"Andy has been having trouble with the starter in his car. Maybe he's stranded," Matt said. "Phillip thought you could go over and check since you're closer and all of the guests are here. I called Andy's cell but he didn't answer. When he spoke to me last, he said he forgot to charge it and the battery was almost dead. I called the gallery but there's no answer there either. I'm worried that something has happened."

"He's probably outside trying to get the car started and hasn't realized the time," Vic said.

"Maybe . . . but I don't know." The worry in Matt's voice sounded so foreign to Vic. "Maybe you shouldn't go. It might not be safe. There's a killer out there, you know. I can call the police."

"No, that's not necessary, besides the police won't go looking for him unless he been missing something like 24 or 48 hours," Vic said. "I'm sure it's just car trouble. He probably tried to get it started, flooded it, or wore down the battery. You know Andy isn't very mechanical. I'll go. If we can't get the car started, I'll give him a lift to your place."

"Thanks. Vic—you'll call me when you find out he's okay?"

"Yup, no problem. Don't worry Matt."

It took Vic thirty minutes to get to the gallery. Ybor was ghostly quiet especially on the side streets. Sunday afternoons didn't bring much activity except for the brunch crowd near the Columbia Restaurant. The gallery was south of Seventh Avenue and off the beaten track, blocks away from the Columbia Restaurant where most of the activity was located. As Vic approached the gallery, he saw Andy's car parked in front, but no sign of him outside. The hood was not up, no signs of any trouble. Vic drove past a blue pickup parked along the road and pulled in front of Andy's car at the curb. The lights were on in the gallery.

Well, he probably gave up on starting his car. Vic figured Matt had already reached Andy by now and he was waiting inside the gallery for him.

The door chimed as Vic entered the gallery and took a couple of steps inside.

"Andy...Andy, it's Vic. You in here?"

Vic took another step forward and his foot slid on something wet. He looked down. A red puddle formed around his foot. It looked like blood. There were drops trailing to the right side of the room where a wall held frame samples and a doorway led into a back room.

Immediately, Vic stiffened his stance, scanned the gallery, and quickly checked behind him, making sure no one was sneaking up from the outside lobby. He saw nothing. Mounted on the wall, next to the door, was a fire extinguisher. Vic slowly backed up and grabbed it. It was heavy enough to make a good weapon, and if swung fast, it could knock someone out with one blow. Holding it with both hands up in a batter's position, Vic moved forward looking for Andy.

A few feet ahead, he saw more blood and a smear on the doorframe of the back room. A noise came from the back area piercing the deadly silence. Vic hurried forward and flattened up against the wall next to the bloody doorframe. He quickly poked his head in and looked for someone, checking the perimeter of the room and then darted his head back out, flattening once more against the wall.

"Andy. Buddy, we were worried about you," he called out. "The cops are on the way." If there were anyone around, maybe if they thought the cops were on their way, it would force them to run out.

Another noise sounded but it was undistinguishable, too soft to be someone trying to make a getaway. Vic listened for a moment. Another small muffled sound, and then, nothing. Someone was back there. Vic readied himself, lunged inside the room and froze at the scene before him. There were blood spatters on the walls, crimson pools on the floor, and bloody handprints streaked across tabletops and cabinet doors. It looked like a war zone.

Tools, wooden pieces of broken frames, and papers supplies were strung about on the floor with smears of blood across everything. The room appeared empty.

Vic headed toward a phone on the wall to call the police. As he passed by the large worktable, an image on the floor caught his eye.

To his left, Andy's blood-soaked body lay motionless in a growing puddle of blood.

"Andy!"

Vic dropped the extinguisher and ran toward him.

Without Vic

Amber finished a salad for lunch and decided to read. She sat on the couch with her legs stretched out. After reading halfway through the page, she found her mind drifting off again for the third time.

Maybe I am stubborn like Vic claims. I shouldn't 't have said he was insecure and needing to have his ego puffed up.

Amber knew that Vic was different. He understood she was an intelligent, self-reliant person. It was rare to find a man who wasn't threatened by an independent and strong woman. She realized that she had become comfortable seeing Vic every night and she missed him now so much.

He cared about her, she knew that, and it wasn't wrong for him to worry about her safety.

The first couple of nights without Vic were somewhat freeing for her. Her mood was lighthearted and almost joyful in the solitude of doing leisurely girl things, like facials. One night she even took a bubble bath. Of course, she kept a watchful eye on the open bathroom door. After that, showers became a regular daytime event. Soon time without Vic left her feeling empty and loneliness crept into her nights.

She thought about Vic and mentally scolded herself because he was the most secure man she had ever known. Not like other boyfriends who needed to prove themselves to her.

He does not need his ego inflated.

After all, he put in the alarm system for her so she didn't have to rely on his protection. She liked that. Their relationship was an equal partnership. No one was boss.

Vic's just a little old-fashioned. Not a chauvinist. Just gallant, a perfect gentleman. I love that about him.

Then the heated words of their fight flooded back and Amber's temper overpowered her again. She visualized Vic storming out of the house like a typical man.

Amber picked up her book and started reading again. A minute later she slammed the book shut and placed it on the coffee table. "This is ridiculous. I don't need Vic," she said and grabbed the television remote. Clicking, she started surfing channels.

Suzanne had warned her to be sure what she wished for. "When the right person comes along," Suzanne had said, "it doesn't mean a woman has to give up her freedom. Freedom doesn't require isolation, either."

Amber realized the question was could Vic be the right person for her. Her heart had the answer. Was it too late?

He's probably moved on and is on a date with a blonde airhead this very minute.

The phone rang. She turned off the television and went to answer it.

"Hello."

"Amber, it's Phillip, something's happened. The sheriff called us. I'm with Matt. We're on our way to Tampa General Hospital. It's Andy and Vic."

"Wh . . . what's happened?"

"The police didn't give us any details. A dispatcher called and said to hurry. An ambulance is in route with both of them on their way to the hospital. It sounds serious. You need to come quickly."

"Okay. I'll meet you at the emergency room."

Amber hung the phone up, riffled through her purse for the car keys. Once she found them, she grabbed the keys, ran, hit the alarm "off" button, and flew out the door.

In the car, she fumbled with the keys at the ignition slot. Her hands were shaking so that the keys slipped from her fingers and fell to the floor. Frantically feeling for them with no luck, she had to step out of the car and bent down to search for them. After retrieving the keys from under the front seat, she jumped back in, shoved the key in the ignition and turned. All the while, she silently begged, *please God, let me get there in time.*

Popping the lever into reverse, she backed out of the driveway. *Why was I so stupid and stubborn?* She sped out down the street. *Why didn't I call him?*

She reprimanded herself the whole time as she raced through town, hoping that she wouldn't be stopped for speeding. Praying she would get to the hospital in time before it would be too late. Why had it been so important to her for Vic to make the first call?

Amber swerved up the ramp toward the hospital. As she ran into the emergency room, she immediately saw Phillip and Matt standing in front of a robust, matronly looking woman in white. Matt's voice was raised in a shrilled yell. Phillip was next to him, trying to talk over him and struggling to settle things down.

"What the hell do you mean they're not here yet?" Matt screamed. "We had farther to come than they had. They should've been here first. Do you even know what you're talking about?"

"Sir, you need to calm down," the nurse said.

"Matt, take it easy," Phillip pleaded.

"Take it easy! No. I'm not going to take it easy—or calm down. You people are all incompetent."

"Matt," Phillip said. "They're not here yet. You're upset, calm down. She'll let us know as soon as they arrive."

Amber joined Matt and Phillip just as a security guard approached.

"Sir, you're going to have to lower your voice," the security guard warned.

Amber grabbed Matt's arm. He spun around, his face contorted with rage and fire in his eyes. A second passed, before a look of recognition came into his eyes and his face relaxed as anger evaporated.

"Moonbeam, the ambulance should have been here already. This woman won't listen to me."

"They probably had to stop in transit, sir," the woman in white said.

Matt whipped around to face her, "Are you stupid or can't you hear. It was urgent that they get here quickly for help, they wouldn't stop unless . . ." Matt's eyes filled with tears, his words froze in midair. He swallowed hard and started blinking repeatedly.

The automatic glass doors to the emergency room swished open and they heard Saffron's voice. "They're here. The ambulance just pulled in."

Phillip, Amber, and Matt turned and raced through the doors as the ambulance pulled up with a police car behind them. The back doors of the ambulance flew open and a paramedic jumped out. Amber peered inside and saw a bag with an IV line leading to a body on a gurney. The large paramedic's body blocked her view of the patient's face. The hospital EMR staff pushed in to help as they rolled the gurney out. Another paramedic, still inside moved through discarded piles of bloody gauze on the floor.

Amber stood crying. *Please God, let Vic be alive.* Her body trembled as she waited to see the face of the man they were transporting. They lowered the gurney . . . it was Andy. Amber looked beyond the men into the empty vehicle where evidence remained of the aftermath of an attempt to save a victim of a brutal attack.

Amber voice cracked as she asked, "Where's Vic?"

"Amber." She heard a call from behind her. She turned and saw Vic, his white shirt-stained bright red with blood and a sheriff was at his side. Vic placed his arm around Amber and led her inside along with the rest of the group in tow leaving the staff attending to Andy outside.

"Vic, you're hurt," Amber said. "You need a doctor."

"No, I'm okay." He paused and then said. "It's Andy's blood."

"What happened?"

"I went to the gallery looking for Andy and found him. The 9-1-1 operator dispatched the police and the ambulance."

More medical personnel rushed past Vic and the group, heading outside to join the others.

"He was alive when I found him," Vic said, "but unconscious. While I waited, the man on the phone had me apply pressure to try to stop the bleeding, but there were too many wounds. I couldn't stop all the blood from gushing."

The glass sliding door swished open again and a mass of people in scrubs and white coats barked out vitals as they rushed Andy by Vic, Amber, and the others. One of the nurses ran ahead and hit a metal plate on the wall to open the automatic solid double doors. The medical team whisked their patient through the doors, disappearing with doors closing behind them.

The forceful woman in white who had been arguing with Matt minutes earlier remained behind. Matt and the others rushed forward and she stepped in front of them turning around holding her hands up to block them. "You all will have to stay here."

"No. I have to go in there with him," Matt said. "You *have to*."

Saffron pushed in next to Matt with Claire behind her. Saffron grabbed Matt's arm. "Matt, he's alive. Let them do what they have to. He'll be okay."

Matt stopped and looked dazed at Saffron.

"They'll come out to talk to us when they can," Saffron said. "They'll let us know something soon. Come on, we'll go sit down and wait."

The matronly nurse turned and disappeared through the same double doors, leaving the group standing frozen in place.

"Matt, Saffron's right," Phillip said. He pulled the six-four tall man like a child. "Come on, let's go over there and sit down."

They all sat not speaking for minutes until they turned to Vic and asked, "What happened?"

"I don't know. Matt called me because Andy went to the gallery to get papers for the meeting. He said all of you had already arrived and Andy hadn't come back. Matt asked if I would go over to check it out."

"Sir," an officer interrupted. We need to get some more information from you and have you sign a statement."

"Yes, of course," Vic said. He and the uniformed officer walked over to the counter near the emergency room check-in. A few feet beyond stood the double doors where Andy's gurney had swiftly rolled away. The doors remained closed, as secure as steel doors to a bank vault.

About five minutes passed. The double doors swished open and a man in blue scrubs with a blue cap covering his head walked out. Vic was still at the counter with the police officer and noticed him before the group. Vic excused himself and followed the doctor to the waiting room where the others sat.

"I'm Doctor Carter."

Matt ejected out of his chair. The others followed, rushing toward the doctor.

"Your friend is alive, but he lost a lot of blood. We need to get him up to the OR. Is a member of his family here?"

"I called his mother," Matt said. "She's on her way."

"Does he have a wife?"

"No."

"Okay. Well, right now, your friend is stable, but he'll need surgery. We'll have to wait for the next of kin to arrive to give consent to operate."

"I need to see him," Matt said.

"Sir, no one can go in except immediate family. As I said he's stable, but he is in critical condition. If his condition changes, we can take him to surgery without the signed consent."

"Wait, you don't understand," Matt said. "I need to see him. He's my partner—my life partner."

Amber looked at Matt shocked, and then gave Vic a questioning look. Vic looked surprised too and shrugged, shaking his head indicating that he had been unaware of Matt and Andy's relationship. Amber held onto Matt's arm and tenderly rubbed it while tears came to her eyes.

"I can give consent," Matt said firmly. "We both carry medical power of attorneys with us in our wallets in case of emergency. But Doctor, I need to see him—please."

Matt's eyes fixed on him, waiting for his approval.

The doctor hesitated, and then, nodded, "Okay, come on."

He turned and Matt followed him though the double doors as they swung open. The two men disappeared into the corridors beyond.

Bloody Scared

The door flew open and slammed against the wall as Samuel stormed into the room. Leroy hurried behind him with Pete following. The door bounced back and crashed into Leroy. He blocked it with his hand before it hit his face, charging into the room on the heels of The Preacher.

"What the hell did you do, Samuel?" Leroy screamed.

The Preacher spun around, grabbed Leroy by his t-shirt, and pulled him close as the sound of the ripping fabric cut through the air. "Don't you curse at me!" he said through clenched teeth as his hot breath exploded into Leroy's face. "I'll not have you question me." The Preacher pushed Leroy with his bloody hand.

Leroy stumbled back into Pete, then recovered his balance and lunged forward, stopping inches from The Preacher's face. He stood there, glared at him as he held his arms straight down at his sides, and balled his right hand into a fist.

"There was so much blood," Pete whined from behind the two men. "If he dies . . . what're we going to do, Leroy? The blood was everywhere."

Leroy broke his stare, turned to his friend and said, "He was still alive, Pete."

"But the blood—"

"Stop it! You need to pull yourself together," Leroy said.

"The both of you, Shut . . .Up!" The Preacher yelled.

Leroy whirled back to The Preacher. "Look, Samuel, gay bashing is one thing but Pete and I ain't never killed nobody."

"We killed him!" Pete wailed.

"No, Pete. He wasn't dead," Leroy said firmly. "I said we never *have* killed anyone and we aren't going to be dragged into killing someone now." Leroy turned back to The Preacher and said, "Samuel you need to get out of here."

The Preacher looked hard at Leroy. "I'll go when I say I'm going." The Preacher glanced over to Pete who was crying and holding his face in his hands and said, "You need to quiet him up. We wouldn't have any problems now if you hadn't pulled me off that faggot. He'd be in hell now where he belongs—instead now his friend is back there trying to save him."

"I may not know the Bible like you, Samuel, but I was taught my Ten Commandments in Sunday school. I remember the one that says, "Thou shall not kill."

"I told you Leroy not to preach to me. Or I'll skin you like one of our opossums back home." He spoke slowly and there was a hint of delight in his tone. "I should've finished my job and done away with his friend too. His soul probably can't be saved—him and that Jezebel girlfriend of his."

Samuel charged toward the bedroom. "I'm going to wash this blood off me." He yelled back to the men behind him, "Shut that sniveling friend of yours up." And he stormed out of the room, slamming the bedroom door behind him.

"What are we going to do?" Pete whimpered.

"I don't know. But I'll not burn in hell for him," Leroy answered in a low voice. "We can't let him kill anybody."

"You think he's killed people?"

Leroy frowned at Pete. "Yeah, I think so. That's why we have to get him out of town before he hurts that pretty girl,

Amber. The one he's always watching.

After the Attack

The doctors kept Andy in the hospital for eight days. He underwent surgery to remove a severed spleen that resulted from the deepest stab wound. While the other punctures were deep, they amazingly had missed vital organs. Doctors ordered a series of MRI scans, x-rays, and a multitude of other tests plus the standard blood work.

Until the results came back, Andy was put in a medically induced coma because of the massive bruising and trauma to his body from the attack. Once the test confirmed no brain trauma had occurred, the doctors slowly brought him out of the coma and moved him from ICU to a regular room.

The medical staff and police credited Vic's fortunate arrival at the gallery and quick thinking as the sole reason that Andy stayed alive until the ambulance got to the scene.

However, it was Lyra, Andy's soul follower, who had intervened and blocked the knife blade forcing it to pass Andy's vital organs. This saved him. The attack was so fast and powerful, she failed to keep the knife from hitting the spleen. Her actions drained and exhausted her. If Vic hadn't scared Andy's attacker off, Lyra wouldn't have been able to continue the battle much longer.

After Andy came out of surgery, someone in the group remained at the hospital with Matt, at all times. Although, everyone urged Matt to go home to rest after the first 24 hours, he refused to leave Andy's side. He stayed in Andy's room during the eight days of his hospitalization.

On the third day, Andy was strong enough to sit up in bed, eat, and visit with Amber and Vic. When Detective Harrison walked in,

211

he looked across the room and couldn't conceal his shock when he spotted Amber sitting with Vic.

"Miss Moon, I wasn't aware you knew Mr. Martinez," he said.

"Yes, he's a very good friend."

Matt glanced at Harrison's badge clipped to his belt, frowned, and looked at Amber puzzled. "You know him?"

"Yes, I received a threatening note a few weeks ago and met the detective then," she explained. "That's the same time I stopped seeing the group. It was *his* explicit instructions to stay away and not tell anyone why, or warn anyone in the group."

Amber sat still a moment and stared at the detective and then she turned to Matt and Andy. "I'm sorry I didn't tell you or anyone in the group but he said I was the only one in danger." Amber turned and glared at the detective. "I guess you were wrong, Detective Harrison."

Vic said, "You need to be truthful with us, *detective*, that is if that's possible. Was Andy's attack connected to The Rainbow Killer?"

"The Rainbow Killer?" Matt shrilled. "Did the police think the note to Amber was from him? Why would The Rainbow Killer threaten Amber?"

"Shhh." Andy grabbed Matt's hand. "Don't get upset, Matt." Andy looked toward Amber and Vic, "Everyone stop this! We need to listen to what the detective has to say. Let him speak."

Andy looked at Harrison and calmly introduced himself. "I'm Andy Martinez—but I guess you already know that. Please tell us why you came. You probably have questions for me?"

"Yes, I do. I'm Detective Harrison, head of the task force. First, let me say that I am very sorry about what happened to you, Mr. Martinez. We weren't aware that the two cases were linked. Not until we conducted a sweep around the neighborhood. When we interviewed the people around there, we came up with witnesses that said they saw a blue pick-up truck outside the gallery around the time of your attack. That linked back to the initial report taken at Miss Moon's residence the night she received the threatening note. That's when the detective working your case turned everything over to my task force. We had released Miss Moon from our protection because we felt she no longer was a target. Weighing these facts, and knowing that you both are friends, we can't make that assumption anymore. No one who knows either one of you is out of danger."

"You think!" Vic raised his voice.

Andy spoke slowly, "Detective, you said a blue pickup truck? The night of Matt's gallery opening some men chased me." He continued as if he was discovering a piece to a missing jigsaw puzzle for the first time. "They had been driving a blue pick-up."

"You didn't tell me about being chased," Matt said.

"I didn't want to upset you. They yelled some crude remarks about homosexuals. I figured they were just guys looking to beat-up a fag."

"My God, Andy," Amber said, "that's awful."

"It's part of life. People are always calling us names. The only thing to do is to ignore it," Andy said. "It doesn't happen often that remarks turn to violence. Most people, well, they're happy to just call us names. Others tolerate us."

Amber sighed, looked down and clasped her hands in her lap.

"Mr. Martinez, my team is going to work very hard to get this guy. Was the man that attacked you, one of the men who chased you the night of the opening?"

"Yes, I think so."

"Can you describe him?"

"I remember the other two men. One was tall and the other short and scrawny. It was a long time ago. I don't think I could describe them any more than that."

"That's all right we don't need to worry about the two from the opening night. It's more important you describe the other man, the one who attacked you three days ago?"

"Three days ago, it was the same three men," Andy said.

Harrison put his hand up to his forehead and said almost under his breath. "The Profile indicates The Rainbow Killer is a loner. He wouldn't have had accomplices."

"A lot of good your profiles are doing us, while you are psycho-analyzing the killer, he's running amuck in town," Vic said. "So much for protecting the defenseless citizens."

"Mr. Richardson, making accusations isn't helping. I think you need to leave the room."

"No, he stays," Andy said firmly.

Amber pulled on Vic's arm. "Sit down," she whispered.

Detective Harrison turned back to Andy. "Okay, tell me everything you can remember about when you were stabbed."

"Well, I'm not sure the other men knew he had a knife. I heard them yelling at him. Begging him to stop, said he was going to kill me."

"I can get a sketch artist down here if you can describe the assailant."

"I didn't really see him. I remember the night of the party he wore black. Three days ago, when they came into the gallery the smaller man was first and then the tall man. He blocked the view of the one I think who had the knife. As soon as I saw them, I turned to run. Then I felt an unbearable pain in the small of my back, that must've been the knife, and I went down. They all were on top of me. I tried to crawl out from under them. They were all yelling. I managed to get free and made it to the side of the gallery near the back room. Then he caught me and started stabbing me and I fell to the floor. I rolled over to protect myself, all I saw was the knife. An enormous knife with blade a mile long."

214

Andy looked at the palms of his delicate hands marred with gashes. "My hands got cut blocking and fighting him. I'm not very strong."

"That's enough," Matt said.

"Wait, there's more. Something I think I heard. They were yelling and everything was going black. I struggled to fight them off. Before I passed out, I think I heard the name, 'Leroy.'"

Nailed

Amber was staying at Vic's house until the police had something more than profiles. Vic's house appeared to be a safe haven since she'd never received threats there. Either he didn't know where Vic lived, or didn't care to pursue her there. Whatever it was, Amber would be safer there with Vic for protection if the killer did show up.

One distinct possibility was the killer might have gone into hiding because of the added attention and security surrounding Andy since his attack.

Amber told Saffron and Claire everything that had happened over the last few weeks. Relieved now that there were no more secrets, Amber told both of them to be alert and that danger to the group may be a real threat. Bennie and Ken were gone and Phillip already knew everything.

At Vic's house, Amber sat in the living room reading when the phone rang. Harrison had Amber's number forwarded to Vic's phone and had a tap put on it. The possibility of the killer calling was a long shot but they had nothing else to work with. Harrison instructed Amber to let the phone ring four times before answering, if the killer did call, she was to keep him talking as long as possible.

Amber looked over at Vic sitting in the chair as the phone rang two more times.

"Don't worry," Vic said. "Even if it's him, he wouldn't dare show up here. If he does, he'll have to go through me first before he gets to you. And that's not going to happen."

During the eight days of Andy's hospital stay Vic had applied for a gun and met the three-day waiting period Florida required. Then he purchased a small but efficient handgun.

Amber got up and went to the phone. "Hello."

"Amber, it's me. Saffron."

Amber let out a sigh of relief. "Oh, hi."

"Anything new?"

"No, there's nothing yet. Detective Harrison is optimistic." Amber heard Vic's "Ha!" in the background.

Amber grimaced at Vic.

"He's going to mess up somewhere and then the police will get him," Amber said. "Now that they have a name that Andy heard, it shouldn't be long. He probably has been in trouble before, so maybe they can find him in the records before he does anything else."

"You must be going crazy held up like you are. I feel so bad that you had to go through what you did by yourself. I know you had Vic, but having to keep it a secret from all of us . . . it must have been hell."

"It wasn't pleasant. I'm glad you and Claire know now. Still, I'll never forgive myself that Andy got hurt."

"It wasn't your fault. Knowing wouldn't have changed anything," Saffron said. "I really believe that you can't avoid destiny."

"Maybe."

"It's true, really. Life goes on—people have to work and go places. It would have happened to Andy no matter what. Claire wants me to cancel all my gigs but I can't do that. However, I'm careful. I won't take any chances."

"Good."

"Guess what. One of the task force guys said he's coming Saturday night to hear me sing. I'll have my own personal *policeman fan* in the audience."

"Really."

"Yeah, Harrison's making him take off to alleviate some of the tension from the case. Harrison found out this guy was a big fan of mine. And Harrison is going to have one detective take off a night each week to come to see my show, as long as I'm here singing. So don't worry, I'll have trained bodyguards, so to speak. Have to go now. Keep me informed."

"Will do."

Task Force Office-Ybor City

Harrison had Detective Stone start running a check for Florida auto tags registered to blue pick-ups. There were thousands. They would first narrow their search to felons with the first name of Leroy. With any luck, their guy had a record. If no leads turned up, next they would work their way down the list to anyone the that owned a blue pick-up who had received any violations in the last five years, even as small as a parking ticket. It was a long process. One that resembled grabbing at straws but they had nothing else to work on and nothing to use from the crime scene at the gallery, either. Blood spatter evidence came up empty, there was so much blood it had destroyed any fingerprints. All blood or useful DNA samples collected were from Andy.

The other crime scenes seemed well planned out. They were very clean of evidence, too. Except for items left like notes that promised damnation and punishment for sinners. The trophies that were delivered to Harrison were of no use either. The name Leroy was the first solid lead. If their search for "Leroy" came up empty, they would be dead in the water again.

The only good thing that came from Andy's attack was that more manpower was allotted to the police and a team was assigned to watch Andy and Matt's house. Orders came for a patrol car to drive by Amber's house every hour in case someone came prowling around again.

Letting these crimes go unsolved was *not* an option. Pressure intensified from the mayor's office to make an arrest before things went cold again.

Detective Stone scanned the computer screen for the name Leroy. Interrupted by the phone ringing, he grabbed it, and answered in a gruff voice. "Stone."

"Detective Stone, this is Amber Moon."

"Hello, Miss Moon." His voice mellowed as the uncomfortable pang of guilt returned to him. The last time she had been in the office he dismissed her as a hysterical female that was wasting the time of the task force.

"I'm sorry to bother you—"

"That's all right, Miss Moon, what can I do for you?"

"I was wondering if you found anything from the check on Leroy."

Across the room, Harrison slammed a phone down, jumped up and yelled, "Stone, let's go. Our guys in town got our man driving by Moon's residence. We've got the bastard, come on!"

"You caught him?" Stone heard Amber's hopeful voice from the other end of the phone.

"Miss Moon, there's a lot of work to do before we can charge him with anything. We don't want him to walk."

"But they have him in custody?"

"Don't worry Miss Moon. We're not going to lose him. I have to go now." Stone hung-up and grabbed his jacket and rushed out of the room.

The Arrest

Saffron called Vic's number for Amber but there was no answer. No answer brought Saffron's positive energy to a screeching halt. She scanned down the list on her cell until she came to Amber's cell number and punched it in.

Amber answered.

"What's going on? Where are you?" Saffron demanded immediately.

"Everything is okay." Amber voice had an optimistic and happy sound to it. So different from the last time they had spoken.

"Why aren't you at Vic's?"

"I would've called you but I thought you were singing tonight."

"I go on in two minutes. The detective that was coming tonight isn't here. Did someone else get hurt?"

"No, it's good news. They caught the killer. I guess everyone is down at the jail where he was taken. Vic and I are going back to my house."

Saffron heard Vic in the background say something about not trusting the detective. "What's Vic saying? Sounds like something about someone screwing up things."

"It's nothing," Amber answered. "He and Detective Stone are so protective of me. They are worse than my mother. Detective Stone comes across as rough but he's really nice. Anyway, I called down there to check on things, and while I was talking to him, I overheard Detective Harrison say that a Tampa Police Officer arrested the killer near my house."

"That's great. Then it's over?"

"Yeah, but of course, Detective Stone wouldn't stick his neck out and say anything. He said they had to be sure everything was in order before they could 'officially' charge him. He wouldn't admit it was over 'officially,' that is—but yes, it's over Saffron."

"Thank God," Saffron said. She paused, as sounds of a knock and muffled voice seeped through the phone line. "That's the back stage assistant. It's my one-minute call. Look, I have to go, Amber."

"Okay break-a-leg."

In Tampa

Harrison and Stone walked into the jail area. After signing in, they were told Leroy Carpenter was being held in interrogation room 2B. His buddy was in 3C down the hall. They would talk to him first so Leroy could sweat it out for a while and wonder what was happening.

Harrison entered the room first and took a seat at the table. Stone followed close behind.

Harrison placed a stack of papers down in front of him while the man across the table sat biting his nails. Stone stood next to the door with his back against the wall.

"I'm Detective Harrison and this is my partner Detective Stone. Looks like you're in a bit of a jam here Pete."

"Leroy told me I didn't have to talk to you," Pete said.

"Leroy doesn't care about you, Pete." Divide and conquer is the best strategy when dealing with the underbelly of the world. There really is no such thing as integrity in the criminal world.

Harrison figured Pete for the weaker of the two. Therefore, he needed to convince Pete to roll over on Leroy to save himself. Usually, the police didn't have much difficulty to get the criminal element to go against one another.

Pete straightened-up in the chair to meet the challenge in front of him. "You don't know Leroy. He watches out for me."

"I'm sure he does but . . . he's got that mean streak in him." Harrison paused and then turned around to Stone. "I'm thirsty.

221

Could you get me a soda?" He turned back to Pete, "Would you like a drink, Pete?"

Pete smiled and giggled, half under his breath. "Sure, if you're buying. I'll have a Dr. Pepper."

Stone left the room and a minute later he returned with two soda cans in his hands.

Harrison took them and turned back to Pete. "Look Pete, I'm not going to lie to you." Harrison popped open the cans and pushed one over to Pete. He nodded for him to go ahead take the drink. Pete stared at the man for a second and then grabbed the can and gulped down a long drink.

Harrison took a drink and then placed the can down. "I know Leroy is your friend but if it came down to him or you? Now that's a *different* story."

"You don't know shit!" Pete shouted at him. "Leroy took a beating for me in school that broke his nose and two ribs. He's my friend—he would die for me. I'm not talkin' to you."

Harrison turned back and looked at Stone, then turned back to the table. They had checked records on Pete and Leroy. Pete came up clean and the only thing on Leroy was he did a month in jail for public intoxication, disorderly conduct, and resisting arrest. Maybe the usually tried-and-true method of putting pressure on Pete wasn't the route to go. Pete and Leroy weren't the standard criminals that were normally pulled in connected to serial killings.

"Well, that kind of friend is hard to find." Harrison said. He took another drink and sat for a minute.

Pete nodded his head in agreement. "Damn right."

Harrison looked at Pete and asked, "You wouldn't want to send your friend to prison because you didn't help us, would you?"

"You're going to send Leroy to prison?"

"We don't want to lock-up a good man. That is, if he really is a good man. But our hands will be tied without your cooperation."

"You don't understand. He's the devil."

"Who? Leroy?"

"No, The Preacher. Leroy is trying to protect me and the others. He wanted to stop The Preacher from hurting that gay fella'. Leroy doesn't even like beating up fags."

"This Preacher guy is pretty mean, huh."

"Yeah, but Leroy won't let him send us to hell. He's going to stop him from hurting anyone else. You can't put Leroy in jail, he didn't do anything wrong."

Out of Jail

Leroy signed his name to the log and grabbed the envelope that contained his wallet, watch, and the loose change from his pockets at the time of his arrest. He moved a few yards away and stood near the wall waiting for Pete to be released.

Pete walked out. A smile spread across his face when he saw Leroy standing waiting for him. He signed hurriedly, grabbed his envelope and rushed toward Leroy. "I knew you'd wait for me. I didn't tell them anything bad, even though they tried to trick me. I told them you wanted to help that fag guy."

"Shhh, Pete. Be quiet. Come on let's get out of here." Leroy turned and headed out the double doors. Pete stopped speaking and followed behind right in step, so close to his heels that Pete looked like Leroy's shadow.

On the drive to the impound lot where Leroy's truck was towed, Pete sat in silence. While Leroy talked to the man in the office and signed the paperwork, Pete watched not saying a word. It wasn't until they were halfway to Leroy's house before Pete spoke again. "Guess the cops believed me cause they let us go."

"They let us go," Leroy answered with an irritation in his voice, "because they want us to get The Preacher for them."

"We can't rat on him. He'll kill us."

"Pete, remember what I keep telling you? Let me do the thinking."

A few minutes later, they pulled the truck up in the front yard at Leroy's house. There were no signs of Samuel. Inside the place was a shambles. During Harrison's "talk" with Leroy, he had shown him the search warrant they had for his house.

"Look at what they've done to the place." Leroy moaned.

The bedroom door opened and out walked Leroy's latest girlfriend, Regina. She hurried over to him, throwing her arms around Leroy's neck. "Sweetie, they released you."

"Guess word's out," Pete said.

Regina pulled her arms away. "Uh, yeah Pete. I heard around town that the cops picked you two up for creeping around a house in South Tampa. Word is that they pulled you in about murders. What's going on Leroy?"

Leroy stared at her for a few second, not answering. "I need a beer," Leroy said breaking the silence. He walked toward the kitchen and Regina followed then Pete. The kitchen was ransacked, cabinet doors were opened, drawers pulled out, and papers and mail thrown everywhere. He went to the refrigerator and grabbed two beers, handed one to Pete, opened his and walked back to the living room.

"Leroy, talk to me," Regina called after him and then followed behind with Pete following in tow.

In the living room, the three sat down and Pete spoke first. "Samuel's gone."

"No, he's not," Leroy said shaking his head. He looked at Regina still watching him, waiting for an explanation. Leroy took a big gulp of beer then put the can down on the coffee table and said, "He's smart enough to stay away. But he's still around. Trust me, bad doesn't go away that easy." He grabbed Regina's hand and stood up. "Let's go to the bedroom."

"Whoa, Leroy needs some lovin' from Regina," Pete said in a singsong voice.

Leroy just shook his head and said, "Yeah, Pete. Stay in the living room." Regina laughed and left with Leroy.

In the bedroom, Leroy closed the door and turned to Regina. "You knew we got arrested because Samuel told you, didn't he" Leroy asked in a low voice. "Did he give you a message for me?"

Regina nodded yes.

An hour later Regina and Leroy came out of the bedroom and went to the living room where Pete had fallen asleep on the sofa.

Regina gave Leroy a kiss and said goodbye. She grabbed her things, disappeared out the front door and down the sidewalk. Leroy started picking up some papers and looked around the disheveled room. *How am I going to stop Samuel and keep Pete and me from frying along with him?* Before he could worry any further, the phone rang. He picked up the receiver.

Pete's face was buried into the back of the couch. He slowly stretched and turned over to face Leroy.

"Hello," Leroy said. "Yeah, Samuel they had to let us go."

Pete sat up and moved to the edge of the couch to listen.

"They had nothing on us." Leroy paused, then he looked over to Pete. He diverted his eyes away and continued to talk. "Don't know, I guess a nervous neighbor called when they saw my pickup. Cops were just fishing because if they had anything they would've kept drilling us for 48 hours."

Leroy eyes darted back to Pete and then away again. "No, he did good. He didn't give them your name. They don't know anything about you . . . okay . . . yeah, the Watering Hole . . . ten o'clock. We'll be there."

He placed the phone down on the coffee table.

"What'd he say?" Pete asked.

Before Leroy could answer, the phone rang again and he picked it up. "Yeah, it's set-up. You heard him ten o'clock. You're going to have your guys inside like you said? Not outside. You have to nab him inside, so there is no chance for things to get screwed up. I told you, I need protection. If he thinks I'm double-crossing him, or he sees anyone he doesn't know hanging around outside he'll stab me and get away before you know what has happened. And this time, he won't leave me bleeding to live like he did that guy at the gallery. That's the deal. Take it or leave it."

226

Pete's eyes widened as he watched Leroy listen and nodded a few more times.

"I'm telling you that's the way it has to be, or I'll warn him, and he'll be gone." Leroy paused and then nodded again. "Okay, I'll get him to go inside. We'll order a beer and I'll scratch my head. That's your cue to nab him then, before he knows what's what."

Leroy hung the phone up.

"You settin' a trap for the Preacher? You sure you can catch him?" Pete said. "You said nobody can catch the devil."

"Don't worry Pete. The Preacher isn't going to hurt any more people in Tampa. I promise you."

Snaring the Devil

Leroy and Pete pulled into the side parking lot of Watering Hole. Motorcycles filled over half of the lot, mostly Fat Boys and Hogs. The rest of the lot had an assortment of trucks and near the back sat a vehicle owned by a man called Skitter that towered over all others known as "King of the Hill." It was a converted Chevy panel truck and a legend because he entered every year in the Monster Truck competition at the stadium and won five years in a row.

If Harrison had his men staked outside, they would've stood out like a poodle in the middle of a pit bull fight. The Preacher would have bolted for sure.

Leroy pulled into one of the last parking spaces and looked around. Things looked normal. Harrison must've been streetwise enough to have kept his word about no cops outside. The set-up was foolproof.

Leroy pulled the keys out of the ignition and turned to face Pete. "Pete remember, let me do all the talking. Don't let on to anyone that there are cops inside. And afterward—don't try to think. Just let me handle everything. Understand?"

"You sure The Preacher won't know somethin's up? We're not going to Hell, are we?"

"No. We are going to protect that pretty girl, Amber *and* stop the killings in Tampa. God will know we did what we had to do in order to save her. Let's go."

Pete opened his door and stepped out. Leroy's hand was resting on the edge of the seat beside his knee holding the keys in his fingertips. He opened his grasp, the keys fell to the floor, and he slid out of the truck slamming the door behind him.

Leroy and Pete walked to the front of the building and went inside. At the pool tables, a bald middle-age man had just sunk the orange ball in the middle pocket, while three other men stood by with sticks waiting their turn. Although they were dressed like bikers, they were new to the Water Hole and Leroy sensed they were Harrison's men.

Leroy and Pete walked over to the bar and took a seat.

"Hey," Harley said, "The usual?"

"Yeah."

"Coming up, Leroy."

Dance with the Devil

Saffron finished her final set of songs and thanked the crowd for coming out to hear her. She gathered her things and headed toward the restroom area to the phones to call Claire. As she moved toward the bar, she saw the familiar face of a man sitting at the bar.

"I didn't expect to see you here tonight." Saffron said stopping.

"Please, join me."

She took a seat on the stool next to the man dressed in black. "I thought you said you had Bible study tonight?"

"No, that's over. I'm leaving town to shepherd a new flock. I wanted to stop in to see you one more time. I've enjoyed our discussions and I wanted to drop off a Bible for you."

"That's so nice of you, thank you. I never did get to tell Amber you stopped in to hear me sing. I never asked you how you know Amber?"

"Actually, we have never met. We have a mutual friend and I was asked to pray for her. I hope I did some good."

"Prayers always do good." Saffron smiled. "I think maybe your prayers for her were answered tonight. You just may have helped more than you realize."

"Helping my sisters and brothers follow the signs is why I was led here. It is my purpose and job. I am the shepherd of the Lord."

Saffron smiled and sat silently not understanding why she suddenly felt uncomfortable with the minister. Then she asked, "Where are you moving to?"

"Georgia." The man in black handled Saffron a glass. "I had the bartender make you a special drink. Had him put in almond flavoring, no alcohol."

"Thanks."

"Strange, that you sing in a bar when you don't drink alcohol," he said. "I wouldn't have thought a Christian entertainer would sing in a drinking establishment."

"I don't drink because I never liked the taste of it. I try to lead a good Christian life. I try not to hurt anyone or judge others, but still, some may not think I'm Christian."

"Why is that, my child?"

"One reason is I don't belong to any specific church. Second is, some people believe only in their rules and ways. If you don't believe their way then they think you're bad."

"No one owns the rules, my child. You need to read the Bible and it will guide you."

Saffron held the Bible up in her hand. "I will," she said.

"Are you going to taste your special drink?"

Saffron put the Bible down on the bar, picked up the glass and took a drink. "It's different tasting. Has a strange taste. What's in it?"

"It's a secret recipe I got from someone in the church back home in the mountains."

Saffron blinked a couple of times as she concentrated on listening to him. His word became distant and her eyes felt heavy as her vision blurred.

"You look tired, it's late and your taste buds are failing you. The flavor enriches after you have a couple of sips. Drink up."

"Yeah, I am tired." Saffron took another sip of the drink. "Your right. It is good but I really need to go call my girlfriend to come pick me up."

"Why don't you let me take you home? You told me your friend works during the day and it's so late. I'm going back to my friends' house, the one that knows Amber. I only came in to hear you sing and say goodbye. Their home is in same direction of yours, I don't mind giving you a lift."

"Well, if you don't mind, I'm really tired all of a sudden." Saffron blinked a few more times and put the glass down hard on the counter sloshing the liquid out onto the bar top. "Wow, I guess I'm more tired than I thought." The room was spinning and she held on to the counter as she slid off the stool to stand. "I don't feel well."

"Let me help you," he said as he put his arm around her and led her toward the door. Saffron looked down, concentrating on walking a straight line. Each step more difficult than the last.

He pushed open the door under the exit sign that opened outside to the parking lot. She looked down at her foot as she took a step, it seemed far away, and the black asphalt looked like a sea of wavy Indian ink. Saffron held her head, took another step, and stumbled but his strong arm around her waist held tight.

"I'm sorry. I don't know what's wrong. I feel so strange."

"Hold on here," he said and pushed her up against something. She groped out in front of her and felt a smooth metal wall edge. Trying to focus her eyes, she saw that she was holding onto the side of a blue pickup truck.

"Everything is spinning," she said as she slumped over and held tight not to fall. The man in black went to the back of the truck and opened the tailgate as she watched. *What's happening?*

He moved slowly like a slow-motion scene in the movies. He walked around to the side where she was standing and grabbed her by the shoulders. His touch was different now. It was forceful and rough. "What's going on—?"

"Shut up," he ordered.

Saffron stumbled, as he pulled her to the back of the pickup and then pushed her forward. Saffron's thighs hit the edge of the tailgate hard.

"Climb up, bitch."

Saffron followed his directions, in a mental fog. She pulled one knee up onto the cold metal surface and placed her hands down on the tailgate, hiking herself up. Moving forward, reaching out in front, she crawled on her hands and knees. She could barely see, things moved and spun in opposite directions at the same time, as if she were on a wild amusement park ride.

Where am I? Is he taking me to Amber? I don't understand.

"Hurry up bitch." Then he pushed her forward, causing her to crash to the bed of the truck as sand and pebbles from the floor grounded into her skin. Saffron looked back to the bumper end of the truck and saw the man grab something shiny and black. Then he threw it over top of her and everything went dark. "No don't. What are you doing? Don't."

The sound of the metal tailgate slammed shut and she heard footsteps move around to the side of where she laid, then the sound of a door opening and slamming shut. The engine started. The vehicle shifted forward. Saffron drifted out of consciousness.

Soon she came to again and heard the drone of the tires in motion on the road. She struggled to move but felt paralyzed. It was dark and the weight of the cover over top of her seemed to hold her down.

Then she lost consciousness for the last time.

Missing

Claire woke up on the couch. "Sunday traffic heading east on 275 will be backed up for some time because of an overturned semi-truck . . . ." blared from the living room television set. She sat up and looked at the clock on the cable box that read six o'clock. *Saffron didn't call me last night to pick her up.*

"Saffron," Claire called out. No answer. She pushed her hair back, yawned, stood up, and walked down the hallway toward their bedroom. "Why didn't you call me? You promised you wouldn't hitch a ride from one of the barmaids."

When Claire reached the bedroom doorway, she stopped dead. The bed was undisturbed. It was still neatly made, displaying the small frilly accent pillows and matching shams with bright yellow and lavender flowers. That comforter and pillow set took Claire six months to find. Saffron hated it. But she told Claire to buy it if it made her happy. Everything was exactly the way it had been left the day before.

Saffron wasn't in the bathroom, either. Claire checked the entire house. Saffron wasn't there. She hadn't come home. A dark feeling settled in on Claire. Something was very wrong.

She stood solitary in the house and her stomach started to heave as the distant sound of the television echoed in the emptiness of the house. "Where is she?" Claire whispered.

She hurried to the spare bedroom at the other side of the house, her converted home office. At the desk, she opened the top drawer and took out a notebook with Saffron's scheduled bookings and contact numbers. Claire slid her finger down the list until it came to the lounge name and number that Saffron was performing at last night. She grabbed for the phone, started to dial, stopped suddenly, and placed the phone down. Then she started to pace about the room.

"Something's wrong. She had to have me pick her up." Claire wrung her hands as fear mounted. "Something's really wrong. What am I going to do? Think. . ..I have to think."

She picked up the phone and punched in Phillip's number. When Phillip answered, she immediately started babbling. "Phillip, I don't know what to do. I didn't know who to call. The lounge won't be open this early—"

"Claire, slow down."

"There's no time, we have to do something Saffron didn't come home last night."

"Did you guys have a fight?"

"No. You know we don't fight. Only that big one five years ago. We didn't have a fight. She's not here!"

"Was she singing somewhere last night?"

"Yes, of course. You know that! She was supposed to call me to pick her up at closing because the jeep is in the shop. I had my car at work and she had an afternoon appointment to go over some new photos with her publicity man. He was going to give her a lift to the lounge after their meeting. Phillip, I'm scared."

"Did you check with him to see if she showed up and he did drop her off at the lounge?"

"No, I didn't call him, but I spoke to Saffron last night. He dropped her off on time and she was warming up for her performance."

Claire closed her eyes for a second, took a deep breath and then opened her eyes again. She tried to push back the tears that were starting to fill her eyes. "This is bad, Phillip. Something's happened. I can feel it. What should I do?"

"Stay calm. You better call the police."

"What if someone grabbed her? Like the men that jumped Andy? They would've killed him."

"I know Claire but we cannot think about that now. We have to keep our heads and act quickly. I've the number for Detective Harrison. He's the one that was in charge with Andy's case. You need to call him and get him to meet you down at the lounge."

"Okay but it will be closed."

"There will be an emergency number near the door for the manager or owner. At least, that will be a place to start. I'll call Amber and Vic. The three of us will meet you there."

"Why are you calling Amber and Vic?"

"If Saffron has met up with the guy who has been stalking Amber, then they can help because they know how he ticks. And Harrison is convinced he was the same guy Andy tangled with."

"The cops thought that guy was doing the killings in town—Phillip, you think Saffron is dead. Don't you?"

"I didn't say that. Remember Andy is alive. There is still hope. Amber said they made an arrest yesterday. If they caught the guy, and he's in jail, then he couldn't have taken Saffron. We'll find her."

Uncovered

When Claire called Detective Harrison's cell phone, it forwarded to a dispatcher's desk in Tampa. The kind sounding officer on the other end of the phone assured her he'd relay the message to Detective Harrison to meet her. Claire hoped that Harrison would get the message and show up at the lounge.

Claire arrived before anyone else, pulled into the rear parking lot, and walked to the front of the building. The emergency number was posted at the door as Phillip said it would be and she flipped open her phone and called it. Dave McCray, the owner of the lounge answered. He sounded concerned after hearing what she had to say and said he'd come right away.

Too tense to stand still, Claire walked back around to her car. She sat in her vehicle for 30 seconds, then got out, and started to pace about the lot. She tried to think of a reasonable answer for Saffron's disappearance but headlines kept flashing in her mind. Familiar ones from the past like, *Another Body Found*, *The Rainbow Killer Hits Again*. They now seemed to address her personally.

Pacing, she stepped on something that crunched ever so slightly under foot. At first, she didn't take notice and kept moving. Her worry consumed her. The real world was a mere fog surrounding her. Nothing existed but Saffron. Seconds passed and the sensation of stepping on something nudged into her thoughts. Her eyes traced over where she had stepped. A small object lay on the asphalt. The morning sun caught a glint of thin gold wire. Claire bent down to see. Her eyes focused on a brown speckled feather on the pavement.

It was a feather earring. Saffron's signature earring.

Amber and Vic pulled into the parking lot and saw Claire standing by her car. She looked a mess, physically and emotionally. She had on a navy-blue T-shirt and jeans, probably Saffron's. Claire's usual attire was "boardroom corporate look." Her idea of dressing casual was no pearls. Today, she hadn't even combed her hair.

Amber watched Claire as they pulled in; the look on her face was a schizophrenic mixture of frantic mania and pure terror. Her eyes moved wildly around, searching about the parking lot, then she would stop, and go into a catatonic stare.

When the car stopped, Amber jumped out and hurried to her. "Claire, Phillip called us. He's on his way."

Claire stood motionless, her eyes blank, fixed and unseeing. Then, she slowly turned toward Amber.

"Did you find the emergency number and call the owner?" Amber asked.

"Yes." Claire answered with a disturbingly calm and slow tone. She held out her closed hand and unfolded her fingers, exposing the feather earring. "It's Saffron's," she said in a monotone voice. "She never takes it off."

Phillip's car raced into the parking lot with another car right behind him. Amber put her arm around Claire. "Phillip's here. We'll find her."

Phillip walked over. "Harrison's not here yet?" he asked.

Dave McCray hurried toward them from the other car. He introduced himself and unlocked the back door. They all streamed in behind him. He disappeared saying he would turn on the overhead lights. Claire looked around the empty room.

The lounge door opened and two uniformed police officers entered and walked over to them.

"Who is Claire Reed?" the heavyset officer asked as he took out a small note pad.

"I am," Claire answered. "I called because my girlfriend, Saffron, is missing."

The officers explained that Detective Harrison had been delayed. Seconds later, the lights flashed on. McCray walked out from the back area, rejoined the group and introduced himself to the police.

"Mr. McCray was Miss Saffron . . . uh." The officer stopped and turned to Claire and asked, "What is the missing woman's last name?"

"She has no last name," Claire said.

"You don't know it?"

"Her name is Saffron, S-a-f-f-r-o-n. That's her full, legal name. No last name."

"Oh, I see. Like Cher and Madonna." The officer turned back to McCray. "Was Saffron here last night?"

"Yes, she was singing. She had three sets. The last one finished around one a.m.," McCray answered. "I noticed her talking to a man at the bar. He ordered a ginger ale for her while she was on stage. I remember him coming in other times and they would talk between sets."

"Do you know who he is, or his name?"

"No, he never came in before Saffron started singing a month ago. He brought something for her this time. She left it on the bar when she went outside with him. When I saw him with his arm around her leading her out, I figured they would be back inside in a few minutes, but they never came back."

"I need to see what he brought for her."

"All right, I have it in the back room. I locked it in the safe when I closed last night. I'll get it. I thought it was a strange gift to give someone singing in a bar."

"Why is that, Sir?"

"It was a Bible."

McCray disappeared to the back again.

Claire had a sinking feeling. Saffron wouldn't let a man put his arm around her—she didn't even let *her* do that. He must've been forcing her to leave. Claire looked across the room. What she saw confirmed her fears that Saffron was not in control when she left. Claire pointed to an area beside the stage. "She left her guitar."

McCray came back holding the Bible, just as Detective Harrison walked through the door. He motioned to the two officers, who stepped away from the group to join him. They briefly spoke in whispered voices and then the uniformed officers left.

Harrison returned to the nervous friends and looked at Claire. "Miss Claire Reed?"

"Yes."

"I'm sorry I couldn't be here sooner. I came directly from a crime scene. I'm afraid I have bad news."

"Is it Saffron? Is she dead?"

"Yes, ma'am. I am very sorry."

Vanished

Amber has started to change from the unyielding person she was before the Rainbow Killer came into town. Her soul has opened to others but she still does not hear me. The deep hurt she feels is not just from grief for the loss of her friend, Saffron. It is more than a wounded heart. Her ache is the result of her soul growing and connecting to others. She is not a "Special One," yet, but perhaps soon she will hear me and believe in Soul Followers.

Kassandra

***

Eight Weeks Later

Amber opened the front door of her small bungalow home. The security alarm beeped as she moved toward the small keypad and punched in her code. The screen flashed and reset to read "armed." Still holding Saffron's memorial pamphlet from the funeral home, she crossed the room to the desk in the corner and put her purse down.

A massive, furry, white cat walked out from the hallway and over to her. It purred and rubbed against Amber's leg.

"Snowball, you miss her too, don't you?" Amber put the pamphlet down on the desk and picked up the cat cradling it in her arms.

"I know you can't understand why Claire can't keep you. You poor thing. Saffron's gone, and you've lost Claire, too. It's not your fault that you remind her of Saffron." The cat snuggled in her arms.

241

The phone rang. Amber grabbed it and sat down petting Snowball in her lap.

"Hi, it's Andy. I wanted to make sure you got home."

"Thanks," Amber said. "The service went nicely, didn't it? I'm glad Claire had Saffron's music playing. I was afraid she wouldn't be able to listen to it."

"Yeah, but she had two months to accept that Saffron is gone. I was so angry at first about the ridiculous delay with the officials not releasing Saf's body, but in a way, it made today a little easier. We all had time to adjust to the reality that she's really gone."

"I know what you mean. I don't think I could've made it through today if it had been right after . . . well, you know."

"The time helped everyone," Andy said.

Amber sat quietly petting the cat for a second or two. "You know I took Snowball." She paused to smile at the cat in her lap. "Saffron loved this cat so much but Claire said she couldn't bear to look at her."

"After Claire, that cat was the most important thing in Saf's life," Andy said. "I'm glad you took her. It would've made her happy." Neither of them spoke for a moment, then Andy broke the silence. "I thought you didn't like cats?"

"I don't," she answered automatically. "Uh, I mean I *didn't* like cats. Snowball is different—or maybe—I've changed."

"I talked to your mom before we left the graveside. She's really a unique person, Amber. She's so caring, like you. She said she's worried about me going back to work too soon, even though I've recovered from my injuries. Said I needed time to heal mentally, as well as, physically."

"She's right, Andy."

"I'm okay. Although, I've decided that I'm going to take a leave-of-absence for a while. To take care of the mental healing thing. I'll help Matt at the gallery."

"Good."

242

"Besides, it will give me time to get *Saffron's Place* up and running. That was another reason I called you. Are you still willing to be my right-hand gal at the center? I'll understand if you've changed your mind. Working with people who are dealing with threats of violence on a daily basis, won't be easy and it may make it difficult to find closure about Saf's death."

"Things won't ever be the same without her," Amber answered. "But helping people who are afraid and don't know where to go for help is the right thing to do."

"What about the closure thing? Do you need more time?"

"It's time to move forward. Working at the center will be the best closure I could ever get."

"The location is not going to be in the best neighborhood, but I'm told that's where we'll help the most. Still, it looks a little rough."

"Andy, I understand that we're not setting up a country club. Rough or not, I'll be fine. But, you know, a year ago I would've been afraid to do this—open a help center. Now, I've never been so sure of a decision in my life. Saffron would be proud. We'll be able to help so many."

"Okay, then we move forward. I'm glad you're on board. What does Vic think?"

"It's fine. Even if he didn't agree, it wouldn't matter. We're not joined at the hip."

"O . . .kay then, it's final."

Amber agreed. The two had already tentatively setup a schedule. Andy would operate the place after his day job and Amber would cover all the day hours. Her design business had slowed down to a dead stop. It seemed like fate.

Andy said, "It'll work out great. You'll be in charge of all the straight people and that will leave the *interesting* gay people for me. The setup is tailor made—everyone and anyone will be comfortable asking for help. We'll make a great team. Andy and Amber—the A-Team."

"You know, Saffron told me she always felt an obligation to give back and make a mark in the world. *Saffron's Place* is happening because of her. She made her mark."

"Yeah, The Rainbow Killer didn't take that from her. I'll talk to you later, Amber. Thanks."

"Okay, bye."

Amber stroked Snowball a little longer, and then put her down on the pink pillow bed she had bought for her and went to the kitchen. In the kitchen she opened a bottle of wine and poured a glass. The funeral had taken its toll on her and she needed to de-stress. She grabbed the newspaper and returned to the living room to read. The front page had headlines about the plans for a new football stadium. After thumbing through the pages, she finally found it—at the top of the obit page. No mention anywhere else. It was old news now she figured.

Rainbow Killer Victim Laid to Rest

TAMPA-Local musician, Saffron, was buried today. The singer was another victim in a string of unsolved murders committed in Tampa over the last several months. Detective Edward Harrison, of the Tampa Police Department, issued a brief statement to the press after the service.

"In the last eight weeks there have been no other murders attributed to the Rainbow Killer. The Chief of Police has officially disbanded the task force. It is believed that the suspect has fled the area and is possibly headed to Georgia. I have notified the authorities in Georgia and have briefed them of the evidence my task force has collected. Tampa's crime spree by the Rainbow killer is over."

The article said that detective thanked the community for their support and said he would remain a liaison for the Georgia authorities.

Amber shook her head, "Oh yeah, just forget about Saffron by sticking a small statement in the obit section. Vic's right about police and cold cases. Out of sight, out of mind."

Amber visualized the crime scene pictures of her friend with the note from the killer pinned to her clothing. She wiped a tear from the corner of her right eye. "Saffron hated having her picture taken—and crime scene photos are going to be the last vision people will have of her."

She took a sip of wine. "I'm sure Harrison and the Georgia authorities are working *hard* together to find out where that evil man went. How dare that killer maniac write a note saying he left to do God's work!"

Snowball looked at Amber, then stood, stretched, and walked over to the couch. She jumped up in Amber's lap, purred, while pushing in close. The cat kneaded Amber's lap, circled twice, and snuggled down tucking her paws into her fur.

"What great police work. Let's not dwell on the fact that the killer got away. Poof! He just evaporated into thin air. Problem solved!"

Home Sweet Home

Georgia Mountains

A small frame building with a cross on top vibrated with music and jubilant voices singing gospel hymns.

Inside, located in front of a plain altar, was a pine table and underneath sat a box with air holes cut around the top edge. Rattling sounds stirred inside.

The music stopped and the congregation took their seats. A plump woman in the last pew fanned herself and leaned sideways to whisper to the elderly women next to her. "Is it true? Has Samuel come back to take his father's place and preach?"

"Yes, he's here," answered the gray-haired woman. "I saw him outside."

At the back of the room, the church door flew open. A man in black came running up the aisle waving a Bible above his head. A silver cross swung back and forth from his neck.

"Praise the Lord! Praise the Lord," he cried as he stepped up and moved in front of the alter turning around to face the packed church. "I feel His Spirit is here tonight!"

"Hallelujah!" cried the congregation, raising their hands. "Praise the Lord."

"God has sent me back home to stand in for my father, Brother Isaac," he said.

Every eye in the room was fixated on him.

"Brothers and Sisters, some of you may have spoken to my sister, Bobbie Sue and learned that I was away doing the Lord's work. I came upon a lost flock of God's children that needed my shepherding. Without God, their souls would have been lost. But even the wretched soul will be saved if he seeks the Lord."

"Praise be the Lord," the women and men shouted.

"We are all lost without Our Lord, but the Bible is here to guide us."

"Amen."

The man in black shouted, "We all must work to spread God's word."

The plump woman fanned rigorously and shouted. "Hallelujah! Praise the Lord!"

Thank You for Reading.
I hope you will recommend my books to
a friend.

Chris Coad Taylor

Two uniquely different series by Chris Coad Taylor are the Amber series of Ybor City and the Havenridge Mysteries series. Pick your favorite. Read one or all of the books.

More books in the Amber series of Ybor City

Danger Amoung Us

Read more of Amber Moon and the people you read about in, *The Rainbow Murders*. The second book picks up where book one ends.

Amber and Andy open a business together called Saffron's Place and experience new challenges. Amber's career and personal life changes dramatically.

The Pied Piper
Evil Returns

Book three in the Amber series of Ybor City takes place three and a half years after the Rainbow Killer took his last victim. Amber's new career as a police sketch artist keeps her life busy. She and Darby, an employee at Saffron's Place, get involved in a crime investigation. Déjà vu hits Tampa and Ybor City residents when several young people go missing. Could there be a serial killer in the area again? Or has an old killer returned? Tensions rise high as each lead goes cold. A young survivor is found but he refuses to talk to any of the police task force, until Amber is brought in to draw a sketch of the bad guy he saw.

Books in the
Havenridge Mystery series

Read about Stephanie Oliver and the intriguing people of Havenridge, Georgia. Cozy. Small towns are full of secrets, a little bit of mystery, and drama of life's ups and down.

Book one: **Secrets of Havenridge**

Book two: **Finding Jacob**

Books are available on Amazon and select independent bookstores
Follow the author on Amazon here or on her Facebook Author page:

Amazon Author Chris Coad Taylor

Connect on Facebook

Some Web Sites of Interest about Ybor City and Related Information on the murders that inspired the writing of The Rainbow Murders.

- Ybor City Chamber of Commerce visitor information
  http://www.ybor.org/ybor-story

- Columbia Restaurant
  http://www.columbiarestaurant.com

- Ybor City Museum
  http://www.ybormuseum.org/

- Pink Pistols is an international gun club. Although it is not required that members are homosexual, the organization supports gay rights. They believe that self-defense is a right.
  http://www.pinkpistols.org/about-the-pink-pistols/
  http://en.wikipedia.org/wiki/Pink_Pistols

YouTube.com has posted a six-part controversial docudrama made by S.P.I Productions; title "Tampa City Held at Bay." It discusses evidence, arrest information and news reports about the murders of Jason Galehouse and Michael Wachholtz.

*WARNING: subject covered is graphic in nature, not recommended for sensitive persons or anyone under 21 years of age.

These links are being provided as a convenience and for informational purposes only; they do not constitute an

www.ingramcontent.com/pod-product-compliance
Lightning Source LLC
Chambersburg PA
CBHW020315200626
46814CB00006BA/2260

* 9 7 8 0 9 8 2 1 8 6 4 2 8 *